A SHADE IN THE MIRROR

Tracey Lander-Garrett

Tracey Lander-Garrett

DEC. 2019

GLASS CAROUSEL PRESS

ISBN 978-1-7334545-1-3 (print) | ISBN 978-1-7334545-0-6 (ebook)

This book is a work of fiction. Names, characters, places, and incidents are either the product of the author's imagination or are used fictitiously, and any resemblance to actual persons, living or dead, business establishments, events, or locales is entirely coincidental.

First printing, 2019

Glass Carousel Press
Pflugerville, TX 78660

Cover Design: Steven Novak, Novak Illustration

FOR SAM

the most unexpected goldfish of all

Prologue
1992

THE GIRL LIES IN BED, THE BACK OF HER HEAD TO the doorway.

Her head rests at an unnatural angle. Straight brown hair partially obscures her face, the rest of its length fanned across the white and black paisley pillow. Her skin is unnaturally pale. It's not a lovely alabaster or creamy ivory; instead there is a chalky, almost gray whiteness to her skin.

Her limp hand dangles off the bed, fingernails gone blue. This much is visible from the bedroom doorway. This is what the landlord sees when he enters the apartment in the morning to fix the leaky kitchen faucet, as he'd promised the day before. The landlord calls the police.

A closer look reveals her eyes are open. A petite brunette with golden brown eyes in her late teens or early twenties. The bedclothes are pulled up to just below her nose. Beneath it, where her mouth and neck should be, runs an angry red and gray ruin of veins and tubes and ligaments that were never, ever meant to see the light of day. It is as if her jaw

1

has been torn off and her throat has been ripped open by some curious animal that then took the time to dissect it.

Beneath this desecration, there are no other wounds. She wears a tank top and shorts. The tank top is white and stained with red, contrasting with the gray of her skin.

But where is the rest of the blood? The paisley sheets . . . the mattress . . . they should be soaked through, sopping with red. There's not a drop on the bed. Hardly any in the girl. Hardly any at the scene. Her lower jaw is found beneath her head as soon as the coroner moves her. The sight is so disturbing to a rookie policeman on-scene, he bolts for the bathroom.

The coroner estimates—based on temperature and the progression of rigor mortis—that she has been dead only four hours.

Soon the detectives will determine she was killed elsewhere, then brought to the bedroom. But not in the tub. Not a drop, not a smear there. There are three drops of her blood in the entryway. Just three tiny drops. No blood of any quantity elsewhere in the apartment, not in the drains, not in the toilet, not outside the windows to the fire escape. No fingerprints found at the scene other than those of the apartment's occupants.

Robbery is ruled out as a motive almost immediately. Her purse and wallet are in the kitchen, her jewelry in plain sight in the bedroom. There are no signs of forced entry, although a lamp in the entryway has been knocked to the floor, presumably as the killer carried her body into the apartment.

Who would want her dead? The roommate is out of the country. A rival at school has a rock-solid alibi. A boyfriend identified as a person of interest cannot be located. They don't even have his last name. There isn't a single lead. Not a single foreign hair or fiber on her body. The lack of evidence baffles forensic experts.

The sun sets, and rises again. Days pass. Weeks. Months.

The case is left unsolved. It goes into a cold case file, forgotten.

Such a violent, unthinkable murder.

Her spirit is left unsatisfied, malcontent, disturbed. Rooted to the spot. Unable to rest.

And when the veil between the worlds of the living and the dead thins . . .

She haunts.

CHAPTER ONE
2017

THERE ARE MANY THINGS YOU TELL YOURSELF when you're afraid of something you can't see, something that can't be there. You tell yourself that you're just imagining things. That you didn't hear or see the thing you saw. And you can forget telling anyone else about it. Why would they believe you? You don't even believe it yourself.

On the night in question, I came home late from work just as I usually did. My roommates were already in bed, also as usual. Because I was hungry, I went to the kitchen. The pull-chain light came on with a buzzing noise that began to decrease in volume, but then the light flickered and buzzed loudly. Not for the first time, I wondered if the halo-shaped fluorescent bulb was about to die.

I'd been living there about a month. I didn't know the protocol. Call the super? Fix it myself? Was there a stepladder in the apartment I could use? And where would I get an old-fashioned halo-shaped bulb anyway?

It was an old building. The water pressure wasn't

4

great. The radiator hissed and clanked. The other lights dimmed and flickered. Kara, one of my two roommates, thought there was something wrong with the wiring.

I poured some cereal into one of Julie's bowls. Ate with one of Kara's spoons. That's how roommate situations work. Everybody adds a little something. Kara brought the TV. Julie brought the couch. I brought a change of clothes and what I'm told is a lovely smile.

I selected a glass tumbler from the cabinet and filled it with water, then took a swig.

I put the glass on the counter, next to Kara's toaster oven and Julie's blender. I couldn't remember which of them brought the glassware. Were the tumblers Kara's and the wine glasses Julie's? Or was it the other way around?

As I stood munching away, I heard the familiar *creak* of one of the kitchen cabinet doors opening behind me. I thought I must not have closed the glassware cabinet door all the way. But the open door was a different cabinet. Strange, but whatever. I closed it and went back to eating my cereal.

Then I heard another *creak*. Did we have mice? It was another cabinet door, this one beneath the counter. I took the last bite of cereal and put my bowl in the sink, then peered in the cabinet. I wasn't brave enough to reach in, but the usual array of pots and pans sat undisturbed without signs of rodents, and that was good enough for me.

I closed the cabinet and took a second drink.

This is important. There was nothing wrong with the glass when I drank from it either time. It was just like any other glass of water. It was just like any other night. Except for the cabinets, of course, but there had to be a rational explanation for that, didn't there?

I set the glass down and washed up. I left the clean things in the dish rack and dried my hands. Then I heard the distinct *plink-plunk* of liquid hitting the tile floor coming from behind me.

I'd left the glass on the counter. I distinctly remembered placing it near the back, in front of the toaster oven. Now it leaned two inches from the counter's edge, tilting on its base at a strange angle. The water slowly dripped from the mouth of the glass, spilling onto the floor in droplets. I couldn't make sense of what I was seeing at first.

Glasses of water don't tilt by themselves. My mind searched for a rational explanation and came up with nothing.

As I watched, the glass leaned more and more, until it was nearly horizontal and the water started to pour out of the glass. My face and hands went cold in fear.

The glass hung, tilting on the counter's edge for several seconds while the overhead light crazily flashed from bright to dim, every change accompanied by a low buzz. Then the light went back to its usual brightness. The glass, seemingly suspended at the edge of the counter, suddenly crashed to the floor, shattering.

I screeched.

Julie's room was closest to the kitchen, and a sleepy, "Everybody okay?" came from that direction.

My mouth was completely dry and it took a few swallows for me to speak. "I'm fine," I said, my voice oddly high-pitched. "I . . . just broke a glass."

She called again. "Need any help?"

"No. Thanks, though," I said. "Sorry I woke you."

"No worries. Goodnight."

No worries. Right. The glass had . . . what? Committed suicide? Gotten tired of the serving life? Could a glass *have* feelings? Ridiculous thoughts like these ticked through my mind while I located the dustpan and quietly swept up the broken bits of glass and dried the floor. The lights in the kitchen flickered again, going dim, bright, and then back to normal.

What the hell was happening? It wasn't just the glass; it was the lights, and the cabinets, and the strange noises I heard in our building at night, and the way the lamp near our front door was always cold to the touch, even when the room was eighty degrees.

Ghost, my mind said.

Kara and Julie, who had been roommates in college, had been living in our three-bedroom Brooklyn apartment for two months longer than I had, but they always had some reasonable explanation for these things: bad wiring, old pipes, a pesky draft.

But how could they explain away what I'd seen the glass do? I was reasonably certain that the laws of physics couldn't cover it. So what could? Psychic powers? I didn't think I had any, and even if I had, I wouldn't be likely to pour *out* the water I wanted to drink. One of my roommates? As ridiculous as telekinetic roommates seemed, the idea of a water-pouring ghost was preposterous. Then I thought of *Poltergeist*, the movie.

Then I didn't get any sleep that night.

Two days later, I was standing in the hallway wearing sweats and an over-sized t-shirt, listening to Kara complaining. She was standing outside her room, ready for work, her light brown hair pulled back in a sleek ponytail, wearing a pair of black slacks and a bell-shaped blouse that hid her just-showing pregnancy.

"Maddy," she said, "I just don't get it. I went to bed last night, and the mirror was on the wall to the left of the bed and the mask was to the right. This morning, it's the opposite. They switched places."

I peeked into the room. The mask on one wall, white plastic with eye holes and a wide, beak-like nose. The mirror dominated the other wall. It was an antique, about three feet by four feet and sixty pounds of glass and gold-embossed wood.

I certainly hadn't moved the damn thing. It was too unwieldy and heavy. I may be tall for a girl, at five-nine, but I'm no bodybuilder. I couldn't move it, so there was no way that Julie, our five-foot-two and maybe one-hundred-pound roommate, could have.

I said as much and, as if on cue, Julie came out of the bathroom wearing a robe, her dark hair twisted up in a towel. "Don't look at me," she said, holding her hands in front of her and retreating to her room. Kara had already interrogated her.

"Dammit, I'm not crazy," Kara said, furrowing her brow.

"Maybe Mr. Delgado moved it during the day yesterday?" I suggested. "And last night you were too tired and didn't notice."

Julie's hairdryer clicked on in her room and the lights in Kara's room dimmed. "I'll ask him, but I doubt it," Kara said. "I should really talk to him about the wiring in this place anyway. Julie using a hairdryer shouldn't do this." She gestured at the flickering lights.

"It shouldn't?" I wondered if maybe Kara had been using a hair dryer the night the glass had jumped to its death. But I hadn't heard any noises like that.

"No. And have you noticed in the kitchen when you make toast? Same thing. I hate to think what putting in an AC unit or two this summer will do."

"Oh, I wouldn't have even thought of that."

"Yeah, well, that's what I'm here for. In the meantime, would you mind giving me a hand?" She stuck her thumb out at the mirror.

Between the two of us, with a couple of rest breaks and several bad words from me, we pulled the mask and the mirror down and moved each back to the spot Kara wanted it. Julie's hairdryer switched off and the lights in Kara's room brightened once more.

"Could Tad and Julie have moved it together?" Kara asked me.

"Did he sleep over last night?" I asked.

"No, he didn't," Julie said. She appeared in Kara's doorway, this time dressed in slacks and blouse, her hair pulled back in a bun. "Look, *Kare*, I didn't move the stupid mirror, and if Madison didn't move it, maybe *you* moved it in your sleep or something. If I remember correctly, it wasn't *me* who pulled pranks when we were at Smith—it was you. Whatever you're up to? It's not funny."

Kara's mouth opened and closed. "You know what? I need to get to work." She grabbed her jacket, keys, and bag. The door slammed behind her.

"Bitch," Julie mumbled, then gave me an apologetic look. "I need to go too, but I'll give her a couple of minutes to get ahead of me. There's nothing more awkward than standing on the platform with someone you're mad at." She pulled a tube of lipstick and a compact from her purse and began dabbing her lips with pink.

"I didn't move it, you know," I said. "It must weigh fifty or sixty pounds."

Julie nodded. "Do you think she has baby brain or something?"

"Huh?"

"Pregnant women. They forget stuff ... Hormones?"

I shook my head.

"When my sister was pregnant, she forgot all kinds of stuff. I guess you never hung out with a pregnant chick before?"

"Uh, I guess not."

"Right, right," she said breezily. "But really. Do you think she's losing it again? Didn't her doctor take her off her meds because of the baby?"

Kara had been hospitalized for a nervous breakdown about six months before. But once she'd been discharged, she'd been fine. She seemed to like her job as an administrative assistant and, since she'd gotten pregnant, she'd been even happier. She was excited about the prospect of becoming a mother to "Little Bean." She and her boyfriend Serge were even talking about getting married.

"I don't think so," I said. "She's been doing pretty good. Plus, I'm pretty sure she couldn't move that thing by herself."

"True. Are you working late today?" she asked. "Will you ask Mr. Delgado about it if you see him?"

"Sure," I said. "How about you? Got a job today?"

"I'm taking my portfolio to an ad agency."

Julie had been temping while trying to get into modeling or acting, but had been having difficulty.

"Let's hope I'm not too *ethnic* this time," she said. Apparently being of Korean descent qualified as "too ethnic" according to one casting agent.

11

I wished her luck and considered going back to bed. Usually when I know I'll be working late, I tend to sleep until noon. I'd woken earlier than usual and had been kept up by the business with the mirror. It was unsettling, to say the least. Was Kara having another breakdown? Had our landlord been moving her stuff around? Could the broken glass be connected? Was either Kara or Julie playing some kind of practical joke? Too many questions with no answers, while a little voice in the back of my head kept saying *ghost*.

There was no way I was getting back to sleep.

On my way out, I saw Mr. Delgado sweeping fallen petals from the dogwood tree in front of our building. I had to ask.

"Hey, Mr. Delgado. Sorry to bother you, but have you moved anything in our apartment recently?"

Mr. Delgado paused in his sweeping for a moment. "Why? What happened?"

I explained about the mask and mirror changing walls in Kara's room and he shook his woolly head when I finished. "I only comes into your apartment with your permission," he said in his thick Brooklyn accent. "You can ask my Marie."

"That's okay. We were just wondering. Maybe Kara was mistaken."

"Does that Kara ever sleepwalk?" he asked.

So much for him.

The next day, I stopped by an occult bookstore in Manhattan called Thirteen Books. The store was in Greenwich Village, just a few blocks away from where I worked. The space itself was clean and small, with books lining the walls and odd posters of UFOs and the Bermuda Triangle on the walls. The guy behind the counter was in his twenties, blond, with a bored affectation that seemed to say either "I've heard it all and seen it all," or "I don't believe any of this crap." I figured he belonged to the latter school, and felt a little spark of triumph when he responded to my inquiries with a tone that was all apathy.

"Yes," he sighed. "We have books on ghosts. Yes, we have books on poltergeists, too." He stood behind the counter and was enormously tall, at least six-four. "They're this way." He moved through the stacks toward the back left of the store and gestured to a shelf marked *Ghosts, Poltergeists, and Spirits*.

"Can you, um, recommend any in particular?" I asked

"What do you want to know?" It was more of a statement than a question, and one that indicated he really didn't want to hear the answer.

Being in retail myself, I wasn't impressed with his idea of customer service.

"I want to know if the weird shit happening in my apartment can be explained by something rational, or if the place is fucking haunted," I snapped.

He raised one blond eyebrow and turned to study the shelf. "We restock two of these fairly often. This one," he said, using a single finger to nudge a book forward on the shelf, "debunks a lot of the common phenomena." Then nudging another forward, said, "This one basically lists the common phenomena, and recounts a bunch of supposedly 'true' haunting stories to back it all up."

"*Supposedly* true?"

"I just work here," he sighed.

"Well, which one would you buy?"

"I guess that would depend on what kind of 'shit' had been happening at my apartment," he said with a hint of a smile.

I explained.

The eyebrow lifted again. "You don't look crazy," he said.

"Thanks. You don't get much business here, do you?"

"Oh, we do okay. Usually people just want to wander around and gawk. Sometimes they buy stuff. Not too many actually ask for help."

"So, which one should I buy?"

"Let me ask you a kind of a weird question. Was there any salt on the counter?"

"What?"

"You ever see someone take a salt shaker and pour some salt on the table, and then stand the shaker up at an angle on the pile of salt? Then they blow the salt away until there are only a few grains left, holding the salt shaker up at a seemingly impossible angle, all by itself." He held his hand diagonally, demonstrating.

I pushed the tips of his fingers until they were roughly at the same angle I'd seen the glass at. "Could it work with the glass like that?" I asked.

"You said there was water in it?"

"Almost full."

He frowned. "Probably not."

He pushed the debunking book back among the other books, and pulled *Apparitions, Ghosts, and Other Haunts* from the shelf. "I guess I'd try this one then," he said.

"Are you humoring me?"

He considered this a moment. "Maybe a little. But you don't seem crazy. A lot of the people who come in here do. You also don't seem to be desperate to believe in ghosts, and you're not interested in getting *me* to believe you. I hate it when they do that."

"Yeah, no. I just want to know the truth. That's all."

He walked with me back to the counter to ring me up. "I'm Derek, by the way," he said.

"Madison," I replied, offering him my hand. "Nice to meet you."

"Likewise," he said, giving it a quick but firm shake.

On my way out the door, he wished me luck. I turned back and wished him the same.

"With what?" he asked.

"Avoiding the crazies." The door swung shut on the sound of his laughter.

"What the *fuck*, Kara?"

Julie was screaming. It had been three days since the water had poured itself out and one since the mirror had been moved.

"I didn't touch it!" Kara shouted back.

Cringing, I slowly opened my door a few inches to see what was going on.

"This stuff was vintage!" Julie yelled from the doorway of her room. Her face was contorted and in one hand she gripped a handful of colorful ribbons. "Tad's going to kill me. Do you have any idea how much this stuff cost?"

Julie's boyfriend was a fashion photographer's assistant with an old-fashioned lingerie fetish. I'm not just talking lacy bras and such, but girdles, garters, stockings, corsets, the whole nine. When she slept alone, she tended to wear pajama sets with cute little holiday or animal themes. When he was sleeping over, Julie would only come out of her room if she was wearing a robe that reached her ankles. We generally didn't ask, but occasionally she'd show off things he'd bought for her. One set had a $200 price tag on the bra, and that was the *sale* price.

"I didn't do it," Kara said.

"*I didn't do it*," Julie spat back. "Were you jealous?"

"Jules, I did *not* touch your lingerie," Kara said.

"I swear."

"Well, did *she* do it? Why'd you invite a crazy girl to live with us anyway?"

"Shhh!" Kara exclaimed.

I slowly closed my door, listening to the dull roar of their lowered voices talking about me.

Things were pretty awkward for the next few days. I tried to be home as little as possible while trying to figure out a way to tell Julie and Kara that we might have a ghost. As if Julie needed another reason to think that I was crazy.

Then I woke to the sound of screams again, shrill and hysterical in the early morning. I flung my door open and ran down the hall, where Kara stood in a nightgown and bathrobe, pounding on Julie's door, shouting, "Jules, unlock the door!"

"Just stay away from me!" Julie shrieked. "I'm calling the cops!"

"What happened? Julie?" I said to the door.

"I don't know," Kara said. "I was making tea and I heard her scream."

The door was locked, and inside the room we could hear Julie talking on her cell phone, presumably to a 911 operator. The words were indistinct, but she seemed to be calming down. Thirty seconds or a minute passed. "Are you guys still there?" she asked. Her voice sounded small and scared, but closer, like she was just on the other side of the door.

Then her doorknob clicked. She came out of her bedroom with her cell phone gripped tightly against her left ear. She closed the door behind her. Her hair was a mussed mess, her eyes were red, and she wore pink pajamas with little cows all over them.

Her outfit was way merrier than she was.

"Are you okay?" I asked.

She nodded.

"That's one of my roommates," she said into the phone.

Kara asked her what happened, and Julie gestured back to her room.

"Can I go in?" Kara asked.

Julie asked the 911 operator if it was okay. She shook her head. "They say there could be evidence in there." The person on the other end was asking her something. "Do we have a doorstop, or anything like one?" she asked. "Or a chair? To wedge under the knob?"

Kara and I looked at each other with wide eyes. Kara went to the kitchen while I searched my room. I returned with a three-ring binder and Kara came back with one of the kitchen chairs, and we used both of them to secure the door. The whole time, Julie gave yes and no answers to questions that we couldn't hear.

After a few minutes, four policemen arrived. Julie thanked whoever was on the phone with her and hung up. One of the cops, a tall older guy, told all three of us to go wait outside in the hall with another cop, a younger guy with really short hair.

We went. Kara tried asking Julie questions, but Julie just shook her head robotically.

A few minutes later, the cop who'd sent us out called us back in.

"Young ladies," he said, "I don't want you to walk into that room, but I want you to look in at that bed and tell me what you see." Kara and I edged closer, and the cop pulled open the door. What I saw horrified me.

Among the rich rose and orange hues of Julie's walls and the colorful watercolor artwork she'd hung on them, one thing stood out. The black handle of a huge chef's knife stood straight up, the stainless-steel blade stabbed deep into the pillow that still held the indentation of Julie's head.

"Oh my God," we said in unison.

CHAPTER TWO

THE POLICE WERE IN OUR APARTMENT FOR HOURS. More uniforms and two detectives, one male, one female, showed up. Photos were taken. They dusted for fingerprints. They bagged the knife.

We were each interviewed separately.

After the female detective questioned Julie and Kara, it was my turn. She sat at our kitchen table, an angry-looking blonde woman with a penetrating stare. She'd given her name as Detective Ramsay.

Before I'd even finished sitting down, she said, "So when did you start using again?"

"Huh? Using what?"

"Well, I see here that you met Ms. Reynolds at a rehab facility. You want to tell me about that?"

"It wasn't a rehab facility. It was a home for people suffering from mental illness."

"Yes, and for addicts in recovery. You didn't answer my question."

I crossed my arms. "I'm not *using* anything."

"So what were you on before you checked in there?"

"On? I wasn't *on* anything. I have a condition. A

dissociative fugue, the doctors called it."

"Right. And you say you lost your ID?"

"No, I don't have any. I didn't have any when they found me."

"Convenient."

Oh, Rice Krispies. She thinks I did this.

"So where did you run away from?"

Great. This again. A lot of cops don't believe me about what happened to me. Detective Ramsay clearly didn't.

"Look, I didn't do this."

"Never said you did. Just trying to clarify your background. Did you run away from a group home? Lots of kids do. Foster family? You'd think there'd be a record."

"I don't know!"

"Uh huh."

The other detective entered the kitchen behind her. "C'mon Fran, give the girl a break. I already verified her story."

He was short—maybe five-foot-six—and good looking, probably in his mid-thirties, with dark hair and a square chin that had been freshly shaved. He was the kind of guy who you might mistake for a model if he'd been taller.

"Why don't you come out to the living room, Miss Roberts. Your roommates are in there."

The female detective scowled at me and the feet of the kitchen chair squealed beneath me as I got up.

Kara and Julie sat close together on the couch

and I plunked into the chair. The female detective leaned against the kitchen doorway while the male detective took the lead.

"I'm Detective Wilson," the male detective said. "I've canvassed your neighbors and landlord and your apartment has been searched. It seems you had some kind of intruder last night or early this morning."

Like that was news.

"Although we're not ruling out the possibility of a jealous ex-girlfriend or boyfriend, we think it's someone who has keys to the apartment, maybe someone who used to live here," he said. "We think this because there are no signs of forced entry. It's possible the intruder entered from the fire escape outside your roommate's room, but we think it's more likely they entered through the apartment and locked her door again before they left."

Kara nodded. It was a logical explanation. Of course, she hadn't seen a glass of water pour itself all over our kitchen floor and then dash itself to pieces.

"You believe that it wasn't one of us?" I asked.

Detective Wilson inhaled and exhaled loudly through his nose. "We're fairly certain, Miss Roberts. There were no fingerprints on the knife nor any foreign ones on the inside doorknob. A number of items have been taken as evidence for forensics.

"Your roommate Miss Moon has not accused you, nor is she pressing charges against either of you. As I understand it, she has already packed a bag . . ." he left off doubtfully and Julie nodded. He continued, "I suggest you get all of your locks changed, make sure the windows are locked, and we'll see what we can dig up on the few leads we have. In the meantime, you and Miss Reynolds might want to find somewhere else to stay for a few days too."

Kara thanked him for his time and he gave each of us his card in case we thought of something that would help with the case. Julie was heading out to go stay at Tad's. Kara had called in late to work, so once the police cleared out, she got dressed and went in. Mr. Delgado said the locksmiths would be over first thing in the morning, and he would take care of letting them in if we weren't home.

Kara wouldn't be; she was planning on staying with her boyfriend in Harlem. I'd be all alone in the apartment. I didn't have much choice. I'd only been at my job for about two months, and while I was friendly with Mac, the owner, I didn't exactly want to ask him if I could sleep on his couch for a few days while his three-year-old twin sons and newborn daughter screamed at all hours.

One of my co-workers, Billy, claimed that he slept on park benches most nights, sobering up after the bartenders at the Slaughtered Lamb bought him one too many shots. He was no help. Likewise, my best work friend Celeste lived in the dorms at NYU and was always complaining about how small her room was and how her roommate smelled like corn chips. There were others, but the store had a high turnover rate and Billy, Celeste, and Mac were the only ones I could even think about asking.

I figured it wouldn't kill me to stay in the apartment for the night. It wasn't like changing the locks was going to keep the ghost out anyway. The knife-wielding ghost.

Suddenly Billy's park bench didn't seem so bad.

After I showered, I threw on a pair of jeans and a long-sleeve black t-shirt with my Converse sneakers and left for work.

I started reading *Apparitions, Ghosts, and Other Haunts* on the subway and found very quickly that our ghost, if that was indeed what it was, was behaving like a classic poltergeist (or "noisy ghost" as translated from German). The moving of objects was basically what poltergeists—well, "lived for" wouldn't be the right term, but you know what I mean.

After coming out of the subway, I passed by Thirteen Books and decided to stop. Derek was there, perched on a stool behind the counter, his long legs at awkward angles.

"Hey," I said.

"Hey back," he said. "How's your water-wasting ghost?"

"It's graduated to shredding lingerie and stabbing pillows."

"Say what now?" he said, putting down the book he was reading.

I told him the tale. He was incredulous, especially when I said I was still staying in the apartment.

"You've got to have some friends or family you can stay with for a day or two."

"Um . . . no."

"No?" The frown on my face stopped him from asking additional questions. "Okay, it's none of my business, but really, you should get the hell out of there."

"I thought you didn't believe in ghosts."

"I don't. But I do believe in psychos. You shouldn't be in that apartment by yourself."

"I'll be fine," I said, mostly believing it.

"I have a couch you can crash on."

"You don't even know me!" I laughed. "And I don't know you."

"So? You have a trustworthy face. And so do I. Plenty of people have told me." I took a good look at his face. Not bad looking, with a hint of freckles across a long straight nose and a wide forehead. His eyes, which I'd thought were purely brown before, had hints of green in the afternoon light and were bordered by blonde lashes and brows that were just slightly darker than his short blond hair.

"Do you have a roommate?" I asked.

"Nope, just me. I live in the apartment upstairs," he said, pointing to the ceiling.

"Seriously? How'd you luck into that?"

"My uncle. He owns this place, the whole building. Asked me if I wanted to be manager when I graduated college. I said sure. And here I am."

"And here you are, asking a strange girl to shack up with you."

"Hey, no one said anything about shacking. I just offered the couch for a night or two until things settle down at your place."

"Well, it's nice of you, but I don't have any of my stuff. I'd have to go back there anyway, and—"

"I'll go with you," he interrupted. "Look—I really don't think you ought to go back into that apartment alone until your landlord has the locks changed and someone goes through and makes sure there aren't any homeless people living in crawlspaces or between the walls or anything."

"You really think it's an intruder, huh?"

"It's a logical explanation."

"And the water?"

"Well, whether it's a stabby phantom or a freaky stalker, I just don't think I could live with the guilt if something happened to you."

"Thanks, that's comforting."

"Good. Then it's settled." I shook my head. I'd clearly lost. I didn't exactly mind losing, though. It wasn't like I relished the idea of spending the night in the apartment alone.

"I close up at seven-thirty," he said. "How about you, are you off work now? On a late lunch break?"

I explained that I was on my way in to work at Christopher Street Comics. Derek knew exactly where it was and said he'd be waiting for me outside when I finished my shift.

"You're sure about this?"

"Never surer," he said with a grin.

I had to admit it. He *did* have a trustworthy face.

Christopher Street Comics was as usual as usual can be when you work among six-foot-tall shelves of comic books with superhero t-shirts arranged on the walls and ceiling. It was slow most days of the week. Serious comics junkies only came in on Wednesdays, which is when the new comics showed up, and the tourists usually came on Fridays and Saturdays. Since the shop was in Greenwich Village, we also got our share of drunks wandering in at night, but this night was dead. Billy, who had recently turned twenty-one, spent most of the night cracking jokes and complaining about the price of drinks in the city, while Mac hid out in the office doing orders or inventory checks or whatever the hell he did back there.

I checked bags and ran the register for most of the night, and right around closing, as Mac was locking the front door, I saw Derek, tall and blond, leaning against the railing in front of the store. He wore jeans and a plaid button-up over a dark t-shirt with some writing on it. I was pretty sure it was what he'd been wearing earlier, but not positive.

Had he changed his outfit for me?

Was this a date?

Derek waved at me.

"We're closed," Mac said.

"Uh . . . he's actually waiting for me," I said, and waved back.

"Oh yeah?" Mac asked. "Got a hot date?" Mac,

a trim forty-something with graying dark hair in a ponytail, usually wore jeans with perfectly ironed dress shirts and ties. He'd been married for however many years and was being hassled at home daily by his wife and kids. He was always asking us if we had any "hot dates" lined up for our weekends. We figured he was living vicariously.

I took my cash drawer out of the register and handed it to him with the register tape I'd already taken out. "Yep, popcorn and a movie," I said. Not that Derek had said anything about movies or popcorn, but it was simpler than trying to explain what was really going on. Mac headed back to the office to count out my drawer.

"What are you going to see?" asked Billy, as he swept the floor.

Crud cakes. I hadn't anticipated that question, so I stalled a minute while digging through my backpack trying to find where I'd stuffed my subway pass.

"I don't know, we're watching something at his place," I said. Billy, dressed all in black with his black hair, piercings, and tattoos, paused in his sweeping, eyed me up and down, then stared outside at Derek.

"What do you think? Is he an ax murderer?" I asked, mostly teasing. Mostly.

"Eh, he looks alright. Tall bastard, isn't he?"

"Yeah, I guess so."

"I didn't know you were into Sasquatch, Maddy. You're a tough nut to crack, aren't you, Miss Mystery Past?"

"Yep, that's me," I said. "So stop asking." I hated questions about my past and never answered any of them. Mostly because I didn't know the answers myself.

"Fair enough. Just be careful with that guy. It's the normal ones you gotta watch out for. If you don't come in tomorrow, I'm going down to the precinct with a description of him."

"Thanks, Billy. I didn't know you cared."

"You're the kind of girl people just want to watch out for."

Before I could respond to that, Mac came out of the office and said my drawer was exactly right, as usual, and wished me a goodnight. Billy put down his broom, and wrote something on a scrap of paper.

He then unlocked the door and held it open, offering me the scrap of paper with his other hand. "Here's my number. Call me if you need anything," he said. Not that I had a cell phone, but it was the thought that counted, I guess.

I suspected he'd said it for Derek's benefit.

I shoved the number in my jeans and said, "Hello."

Billy locked the door behind me. The night air was chilly, though the street was still vibrantly lit and busy with several passersby.

"So where do you live?" Derek asked as we began walking down the street.

"In Dumbo," I said, referring to the name of my Brooklyn neighborhood. Dumbo stands for "Down

Under Manhattan Bridge Overpass." I didn't believe that was its actual name either until I saw it on a map.

"Excellent," Derek replied.

"Why is that excellent?"

"Because my chariot awaits," he said, gesturing toward the end of the block.

Several cars were parked in the metered spaces on Seventh Avenue. "Which one is yours?"

"The little white one," he said.

The little white one was an antique sports car I recognized, not in prime shape, but still cute.

"Nice Karmann Ghia," I said.

"Hey, a girl who knows her cars!" he said. "Are you a car buff?"

"Not really." I wasn't sure how I knew. It was just one of those things.

Derek chivalrously opened the door on my side first, then went around to his.

I climbed in. The seats were scuffed and cracked leather. A blanket and some books lay on the tiny back seat, but I didn't get a good look at the titles.

"Do you want the blanket to sit on?" Derek asked me as he got in. "I know the seats can be a little rough if you're not used to them."

"How do you even fit in here?" I asked, my knees bumping the glove box. I'm five-nine in flats. He had to be at least six-five.

"Ah, sorry about that. The seat moves back," he said, reaching over as if to dig under my legs and then stopped, awkwardly. "Right. So . . . there's a knob and lever under the seat. Just pull it and push with your legs."

I did what he said and was immediately rewarded with more legroom. "Ahhhh," I sighed. "Much better."

"I haven't had anyone else in here in a while," he said.

"Do you know how to get to Dumbo from here?"

"Sure," he said and started up the little engine.

My apartment was completely dark when we got there. I turned on the hallway light and noticed that the floor lamp in the living room—the one that was always cold to the touch—was lying on its side.

Pointing, Derek began asking, "Was that—?"

"No."

We stood there staring for a few seconds.

"Um, maybe we should—" I began, but he held up a hand and put a finger to his lips. He then grabbed a large golf umbrella that Kara kept near the front door.

"Which room is yours?" he asked.

I gestured, and he went and checked it.

I reviewed the contents of my room, trying to imagine what it would look like to his eyes. Boring, probably. Futon bed, desk, laptop, a small bureau. Nothing on the walls except a bulletin board with a calendar tacked to it I got free from a drugstore. Make that *super* boring.

He emerged and declared it safe, then checked the bathroom across the hall. I heard the jingling of the shower curtain hooks as he checked the shower for psychos.

While he secured the bathroom, I went to my room and packed my backpack with two days' worth of clothes. I again lamented the room's anonymous drabness. By comparison, Kara had masks and the mirror and framed prints of Broadway shows on her walls, with moss green and violet bedding. Julie had her paintings and beads and colored lanterns hanging from the walls and ceilings, with orange and rose sheets and comforter. My sheets were white and my walls were empty, except for the bulletin board and an old key hanging from it. It might as well have been my hospital room.

My roommates' rooms were reflections of who they were. But who was I?

Nobody.

After Derek came out of the bathroom, I went in and quickly packed a few more necessary items, and we got the hell out of there.

Once we were in the car, we were laughing, or maybe I was laughing at myself, and he was laughing at me, but either way, it suddenly seemed very funny. Running from ghosts. Who does that?

Twenty minutes later, we were back in Manhattan and he'd parked in a long-term garage and handed his keys off to an attendant who called him Mr. Miner.

"Miner? Is that how you can afford that fancy car? You struck it rich during the gold rush?"

"Not that kind of miner. M-I-N-O-R."

"Derek *Minor*?" I asked, trying not to laugh as we walked down the block. "But you're so tall!"

"Yes, yes, it's very funny, Madison . . . what's your last name anyway?"

"It's . . . Roberts," I said. It still felt so foreign that I almost forgot it that time.

"You sure?" he asked, an amused look on his face.

And here was where it got tricky. Did I tell him the truth? Or did I play it off? If I told him, would he regret asking me to stay with him?

I gave him a look from under my eyelashes. "If I told you it was an assumed name to protect my identity, would you believe me?" I asked sweetly.

"Have it your way. I'll get it out of you some other time," he said.

We reached the building where Thirteen Books was located. A metal security fence had been pulled down over the front glass and door, so that you could still see the book display in the window behind it, but there was no way you could get in without bolt cutters.

Derek unlocked the door to the left of the store. "After you," he said. Inside, a short hallway extended back with a set of stairs going several floors upward, lit by a ceiling lamp. He led me up the stairs, taking them two at a time. And yeah, I checked. He had a nice butt.

On the second floor, his keys jingled as he unlocked his apartment. "Come on in," he said, moving forward and hanging his keys on a hook near the entryway.

"The living room's through there," Derek said.

I moved through the archway at the end of the kitchen and stood amazed, facing a huge swordfish mounted on the wall of the living room over a futon couch. The fish had to be about six feet long, including the "sword" part.

"Holy carp!" I exclaimed.

"Yeah," Derek gave a short chuckle. "Meet Charlie."

"Charlie?"

"You know, like the tuna mascot?"

"Oh, right," I said. Some dim memory of a cartoon fish in glasses that talked like Mr. Delgado flit through my mind. A commercial.

"You're not a member of PETA, are you?" Derek asked, after I'd been silent maybe a beat too long.

"A member of what? No, no, sorry . . . just lost in thought. I don't think that guy's a tuna, though."

"Yeah, but there aren't any celebrity swordfish."

"You like fishing?"

"I used to go with my granddad down in Florida when I was a kid. Loved it."

I turned to take in the rest of the room, which was dominated by an enormous flat screen TV surrounded by shelves and shelves of DVDs.

I whistled a low whistle. "My, my. I guess I was right," I said.

"About what?"

"Wanna watch a movie?" I asked.

Ten minutes later we were sitting together on the futon, sharing a bowl of buttery microwave popcorn, watching a movie he'd just bought. In it, two conman brothers convince an eccentric heiress to join them in a heist, planning to rob her as well. What they don't plan on is one of the brothers falling in love with her, or for the guy they swindled to seek revenge.

My hand brushed against Derek's twice when we reached for popcorn at the same time. And I was abnormally aware that his leg was less than a foot away from my leg. I felt both awkward and comfortable with him. It was a weird feeling.

The movie was romantic and crazy and fun and sad all at the same time. As the credits rolled, I found myself wanting to rest my head on Derek's shoulder, so I did.

"Oh, hey," Derek said, and abruptly stood up. "I should probably get you some sheets and a pillow and stuff."

Did he think I'd fallen asleep on him? I swallowed my embarrassment and thanked him. He disappeared through a doorway and came out a few minutes later carrying a bundle of blankets and linens.

"You know, I could sleep out here if you want the bedroom," he said. "It wouldn't be a problem."

"No, this is fine, really. Thank you."

"The bathroom is through there, on the right," he said, "and there are fresh towels on the rack if you need one."

He seemed to be going to a lot of trouble to make me feel welcome. It was nice, especially after feeling so unwanted at home.

"You've been really sweet," I said. He sighed. My comment seemed to have deflated him somehow.

"You must be tired," I said. "Just leave the sheets and stuff, I'll make up the bed."

"Do you know how to open the futon?" he asked.

His futon was different than mine, so he opened it for me and I thanked him. Again. I seemed to be doing that a lot.

"Goodnight," I said. I had already kept him up late as it was. I didn't even know when he was supposed to open the store.

He wished me a goodnight too and closed the door to his room.

Damn, I thought as I wrestled the sheets onto the floppy futon mattress. *Damn, damn, double-damn.*

I shimmied out of my clothes and pulled on an extra-large t-shirt. I wasn't even slightly sleepy, so I just lay on my back and looked around the room. My eyes fell on a shelf of liquor bottles. *Damn, damn, double-damn, butterscotch schnapps?*

A dusty bottle of butterscotch schnapps stood

next to a bottle of Bailey's Irish Cream. That made me think of Kara's mom.

I'd met Kara while at Spring House, the name of the center for people with various mental health issues that I'd been sent to after my diagnosis. Kara was a "member" there too, not-quite recovering from the nervous breakdown she'd suffered after her mother's death. She just sat and stared most of the time, moving through the cycle of meds and meetings and group therapy sessions like a zombie. Then one day, during group, she said she was supposed to go to Ireland with her mother, and then got quiet again.

Later that afternoon, I asked about her mother. I didn't remember mine, so I was curious about what moms were like. She told stories of her mother the beauty queen, who loved Broadway shows, and Bailey's on the rocks. She told me stories about her mother reading "The Frog Prince" to her when she was little, and taking her shopping for her first bra when she was fourteen, and plenty of other stories. And while Kara talked about her mother, that zombie face lost some of its blankness, and her blue eyes took on a personality for the first time since I'd met her.

It was Kara's breakthrough. The therapists and doctors had asked her to talk about her mother plenty of times, but for some reason, she chose to talk to me. We became friends, and when it was time for her to leave, she told me she'd be getting an apartment in Brooklyn, and if I needed a place to stay, I should stay in touch. A couple of months later, job at Chris Street Comics secured, I called her and moved in that weekend.

And everything had been fine, mostly, until all the ghost stuff started.

I wondered how Kara and Julie were. I felt like a bad roommate for not trying to get in touch with them. But their cell phone numbers were written on that free calendar back in my bedroom and there was no way I was going there again until the sun came up.

I looked at the bedroom door, just a few feet away.

I wondered if Derek was still awake. I wondered what he wore to bed. Boxers? Briefs? None of the above?

Sleep didn't come easy.

CHAPTER THREE

KARA, REMEMBERING THAT I DIDN'T HAVE A cell phone, called me at work the next afternoon. She'd heard from Mr. Delgado, who told her that the locks on all the doors had been changed. She was planning on going home tonight. Would I be there?

That was a good question. Maybe there was something to this whole intruder idea. Maybe I'd just been imagining things when I thought I saw the glass of water pour out. It's not like my brain never played tricks on me. But did I really want to go back to an apartment that some crazy person was trying to get into?

"What about the windows next to the fire escape?" I asked.

"Mr. Delgado says he's going to cut some pieces of wood for us to use to wedge them closed."

"That's nice of him."

"Oh, he'll probably charge us for it eventually. So will you be there?"

"Well . . ." I said, "I kind of sort of have a date-type-thing after work and—"

"Shut up! You have a date?"

Kara had been after me for weeks to "get out there." She thought it would help me feel more "normal."

"What's his name?" she asked. "Where'd you meet him?"

"Derek. He—"

Just then I noticed Mac watching me. I realized I was talking on the store phone about my personal life, which was a no-no. He didn't mind if his workers periodically sent text messages, but conversations were off-limits. I made an apologetic gesture and said into the phone, "You know what? I can't talk right now. At work and all. Tell me your cell number and I'll call you later when I get a break." Holding the phone against my ear with my shoulder, I scribbled the number she gave me on the back of a receipt and hung up.

"Sorry about that," I said to Mac. "That was my roommate."

He frowned. "You still haven't gotten your own phone?"

"Of course she hasn't. Because you don't pay us enough," said Celeste, who was handing a customer's bag back to him.

Every store in New York City doesn't demand you check any large bags or backpack you're carrying, but it's a pretty common practice in comic book shops as far as I can tell. Another common practice in comic book shops in New York City is to hire pretty girls with weird colored hair.

This week, Celeste's hair was bright pink, and as usual, she was wearing clothes that matched her hair. The previous month her hair had been blue, and she'd worn several variations of the shade: royal blue shirts, sky blue plaid skirts, azure dresses and even blue suede boots. Today she was in neon pink overalls worn over a bubble gum pink t-shirt along with a pair of pastel pink combat boots. "I think we should all get raises, don't you?" Celeste asked me, wrinkling her nose. She had a small, heart-shaped face, with brown eyes and a small mouth. Along with her slight stature and monochrome style she seemed like a character out of those weird Japanese cartoons we kept behind the counter.

"What do you care?" Billy asked, emerging from the back of the store.

"What's that supposed to mean?" Celeste asked.

"You go to NYU. NYU isn't cheap. Your parents must be loaded," he said.

"We're maybe well off, but we're not rich, if that's what you mean."

"That's what rich people always say."

Celeste's face turned a bright pink that almost matched her hair. She opened her mouth to say something back, but I interjected quickly. "Where did you go to college, Billy?"

"Pshh," he said. "I didn't. College is for suckers."

Celeste huffed a mighty sigh and announced she was going on her break.

With the class warfare temporarily de-escalated, I went back to what I had been doing before Kara called. The 11a.m. to 7p.m. shift was usually pretty slow, so I passed the time leafing through a *Captain America* graphic novel that Billy had insisted I read. In it, Cap learned that his long-thought-dead partner had returned, mysteriously unaged, as an enemy operative.

"How far have you gotten?" he asked.

"I'm almost done," I said. "But I want to go back and read the other parts about Bucky."

"So you found out who he is?"

"Yeah—but what happened to him?"

"Brainwashing," Billy said. "It's pretty fucked. Imagine finding your best friend after all those years and then he doesn't even know who you are."

"Imagine," I said. I wondered if I was anyone's Bucky.

"I'd rather be dead than be brainwashed, you know? Not in control of my own destiny? What if I hurt someone I cared about? Fuck that."

I nodded, and went back to reading, not trusting my voice not to give me away.

Confession: I don't hate comic books. In fact, I kind of like them. I guess I used to read them when I was a kid, because I know a little bit about a lot of different ones—old ones, though, not recent issues. When I'd seen the HELP WANTED sign in the front window, and Mac had interviewed me and asked me if I knew anything about comics, like different titles for Spider-Man, I'd rattled off *Amazing*, *Spectacular*, and *Web of*. Some of those hadn't been published in years. Impressed with my arcane knowledge, he hired me on the spot.

The other thing—and the main reason why I'd accepted the crappy pay—was that Mac didn't care that I didn't have any previous experience working in a comic book store, or any work experience at all, for that matter. Every other job I'd applied for wanted applicable experience among many other requirements I didn't meet.

So, I worked for Mac, despite the not-great hours and minimal pay. It was the best a non-entity like myself could hope for in a world where you didn't exist if you weren't in the computer.

When I took a quick break later in the evening to call Kara back from a kiosk on the street. First, I asked how she and Little Bean were doing, and she said they were fine. I told her I had the next day off and could meet her at the apartment whenever she wanted.

"Who cares about that?" she said. "Tell me about Derek."

I told her I'd fill her in when I saw her, which did nothing to do satisfy her curiosity. Then I grabbed a slice from the pizza place on the corner and went back to work.

When my shift ended, I went to Derek's store. I could see him through the window, perched on the stool behind the counter, reading a book. He was dressed in jeans and a striped dress shirt unbuttoned over a gray tee.

"Hey," I said as I entered. Derek looked up and smiled.

"Hey," he said. "I was wondering if I was going to see you tonight."

"And here I am. When are you closing?"

"At 7:30. Did you want to go up to my place until I'm done?"

"No, that's okay, I'll just look around the store if you don't mind."

"You sure?" he asked, as if he couldn't believe I'd find anything interesting to pass the time.

"Sure I'm sure," I said. "Look around, the posters, the books, this bulletin board—holy crap, do people really still hold séances?"

Multicolored flyers were tacked all over the old corkboard across from the counter, featuring ads for psychic readings, new age healers, and yes, séances, among other oddities, like ads for a "genuine" crystal ball, or someone who would pay for "REAL EVIDENCE OF UFOs!" The word "real" was underlined three times. Another flyer wanted volunteers for a ghost hunt at a historic house in Tarrytown, which was north of the city.

I wasn't sure how I knew that, like many odd bits of information my brain coughed up.

"Yep. Séances, voodoo, witches, we get 'em all," Derek said with a disgusted sigh.

"How do you stand it?" I asked.

"Can't," he said in what sounded like an English accent.

"You can't stand it . . . but you still work here?" I asked, puzzled.

He laughed. "No, no. Not 'can't.' Kant, K-A-N-T.

The philosopher," he said and held up the book he was reading.

"Never heard of him," I said.

"Too bad. You might be interested in his definition of enlightenment."

"Would you hate me if I said I wasn't interested?"

"No, not at all. Most people aren't interested in philosophy. I was dumb enough to major in it."

"I don't think it's dumb."

"Well, it didn't exactly prepare me for a job on Wall Street," he said, perhaps a little bitterly.

"Do you want to work on Wall Street?"

"Not really. Just . . . parents. You know how it is."

I wished I did. I gave a non-committal nod and picked up a book on one of the nearby shelves. It turned out to be about dowsing—the practice of finding underground water deposits with a forked stick—a subject I had even less interest in than Kant.

"Nevermind my white people problems," he said. "Go ahead and browse. I'm going to pre-count the register and if no one comes in, I'll close up a little early. You feel like Chinese delivery tonight? My treat."

One thing that you learn when you're poor: Never turn down free food.

Approximately half an hour later, we were eating sesame chicken and mu shu pork in his living room. Derek asked me how long I'd been working at

Christopher Street.

"Just over two months."

"You like it?"

"Yeah, so far. The pay isn't great but it's casual and the owner is nice."

"That's cool," he replied. "So how long have you been living in Dumbo?"

Uh-oh, Spaghetti-O. "About a month," I said, immediately stuffing an enormous piece of chicken in my mouth. This was the conversation I'd been dreading most of the day.

It was one thing to hang out and watch a movie for the evening and sleep on the guy's couch. It was another to sit down and eat food together and chat like we were on a date and might conceivably see one another again. And that was the problem; I thought that maybe I did want to see him again.

"Mmm," I said, as I speared a piece of broccoli. "This is really good."

"Mine too. So, where'd you live before that?" *Rat heads.*

I chewed my broccoli a little longer than I needed to. "Why do you ask?"

"Well, you don't have a New York accent, so I guessed you probably weren't born here. Yesterday you said you didn't have friends or family to stay with, and if you've just been living in that apartment for a month, I figured you just moved here."

Double damn, he'd been paying attention.

I exhaled. "You could say that."

"I could say that. I could. But *should* I say it?" he

46

asked nonchalantly, rolling bits of pork and vegetables up in a sort of tortilla thing that had come with his food.

"Probably not," I said and frowned.

"So you didn't just move here?" he asked, then took a bite of the mu shu pork burrito he'd made.

"Wellll . . . if I tell you," I paused, trying to figure out what to say next.

"You'll have to kill me?" he asked.

"No. Yes. I mean—no. No literal killing. It's just complicated."

"Did you run away from a cult?"

"No?" I didn't think I had. But it was possible, I supposed.

"You don't sound sure of that."

"What if I'm not?"

"Not sure? Not sure if they were a cult, not sure if you ran away, or not sure about something else?"

"Something else."

"You really don't want to answer this question, do you?"

No. I really didn't. But if we were going to date, it would have to come out some time.

"Would you believe me if I told you that I don't actually know?"

"Don't know what?"

I took a deep breath. "I don't know where I lived before."

He'd put down his fork and gave me a critical look.

"You're not kidding, are you?"

47

CHAPTER FOUR

THE DAY IS GRAY, WITH A CHILL IN THE AIR. I'M standing on a sidewalk in New York City and I have no idea how I got there. I don't know what day it is.

I'm wearing jeans, a large black V-neck sweater over a hot pink tank top, and a pair of black Converse sneakers. I see my reflection in a shop window: bobbed blonde hair, high cheekbones, a wide mouth, and I know that I'm seeing my own reflection. But who am I? What name goes with this face? I check my front and back pockets, and find only a matchbook for a restaurant called Raoul's. I see my hands, and I know that they're my hands. But I'm not wearing any jewelry on them, no rings, watches, or bracelets.

Scared, confused, I look around and see a sign for Madison Avenue, and beneath that sign, I see a man in a dark blue uniform with a shiny brass badge. I approach and ask him to help me. And he does, calling an ambulance because I'm an EDP, Emotionally Disturbed Person, even if I'm not so much disturbed as confused and upset, because shouldn't I remember who I am?

They drive me over to Bellevue, because that's where the EDPs go, and that's where I remain for the following week. The first couple of days involve tests of all kinds. MRIs,

CAT scans, blood tests, psychological questionnaires, along with physical examinations. The doctors have difficulty diagnosing me. I have no brain trauma, no physical trauma, not even a single bruise or bump on the head. No drugs or alcohol in my bloodstream. As far as my body is concerned, I'm perfectly healthy.

When it's determined that I am not a danger to myself or others, a case worker escorts me to the local precinct, where my face is compared to hundreds of missing persons photographs. Nothing matches. I don't have any tattoos or distinguishing marks for them to go on. They ask if they can fingerprint me and I say yes, but my fingerprints don't turn up anything useful either. They even send my info to Interpol and Canada, without any results.

I pick up the name "Madison" when one of the interns, on hearing my "oldest" memory, says it reminds him of a movie. "Just like in Splash. Tom Hanks falls in love with a mermaid. He names her 'Madison' because he found her on Madison Avenue."

It's better than Patient 551236, or Jane Doe, which is a bit too corpse-like. After that, everyone calls me Madison. We pick the last name Roberts because I smile really wide, which one of the nurses says made me look like a famous actress I've never heard of.

Now that I've seen a couple of her movies? I don't really see the resemblance.

Or maybe I just don't smile very often.

I have all of my wisdom teeth, which probably puts me, based on other physical characteristics and my appearance, anywhere from eighteen to twenty years old. My natural hair color is strawberry blonde.

I am not a virgin.

I speak French, almost fluently. Though my accent is not that of a native speaker, it's good enough to pass. I know my multiplication tables. I can read and write. I know traffic laws, and it seems likely that I know how to drive, but I have weird blind spots. Mostly technology related.

I know essential things about the world I live in, like the names of cities and general rules of etiquette. But as far as my cultural and personal memory? A book missing half its pages seems to be an apt description.

A reporter writes a story about me, then a couple of others, and I'm interviewed on a morning TV show. The hosts implore any viewers with information concerning my identity to call in, but no one does.

I take a polygraph test and pass, then another one and pass. I agree to try a dose of sodium pentathol—popularly and erroneously known as truth serum—to see if it will help me remember. It doesn't. We even try hypnosis, but it doesn't conjure up a single detail about my identity or past.

At that point, the psychologists feel they've exhausted all options. My official diagnosis is dissociative fugue, a condition in which a person who has experienced trauma loses all sense of their own identity. Personal information—including memories—are inaccessible. Unexpected travel is part of the diagnosis as well, as the person flees the inciting traumatic event.

So my brain is trying to escape . . . something. They said it should go away on its own one day, and I'll just suddenly remember who I am.

The only other clue to my identity I have—although I hadn't noticed it at first—is a key. Once I was at Bellevue *and changed into the backless hospital gown they gave me, I found a weird skeleton key hanging from a chain beneath my shirt. It's oddly shaped, with not one set of teeth at the end, but two that mirror each other, like the silhouettes of two hands, side by side. It's engraved with the word FICHET. The police don't know anything about the key and suggest I see a locksmith.*

I see three different locksmiths at hardware stores. Each one says pretty much the same thing. There are thousands and thousands of antique keys that no one knows anything about—they're just curiosities and decorations, sold in estate sales to dealers who in turn sell them to collectors. Some are just made as decorations. Without a serial number, there's no way of knowing what my key goes to, if anything. None of them recognize the brand name of the key, Fichet, either.

In the meantime, the police and doctors tell me I'm supposed to go on and live my life.

So I do. I get a job and a place to live and friends. I get a life. But is it my life? And if it isn't, whose is it?

Derek looked across the table at me, a mixture of confusion and concern on his face.

I moved my fork around inside the white carton I'd been eating from. I hadn't eaten anything since that last bite of broccoli, and didn't feel much like eating more now.

"You really *aren't* kidding about this."

"Not even a little bit," I said.

"That's why you're weird about your last name."

"Well, yeah, because I don't have one. Not a legal

one, anyway."

"Huh."

"Huh? That's it?"

"Well, it's a lot to process. This is crazy. How do you survive? Do you even have an ID?"

"Not really. Without a birth certificate, social security number, or passport, it's pretty much impossible to get one. My social worker took me to the DMV to get a state ID, but we couldn't. All I have is my ID from Spring House."

"Then how do you have a job?"

"He pays us under the table. A tax thing, he says."

"So . . . there just aren't any clues at all to who you really are?" Derek asked.

"Nothing useful."

"What about that matchbook?"

"The matchbook was for a restaurant that's been around since the 1970s, but no one there recognized me."

"Man. That's got to be hard," Derek said.

"What?"

"Not knowing who you are. Where you come from."

"I don't know. I mean, it was scary at first. But after a while, I got used to it. Whoever I was is gone. I'm just me now."

"But don't you wonder? Doesn't it bother you?"

"Should it?"

"It would bother me."

"I guess I just felt like I had a choice. I could

either go nuts wondering and trying to find out, or I could just live my life. That's what I'm trying to do," I said. "You're taking this pretty well."

"Well, my last girlfriend had three suicide attempts over two years. Two of which were before I started dating her. The other was during, and that was when I found out about the first two."

"Yikes."

He agreed that *yikes* was an appropriate response. "By comparison," he said, "a little dissociative fugue is nothing."

"Nothing?"

"Well, not nothing. Poor choice of words. You just seem pretty stable, is what I mean."

"I feel pretty stable. Except for the whole I don't know who I am thing, oh, and the creepy stalker in my apartment thing, yeah, everything's peachy." I sighed. "Damn. I knew I should have told you I was in the Witness Protection Program."

He laughed. "It's okay. Thanks for trusting me."

"You're welcome," I said. I tried taking another bite of sesame chicken, but it had gone cold. So had my appetite. Derek took our food boxes and the takeout bag into the kitchen.

"You want to watch a movie?" he asked as he returned.

I said I did, and he began rattling off titles of things he wanted to watch. I hadn't heard of most of them. Derek found that interesting and wanted to do a comparison of what movies I had heard of and which ones I hadn't. He thought it might reveal something about my past.

"Another night, maybe?"

"Sure. But for now, how about a movie about a guy with amnesia who finds out that he's really an assassin? Could be your life story."

"Yeah, right."

Almost two hours later we were both slouched low on the futon, inches apart and watching the credits roll for *The Bourne Identity*. I was intensely aware of the few inches that separated us and almost felt as if there were an electric current running from my hip to Derek's leg. I found myself wanting to rest my head on his shoulder again, but didn't want a replay of the other night.

I tilted my head towards his shoulder and said, "Hi."

"Hi," he replied and slid his arm around me. I sighed and put my head on his shoulder.

"This is nice," he said.

"It is," I said. Some of my hair, which I'd freed from its ponytail during the course of the movie, was drifting across my face. Derek brushed it away. I was breathing a little funny.

"I don't want to presume," he said, tucking the piece of hair behind my ear, "or make things awkward, but I want to kiss you." I felt my cheeks getting warm and I bit my lip, looking down. I suddenly felt very self-conscious, so I looked away.

"Is that a yes?" he asked. I nodded, shyly, and his

hand carefully lifted my chin and his lips met mine.

It was a funny, tentative sort of kiss, and his lips were dry at first but they hovered over my mouth and kissed me again, just as tentatively as the first time, but softer, somehow, and I found myself kissing back.

So this was kissing. I had no memory of ever doing it before, but I knew how to do it all the same. In fact, I was pretty sure I was good at it.

Kissing. I liked kissing.

After a minute or three, kissing evolved into me somewhat-unconsciously moving into Derek's lap. He broke off the kiss, taking a deep breath. "I . . . need some air," he said, and gently helped me back to the other side of the futon. He stood up awkwardly, straightening his pants.

"I'm sorry, I—"

"No, Madison, I'm sorry. I didn't want to rush things."

"Right, no, I mean, rushing is the last thing I want to do," I lied.

"Yeah, me too." His face was flushed. "I don't want you to feel pressured or uncomfortable in any way. You're sleeping here tonight and I don't want you to think I expected—" He stopped and gestured vaguely with his hand toward where he'd been sitting. "—that."

"No, not at all. I didn't think you expected anything," I said. If I was being honest with myself, I hadn't expected anything either, but I'd been *hoping*.

An awkward silence prevailed.

"I should get some sleep," Derek said.

"Me too," I said.

He asked me if I needed help with the futon and I said I didn't, and then he went to bed. I set the futon up and put the sheets on again, but couldn't seem to fall asleep. I kept wondering if I'd screwed up by climbing into Derek's lap like that. Maybe I'd been too aggressive. I heard some guys don't like that. I wasn't even sure how it had happened. It'd just felt right.

Not for the first time, I wondered about my past. What kind of girl was I?

Doesn't it bother you? Derek had asked.

Who had been my first kiss? And what about my first everything else? The doctors told me I wasn't a virgin. I must have slept with someone at some point in my past. But who? A first boyfriend? A second or third? Had I slept with loads of guys? I didn't seem to be into girls, as far as I could tell, so girlfriends seemed improbable. When it came down to it though, I just didn't know.

Maybe it was time to start looking again. See what, if anything, I could find about myself.

The morning was sunny as I walked up the steps of the main branch of the Brooklyn Public Library. The front of the building is rather majestic, with a tall brass entry flanked by two massive stone pillars embossed with gold figures like Zeus and Athena. I'd become familiar with several branches of the

New York and Brooklyn Public Libraries while I'd been at Spring House. Though my lack of ID prevented me from checking out books—a fact I lamented every time I visited a library branch—I could still use other library resources. My social worker Linda (after accusing me of being a Luddite and then having to explain what that was) encouraged me to sign up for various free programs at several locations, including basic courses: how to use computers, do internet searches, email, social media, and more. Some processes had seemed familiar, others utterly alien. As I got more comfortable online, I spent hours searching newspaper databases for missing persons records, not just in New York, but the tri-state area, followed by the rest of the U.S. Since I spoke French, I even tried Canada. Nothing turned up.

I also researched Fichet keys, since the locksmiths I'd talked to weren't any help. Fichet was a French company that made safes, safety deposit boxes, vaults, even jail cells. They'd been in business since the mid-1800s, but there wasn't much to go on as far as my key went. I found lots of images online of different kinds of Fichet keys, even one like mine with the two separate sets of teeth side-by-side. The teeth were also called "bits" and the double bit on this key was pretty rare. Because the key would work from either side of the lock, Fichet referred to it as a *sans souci clef:* a "without care" or "carefree" key. Wasn't that ironic.

I sat down at a computer in one of the Wi-Fi

rooms and searched the newspaper databases. Nothing, as usual. Plenty of missing people, but no one who looked like me.

Maybe Derek was right. It was depressing, really. Not just the thousands of missing people all over the country, but not knowing who you are. Not knowing if you like eating fish, or are allergic to bee stings, or whether you know how to swim. Not knowing what your favorite color is, or the name of your favorite teacher. No friends, no family. No history. Just a bunch of random skills, odd trivia, and a wide smile, owning only a weird antique key to nothing, clothes from secondhand shops, a used laptop purchased from a co-worker, and a futon from Housing Works. Even the bulletin board in my room had come with it. Like the mirror that had come with Kara's.

The whole haunting or intruder thing had been excessively weird. Did I really believe we had an intruder? It was easier than believing we had a poltergeist. Besides, everything I'd read claimed that poltergeists usually focus on individuals, not on places, and usually those individuals are children or teens. Julie was twenty-four and Kara was twenty-five. It couldn't be them.

I wondered how old I was. *Could* I be a teenager? But then, if it had been a poltergeist, why hadn't anything weird happened to me at Derek's, or at work, or even in my room? *Because*, I told myself firmly, *there is no such thing as a poltergeist*. Yet I found myself flashing back to the night that I saw the glass of water splash and smash on the kitchen floor while the lights blinked from bright to dim, and I knew that there was no rational way to explain what had happened. If it wasn't a poltergeist, then it must be a ghost, I thought. The book I'd read said that ghosts usually have some kind of connection to the place they're haunting. Why not search the newspaper databases for my address and see what came up?

Ten seconds later, a headline popped up in my search window: JUILLIARD STUDENT FOUND DEAD IN BROOKLYN APARTMENT.

I clicked on it.

> The scene was one of tears at 68 Young Street in the DUMBO neighborhood of Brooklyn today, as the mutilated body of Tamara Meadows, 20, a Juilliard student majoring in music, was removed from her third-floor apartment in front of a crowd of horrified onlookers. "We didn't hear anything," said Esther Jones, 37, who lives with her family in the apartment below the victim's. "She was a nice girl. Such a pretty voice. She loved music so much. Her and her roommates all did."

The article went on to describe how police believed that the girl had been killed elsewhere and her body dropped off where she lived, since there was hardly any blood at the crime scene. Her roommates were wanted for questioning, though they were believed to be out of the country when the crime had occurred.

How convenient for them. The date on the article read April 12, 1992. Twenty-five years and one week ago. I counted back and realized April 12th was the same day that the water had poured itself out.

My scalp prickled like a hundred ants were marching over it, then over my arms and legs.

Derek would have dismissed it as a coincidence, I knew. He would have told me that examination of "the real" outweighed "theoretical belief in the unreal," which was what he'd said when he had again tried explaining his philosophy stuff to me. But my entire sense of self could be described as "theoretical." What "real" did I have to hold on to? No name, no memories of birthday cakes or candles or Christmases or Hanukkahs.

Maybe considering the possibility of ghosts was a little crazy. My life was a little crazy too.

After the library, I went home. I got as far as our door and tried to use my key, then realized the futility when I saw the new lock. I trudged all the way back downstairs to ring Mr. Delgado's apartment on the first floor.

He answered the door in jeans and a dark blue t-shirt, his salt-and-pepper hair mussed, with a smoking cigar bobbing beneath his impressive gray mustache. "Locksmiths are all thieves," he said as he gave me the new key. "It's not cheap changing alla these locks, you know."

He seemed genuinely cranky. So far, Mr. Delgado had been a pretty decent guy who was very dedicated to his wife, Marie, who I'd only seen twice in the hallways since I'd moved in. The lock change must have been expensive.

"We appreciate you arranging the lock change for us," I said quickly. He nodded his head wearily. "I think Kara said you would add the cost to our rent?" As he continued nodding, I babbled on, "I mean, how horrifying to think one of your former tenants might have kept his keys and went into our place. Do the other tenants feel unsafe?" I kind of hoped if he felt responsible in some way for the security issues, maybe he'd charge us less.

"Yeah, well, the other tenants didn't have any problems like you did in yours. We just changed the locks on your place and put new doorknobs on the bedrooms. Also, we got some wood slats in the windows for you to use. So yeah, I don't know. I'm talking to Marie about it and we'll settle out an invoice before the first of the month for you girls." There was hope yet. From what Kara had said, Marie had Mr. Delgado wrapped around her finger. Maybe she'd feel sympathy for us and get her husband to charge us less.

I let him know that Kara would be by soon, and went up to the apartment.

On the stairs, I passed our downstairs' neighbor, a woman with close-cropped hair I'd only seen a few times since I moved in. According to Kara, she'd lived in the building for years and years. The woman was locking her door on her way out. We said hi, as friendly-but-not-nosy neighbors do, and I continued up to my apartment.

The floor lamp that had been knocked down the last time I'd been there had been set back to rights, and three separate sets of keys dangled from the shiny brass doorknob of each bedroom. The kitchen garbage smelled. I took the bag out to the trash cans in front of the building, then changed the sheets on my futon while I waited for Kara.

Every little sound in the building spooked me until she arrived. Footsteps in the hallway, the clank of the pipes, and ghostly thumping music from the downstairs apartment. It didn't help that the lights flickered every once in a while. But that *had* to be power fluctuations, didn't it? By the time Kara arrived, about thirty minutes after I did, I practically wanted to hug her. She was dressed in business maternity wear, looking very professional in khaki slacks and a fitted indigo blouse that stretched over her baby bump.

We exchanged greetings and I explained about the keys and confirmed that Kara had heard the same as I had from Mr. Delgado. Then the grilling began.

"So who is this . . . damn, what's his name? Don't tell me, it starts with a D, right? Donald? David? Or was it Darrin?"

"Close," I said. "It's Derek."

"Derek, right! Spill! Where'd you meet him, what's he do, and have you kissed him yet?" she squealed, taking her shoes off and curling up on the big couch in our living room.

I explained that Derek managed a bookstore near the comics store, leaving out the occult part, and that he liked movies and philosophy.

"He put the moves on you after a movie, am I right?"

"Well, the first night he was a perfect gentleman . . . and then, even when we kissed the next night, he was the one who broke it off and went to bed."

"You kissed? Give me deets!"

I explained in detail.

"Hm. Dry lips, huh?" she mused. "Get that boy some Chapstick. I like that he asked if he could kiss you, though. That shows he understands the importance of consent. So what else?"

"Well, his last girlfriend was kind of . . ." I hesitated for a moment, "well, she would have fit in at Spring House."

"So what have you two been doing?"

"Well, mostly? Just hanging out at his place, watching movies."

"With all there is to do in New York City, he just wanted to watch movies at his place? Madison, tell me you didn't sleep with this guy."

"I didn't!"

She tapped her chin while thinking. "He's either

broke or boring," she declared, crossing her arms.

"I don't know, it wasn't like that. I was the one who got us watching movies. It wasn't like he planned it. We were just hanging out, I guess."

She smiled a little. "Okay, okay. You like just hanging out. You like him. Is he cute?"

"I think I like him? I mean, I do like him. I think. He's really tall. Like six-five or six-six. Blond hair. Green eyes. Nice butt."

"I'm sensing another 'but.' One that's not so nice."

"Well . . ." I explained I *did* like Derek. It was easy being around him, and I was definitely attracted to him. I supposed what I didn't really like was his insistence that everything that people thought of as supernatural could be explained by something rational. I particularly didn't like the way he regarded the patrons of his uncle's store as a bunch of crazy people. Not that I could entirely blame him, after seeing the ads for UFO photos and ghost hunts, but still.

People experience weird stuff sometimes. And not all of them are crazy.

Kara got up to call Julie and tell her about the locks, and I went back to my room. I emptied my backpack and tacked Derek's cell phone number onto the bulletin board next to my Fichet skeleton key and then found Billy's number and put it up there too.

I wondered if I should feel guilty somehow. I mean, how did I know that I didn't already have a boyfriend? Maybe out in the world somewhere there was a guy who was sick with worry trying to find me. Maybe he and my parents were on the road, following my trail, leaving MISSING posters featuring my photo at bus stops and gas stations. REWARD, the poster would read. My name would be there, and so would my age. My real name. My real age. A series of tips would lead them to Christopher Street Comics, and they'd walk in the door, and my mother, a redhead in her fifties, would say my name. It'd be something like Emily, or Amy, something normal, and I'd turn, just to see who was speaking. I'd see her, but I wouldn't recognize her at first, but then suddenly all of my memories would come rushing back. I'd drop whatever I was holding and say, "Mom?" and run into her arms to be held.

Ugh. Pathetic. More than likely I'd run away from a clan of demented Luddites who abused me until I snapped. Maybe not having memories was a good thing.

CHAPTER FIVE

THE NEXT MORNING, I WOKE UP EARLY. IT WAS A sunny day with tufts of white cotton clouds drifting across a blue sky.

Sleep hadn't come easily the night before. Various building noises that I hadn't paid attention to while Kara was up were once again scary and ominous while I lay there in the dark wearing only an over-sized t-shirt and underwear. I was hyper-aware of the sound of a door in the hallway opening and closing, then footsteps as Kara (at least I hoped it was Kara) went to the bathroom. After tossing and turning for an hour, I had gotten up, locked the new lock on the door, and turned my reading lamp on. I fell asleep in minutes.

I'd just gotten out of bed when I heard heavy footsteps in the hallway approaching my room. Kara, on her way to the bathroom, I figured, but then the footsteps stopped and the bathroom door didn't close. Did she need something from me? I waited for her to knock. Instead, I heard my doorknob rattle. My mouth went dry.

I wanted to say, "Kara?" but my voice caught in

my throat. The doorknob rattled again. Could that be Kara, trying to get in my room?

No. Roommates knock. She'd always knocked on my door when she wanted something, even before the new locks. Thank God I'd locked the door.

The doorknob rattled once more. Was it the stalker? Was *Kara* the stalker?

For the first time since I'd moved into the apartment, I wished I had a phone.

I stood very still, still in my t-shirt and underwear, watching the door. I glanced at the fire escape outside my window, wondering if I had time to make a break for it. The doorknob rattled a third time, insistently. My eyes darted back to it, and I saw the door tremble in its frame as whoever was on the other side gave it a shove. I pressed my lips together tightly to stop myself from screaming.

Then the heavy footsteps moved away from my door. I heard a door open. I thought it was Kara's door. It closed. I didn't hear footsteps again.

I didn't know what to do. Should I investigate? *Only if you're stupid.* Should I get dressed? *That'd be a start.* I pulled on jeans, socks and sneakers. Didn't I have anything to use as a weapon? The room was bare: bed, bulletin board, reading lamp, desk, chair, and laptop. What I needed was a baseball bat. Or a frying pan. Too bad I didn't keep those in my room. The door down the hall opened again and the sound of heavy steps moved toward my room again.

Once again, my eyes strayed to the fire escape.

Screw this. I removed the newly installed wooden slat and opened the window. The metal fire escape seemed sturdy enough. I climbed out onto it. It held my weight. *So far, so good.* My feet made scraping noises as made my way down the stairs. A cold wind moved through the leaves of the trees on the block and blew my hair in my face, pricking up goosebumps on my arms. The sun was now behind a cloud.

The blinds were drawn in the window facing the second-floor fire escape, and an ashtray with butts sat on the outside sill. There were no more steps down. There was a rectangular hole, with a ladder, but the ladder was pulled up beneath the metal grating, and held in place with a rusty hook. I imagined the sound the ladder would make when released, a high screeching whine worse than the brakes on city buses.

Did I want to alarm the woman who lived on the second floor, if not the whole building? How hard was it to put the ladder back afterward? Were fire escapes just for escaping fires? Or could you use them to escape anything? I didn't know. What I did know was that I was afraid of whoever was in my apartment.

It had to be Kara in the hall. Had she snapped, or something? As far as I knew, she was happy. As far as I knew. But what did I know, really? How long had I known her? Four-plus months. And I had met her in a home for the mentally ill.

Another cold wind blew across me. I wished I'd

worn my jacket. It was only one floor up. In an apartment with a crazy person. In a locked room, though. How dangerous could it be?

Trying not to make much noise, I walked carefully up the stairs, lifting and setting my feet gently on every metallic step. Standing with my back against the building, I peeked in the window to my bedroom. Empty. I reached in and grabbed my jacket off the back of my chair and shrugged it on.

The window in our living room that also led to the fire escape was ten feet away. I don't know why I crept over to look inside, but what I saw tightened my stomach into a lump of fear and gave me chills as the blood in my body left my extremities.

Kara was standing there, still in the pale blue nightgown she'd worn to bed the night before.

She was standing right in front of the window, with her light brown hair floating around her head, blown back by the wind.

Except the window was closed.

Her eyes, which held an odd, vacant look I'd never seen before, suddenly focused on me. Her voice was faint through the window pane, but got louder. "Where is he?" she asked in a high, clear voice with a Long Island accent. "Where *is* he? *WHERE*?" The last word was a scream, resounding with frustration and anguish.

I opened my mouth to answer, to say something, anything, but nothing came out. I watched her eyes roll back in her head and saw her drop to the floor in one motion, like a curtain cut from the rafters. I gasped and tried the window. It was locked.

I scrambled back through my own window and threw my door open. I sprinted down the hall to find Kara crumpled on the floor in front of the living room window, the swell of her stomach exaggerated by the angle of her back and the way the nightgown was stretched.

Two words rang in my head: *the baby.*

I got down onto the floor and hauled her into a sitting position. "Kara," I said, pushing her bangs out of her eyes. "Kara, wake up."

Nothing.

I felt her wrist, but couldn't feel anything. I knew there was some specific way to check for a pulse, not to use the thumb or something, but in my panic, I couldn't think of it. Was she breathing? I put the back of my hand up to her nose and felt a gentle brush of air across one knuckle. *Thank God.*

Her breath was faint but at least she was breathing. I patted her cheek several times, at first gently, then harder, trying to get a reaction. Nothing. Was passing out dangerous for a pregnant woman? Probably? Then I saw it, around thigh-level on her nightgown: a wet spot of red.

Leaning back, I grabbed a throw pillow from the couch and lowered Kara's head onto it, then ran to her room to find her phone. I spotted it on her bedside table and dialed 911.

Ten minutes later, we were in the back of an ambulance racing to the hospital. I found her boyfriend's number and called him, and he said he'd call Kara's sister and meet us at the hospital.

The paramedics wheeled Kara's stretcher into the emergency room. Pale and fragile in the harsh overhead lighting, she still hadn't woken up. We passed through a set of double doors, and two women in scrubs joined us and began interrogating the paramedics about Kara's condition. One turned to me and asked, "Family?"

"No. Roommate," I responded.

She gestured toward a sitting area stuffed with orange and blue plastic chairs. "You'll have to wait over there," she said as they pushed the stretcher though the next set of double doors. I watched them swing closed with a thud.

I sank down into a blue seat under a blaring TV, trying to make sense of what had just happened. Kara had fainted, that much was clear, but what about *before* that? She'd asked "Where is he?" but who was she looking for? Her boyfriend, Serge? The stalker? I also considered the possibility she'd had a schizophrenic break and was talking about someone imaginary.

But one image kept coming back to me: her hair floating around her face, the blank look in her eyes, the way her face contorted into a panicked grimace when she screamed "WHERE?"

Even her voice had been different. I rubbed my eyes and then the rest of my face. What was I thinking? I wondered if Kara would remember any of it.

The meteorologist on the TV over my head was

talking about all the rain we could expect. I changed seats so I could watch and not have to think.

Serge arrived about thirty minutes later, a look of panic on his face, his wavy brown hair mussed, wearing a dress shirt and tie beneath a blazer with jeans. "How is she?" he asked, breathlessly. I told him I hadn't heard anything since we'd gotten there.

Not long after Serge arrived, a doctor came out through the double doors to tell us that Kara was awake and that we could see her. "The baby?" Serge asked at once, a tremor in his voice.

"You're the father?" the doctor asked.

He nodded emphatically. "Yes."

"The baby is okay. We're going to keep Kara here for a few days to do some tests, but you can come in and see her now."

In a corner of the ER, surrounded by sea-green curtains, wires, and beeping machines, Kara reached for Serge as soon as we were in sight. I stared at my feet for a few moments until Kara said, "Maddy."

She was smiling and holding a hand out to me. I walked forward and took it. "Thank you. Thank you for getting me here."

"It was the least I could do," I said.

Serge was sitting partially on the hospital bed with his arm around Kara. "We both appreciate it," he said, and squeezed Kara's shoulder.

I had to ask. "Do you remember anything? I found you lying in the living room."

"The living room?" she asked. "No. I . . ." She bit her lip. "The last thing I remember . . . I was standing in front of the mirror in my room . . ."

A strange look passed over her face.

"What?" I asked.

She shook her head. "I just remembered. I thought I saw someone standing behind me in the mirror, but when I turned around, there was no one. I thought it was the stalker, but there wasn't anyone there."

Yikes. "That's . . . weird," I said. "Do you remember how you got to the living room?"

"No idea. I kind of remember feeling lightheaded after that. I must have crawled out there or something."

Or something really creepy, I didn't say.

"Oh!" I said, reaching into my pocket. "I have your phone."

Kara took it from me and sighed, saying that she should probably call work, her father, and sister. I agreed and said that I needed to go home and get ready for work anyway, so I made my exit. As I headed out, I glanced over my shoulder, and saw Serge kiss Kara's forehead while she held her phone to her ear.

The whole time I was on the subway, I kept replaying everything that had happened in the past couple of weeks. Kara being crazy could explain the knife and shredded lingerie, but nothing could explain the glass of water or the way Kara's hair had been flying around her face.

Unless I was the crazy one.

I decided not to rule that out.

The stoop of my apartment building was cold.

I could just see the Manhattan Bridge from the front steps, on the other side of a huge brick building. Every now and then a low rumbling sound came from a subway train passing over it. Lots of low warehouse buildings were crowded together on the opposite side of the street, with cobblestones and old streetcar tracks showing through the asphalt. I wondered how old the neighborhood was. One hundred, two hundred years? Older?

A few trees were in bloom, including the dogwood tree in front of our building. Every now and then a white petal floated down and landed in front of me. The sun was shining, but it was still windy. For some reason, I just didn't want to go inside. I was glad I had my jacket. I sat down in the slice of sun playing across the steps, pulling the ghost book out of my backpack for something to do.

Sometime later, a voice said, "Locked out?"

I looked up, startled, to see my downstairs neighbor, the woman with the very short hair, standing at the bottom of the stoop with a sack of groceries.

I closed the book quickly. "What? Oh. Um, yes," I amended. I thought I was telling a convenient fib, but then I realized that I actually *had* left the new key to our apartment in my bedroom. Technically, I *was* locked out, though not from the building, just from my apartment.

"Lost your keys?" she asked, unlocking the door. She started climbing the stairs and I followed her. Beneath her coat she wore dark pink pants and soft white shoes.

"No, just left them behind this morning. My roommate went to the hospital and I went in the ambulance with her."

"Which one, the Asian girl? Or the other one?"

"The other one."

"Isn't she pregnant?" she turned mid-stair and asked, a look of concern on her face.

"She is. Baby's okay, but they're keeping her at the hospital for a day or two to make sure."

She made a "tsk" sort of sound. "Which hospital did they take her to?"

I told her and she *tsked* again. "They're alright. Should have brought her to Methodist, though. That's where I work."

"You're a nurse?" I asked, then realized how sexist that was. "Or a doctor?"

"Nurse," she said. "Neurology ward."

We got to the second floor and she began opening her door. I hesitated on the landing. "You want to come in?" she asked. "Better than sitting on the stairs with your butt falling asleep. I have peppermint tea."

"I'd love some peppermint tea," I said.

"I'm Theresa, by the way."

"Madison. Nice to meet you."

She led the way through a short foyer into a

living room where she took off her jacket, revealing a short-sleeve dark pink V-neck that matched her pants. Her apartment was basically laid out the same as ours was, with the kitchen through an archway off the living room and a number of doors that must have led to bedrooms and bathrooms.

The furniture and decorations were distinctly different, however. The walls had been painted in varying shades of tan, and the biggest feature of the living room was an old-fashioned couch made of green velvet or velour. A rocking chair with a draped knit blanket sat near the couch in front of a glass-topped coffee table, all surrounding a large television.

"Come on in," she said, gesturing with her head toward the kitchen. "Have a seat."

"Thanks," I said, seating myself at a round kitchen table. The table had a bowl of fruit in the center, with light green cloth place mats at each of the seats. A colorful, ornate platter hung on the wall over the archway, reading "Trinidad + Tobago," painted with palm trees and blue ocean. Theresa filled a kettle with water and put it on the stove.

"Do you live alone?" I asked.

"My sister *says* she lives here, but she's a stewardess, *excuse* me, a *flight attendant*, and she's traveling four or five days out of the week. She was here yesterday, but I won't see her again for a bit."

"How long have you lived here?"

"Since I was a little girl, five years old. It was our mother's apartment."

"I'm sorry," I said, noting her use of past tense.

"Sorry?" she said, turning from the two mugs she'd placed on the counter. "What for?"

"Your mother? She . . ." I let the sentence trail off.

"Oh! No, my mother, she's in West Palm Beach, living the good life!"

"Oh!" I felt my cheeks flush in embarrassment. "Now I *am* sorry."

"That's alright," she said with a smile. "No harm done." She busied herself with a teapot and tin of tea leaves for a few moments while I said nothing. The water in the kettle began to bubble and eventually whistle, and she whisked it off the heat, turned off the burner, and poured it into the pot, which she placed on the table along with the mugs.

She then sat down opposite me. She had a very direct gaze, large dark eyes with long eyelashes that curled at the ends and expertly arched eyebrows. "So how do you like living here? Is Mr. Delgado treating you alright?"

"Yeah, he's been good so far," I said.

"He's only owned the building for two years. Did a lot of work on it after he bought it. I thought it was just so he could raise the rent, but it didn't go up too much. Stabilized, you know. Your apartment's nice?" she asked.

"Yeah, it's . . . nice," I said. Except for that whole ghost thing.

"You had the police here the other day, though, didn't you? And then locksmiths came?"

Man, she sure knew a lot about what was going on. "Well . . . yeah. How did you—"

"Oh, that man was cursing up and down those stairs about the cost of locksmiths. Plus, cops are hard not to notice when they come. They asked me if I'd heard or seen anything. Which I hadn't. I guess you had some kinda trouble up there, huh?"

"Yeah," I said. I didn't really want to get into the whole intruder story with her, especially since I didn't really believe it myself.

"That apartment has always had trouble," she said with a frown, almost as if she disapproved of the apartment more than the trouble. She checked on the tea and made a small sound of satisfaction as she poured some into our cups. The liquid steamed with the fragrance of mint and the cup was warm when I put my fingers around it.

"Seems like someone's always coming or going, moving in or moving out, complaining about noises, things breaking or going missing," she continued.

"Really? People have complained before?"

"Sure they have. Nothing could be proved though. One guy told me he thought the place was haunted."

I inhaled the scent of peppermint as I took a tiny sip, but it was too hot to drink. "I . . . kind of thought that too," I admitted.

"I saw the book you were reading," she said with an apologetic incline of her head. "The guy—he said he told the ghost to leave his things alone. Said one of his books went missing, a dish broke, things like that."

"Did telling the ghost to leave his stuff alone work?"

"He didn't complain to *me* again. Then again, he moved out a few months later. So you can never tell."

I shook my head in wonder. Here it was, evidence . . . well, maybe not evidence, but at least some kind of corroboration that someone else thought the apartment *could* be haunted.

Theresa periodically took sips of her tea while speaking. "You heard about the murder that happened up there years ago?"

"I read about it," I said. "Did you . . . you were living here then?"

"Sure I was. Remember it like it was yesterday. I was watching the TV movie about that Baby Jessica—when the police came knocking on my door. I guess I always get a little nervous when the police come into the building like that ever since they found that poor girl up there."

"Baby Jessica?" I asked. Why did that ring a bell? "Oh right, I know. That was that little girl who fell down a well, wasn't it?"

"I'm surprised a young girl like you would even know that story. But yes, that little girl down in Texas. They made a movie about it. I was watching that when the detectives knocked at my door asking about poor Tamara."

"You knew her?"

"Sure I did. Me and Colleen—my sister—we used to take piano lessons from her and her roommate. Both of them were studying music at Juilliard."

"Did the police ever find out who killed her?"

"Well, that was the funny thing. Her roommate, Rebecca, was out of the country up in Canada when the whole thing happened. She came back and just went to pieces. Had to move back home with her mother. Story was there was a third roommate, a boyfriend, but *I* never saw him if there was. Police never got a lead."

A roommate out of the country and mysterious third roommate who disappeared. One dead girl who was haunting her old place.

The tea had cooled enough to drink and I took a long pull of it. Even without sugar, it was surprisingly sweet, and I liked the mint flavor. "Theresa?" I asked.

"Yeah?"

"Do you believe in ghosts?"

She pursed her lips a moment before she spoke. "I don't *not* believe in ghosts. I don't know if I believe *in* them, but I don't know enough about this world or the afterlife or any of that to say for sure. Seems there's been enough stories about them that maybe there's something to it."

"If you did believe in ghosts, do you think it's likely that a ghost would haunt a place where it had been killed?"

"Sure. It makes sense. *If* you believe in such things."

"Why, though? Does it want revenge? Does it want to tell someone what happened to it? Is it just angry?"

"I guess it could be any of those things."

"The girl who died—Tamara—you said she had a roommate? What was her name again?"

"Rebecca."

"Do you know her last name?"

"Yeah, it was Black-Pitt. Black like the color, then dash-P-I-T-T. We thought that was funny as hell. She hated it."

"Did you ever hear from her again?"

"Nope, can't say I did. Like I said, last I'd heard, she moved back home with her mother." Theresa took another sip of tea. "Why? You thinking about trying to get in touch with her?"

"Maybe?" I said. "I mean, if her old roommate is a ghost, haunting their old apartment . . . and they say that ghosts hang around because of unfinished business . . . I'm just thinking that maybe Rebecca would know if Tamara left anything unfinished."

"Well, good luck with that," she said. What might have been a sarcastic remark didn't seem so coming from her. "All I can say is that I wouldn't be messing around with *any* of it." She shook her head with finality.

I drained my mug and Theresa lifted the pot as if to fill it again. "No, thanks," I said. "Hey, can I use your fire escape? My window might be unlocked. Maybe I can get in that way."

"You're going back up there, huh? Sure, come on

through this way. I'm wanting a cigarette anyhow."

"You smoke?"

"Surprised that a nurse smokes? What can I say? It calms my nerves."

The door to my room was ajar, the new keys hanging from my bulletin board, right where I'd hung them the night before, next to the Fichet key on its chain and Derek's and Billy's phone numbers. I snatched the new keys up and changed the old one on my key ring out for the new one. Stupid locksmiths. Not like a new lock was going to do any good anyway. I folded the numbers and tucked them into a pocket in the backpack, and on a whim, hung the Fichet skeleton key around my neck and tucked it inside my shirt.

There was only one Black-Pitt listed in the New York White Pages: Black-Pitt, Elizabeth. The address was on the Upper East Side in Manhattan. I wrote it down along with the number and the first name: Elizabeth. It had to be Rebecca's mother, I thought.

What should I do? Call? And say what? That I'm looking for Rebecca? That we went to school together? If either of them asked to meet with me, that'd be the end of that. Maybe I could say I was Tamara's daughter. Yeah, real smart there, Maddy. She was nineteen when she died. What if I said that Tamara had been my aunt? That could work, as long as she hadn't been close with the family afterward.

This could work. It *had* to work. Somehow I understood that it was up to me to fix it.

I could try to catch Elizabeth Black-Pitt at her building, I supposed, but a phone call seemed less intrusive.

I showered and ate quickly, nervously listening for weird noises the entire time. I checked the clock. I had to be at work in three hours. Time enough.

CHAPTER SIX

GETTING OUT AT THE 77TH STREET STATION, I found a kiosk and dialed the number I'd jotted down.

A female voice on the other end said, "Hello?"

"Hi. May I speak to Rebecca Black-Pitt?" I said, in a high, polite voice.

There was a pause on the other end. "Who's calling, please?" She had a clipped British accent.

"My name is Madison. Um . . . she doesn't know me."

"And what's this regarding?"

"Well . . . my aunt, actually."

"And who is your aunt?"

"Tamara Meadows."

Another pause. "I see. Well, I'm sorry, but Rebecca isn't available—"

"Could you tell me when she'll be in? It's very important."

An ambulance went by, siren blaring.

"Where are you calling from?" she asked.

"77th and Lexington," I said.

"That's just a few blocks from here."

I waited, biting my lip.

"Perhaps you should come up," she said.

"That would be great!" I said. "Thank you."

The address she gave was the same as the one in the phone book, and she told me to ask the doorman for apartment 40-J. After hanging up, I checked my watch. I had two hours before work. Plenty of time.

The doorman, in his gray uniform, told me I was expected and pointed down the hall. The foyer of the building was done up in marble and mirrors, with plush gray carpets matching the doorman's suit and black leather couches. The elevators were sleek, quiet, and fast, with digital numbers counting the floors. As the floors flew by, I tried to get my story straight. I was Tamara's niece. Her sister's daughter. My mother . . . was dying? Too dramatic. Had been dreaming of Tamara? Maybe. Maybe my mom was sick. That was why she hadn't come herself. Maybe she was dead already? Why hadn't I decided any of this before I'd gotten here?

I got out on the 40th floor and walked down the hallway, looking from door to door until I found the right one. There was a welcome mat outside with an ivy leaf design around the word for welcome in French, *bienvenue*. We didn't have a doormat outside our apartment. I wondered if we should get one.

I pressed the doorbell and heard a cascading melody of notes. Fancy. On second thought, maybe we weren't fancy enough to have a doormat outside.

A shadow crossed the peephole in the door, and then it opened. The thin woman in her sixties standing on the other side wore beige slacks with a cream-colored sweater. A pair of reading glasses hung from a long chain around her neck, and her gray hair had been twisted into an elegant bun.

"You're Madison?" she asked with the same British accent I'd heard on the phone. "Tamara's . . . niece?" She seemed hesitant. I guessed I didn't look much like Tamara.

I nodded vigorously. "Yes, and you must be . . . Rebecca's mother?" I asked.

"Yes, call me Elizabeth. Come in, please."

The apartment matched the doorbell and mat. Fancy. It was the only word I could think of to describe it. A chandelier hung from the center of the large room she brought me into, a crystal construction that sparkled in the afternoon light coming in through the tall windows. We passed through a formal dining room into a living room with polished hardwood floors and a large, brightly colored oriental rug. A low-slung gray corner sofa was surrounded by built-in bookshelves full of hard covers, pottery vases and photographs, with a burnished wood and leather trunk serving as a coffee table in the center.

Elegant. *Elegant* was a much better word than *fancy*.

"Can I offer you a glass of water?" she asked as she gestured toward the couches.

"Yes, thank you," I replied, sitting down. My mouth felt dry.

After she left the room, I let out a breathy sigh, and imagined myself saying, "My mother's name is . . . " *Pick a name, any name.* ". . . Michelle. She and Tamara didn't get along. She felt guilty for not doing more after Tamara's death. She was hoping to get in touch with Rebecca."

No, maybe she was the younger sister, and hadn't understood what was going on because she was too young? Ugh, no. Simplify. Don't tell anything you don't have to.

Among the photographs on the bookshelves, I noticed several images of a girl with short, curly red hair at different ages. In one, she was laughing, maybe eight or nine years old, dangling a fishing rod over some body of water. In another, she was twelve or so, dance recital, ballet. Then she was in her teens, posed with a blonde with braces, both dressed in ski gear amid snow and blue sky. Finally, she was a young woman, dressed in black and playing a piano on stage.

Rebecca's mother returned, handing me a glass of water. I took a drink from it and set it down on a coaster on the trunk as she sat across from me.

"I found your name in the phonebook," I said. "I hope you don't mind."

"No, of course not. Why have it there unless it's to be found?" she said.

Right. "So—" I began, at the same time she said, "Tell me—" and we both paused.

I felt a smile of embarrassment appear on my

face that was echoed on hers.

"Please, go ahead," she said.

"Are you sure?" I asked.

"Please," she said, assuming a listening pose: leg crossed at the ankle, hands in her lap, alert expression.

"Will Rebecca be here soon?" I asked.

Something like a shadow flickered through her eyes. "I'm sorry to say that Rebecca doesn't actually live here with me. She lives . . . on Roosevelt Island." A pause. She seemed to be waiting for me to say something. Roosevelt Island. It was a tiny islet in the middle of the East River, with a tramway going to it from the Upper East Side.

"I don't think I've ever been there," I said. "Is it nice?"

She pressed her lips together thinly and spoke in a well-modulated voice. "Rebecca is an inpatient at Holmwood Hospital."

I'd heard of Holmwood, a private facility for substance abuse and the mentally ill, while I was at Spring House. It had a good rep among the crazy crowd.

"She has been in treatment for over twenty years now," Elizabeth continued. The words were spoken carefully, without emotion or affect. "I don't like to talk about it over the phone," she finished with a slight shake of her head.

"I'm sorry," I said. What else are you supposed to say when a woman basically tells you that her daughter is locked away from everyone because she's a danger to herself or others?

"Thank you," she replied. "So, you see, it's not particularly easy to get in touch with her. She has a particular schedule," she pronounced it *shed-yule*, "and it's best for her if we keep it that way." Beneath her surface pleasantries, she seemed inflexible and unemotional.

"Then . . . I guess I can't really talk to her?" I asked. *Come on, Maddy, look pathetic.* I opened my eyes a little wider and tried to look worried.

"I suppose that would depend on what you wanted to talk to her about. It was Tamara's death that drove her there in the first place, after all." She frowned, as if she blamed Tamara for dying.

I bowed my head a moment. "It's just . . ." I bit my lip. *Here goes.* "My mother died last year. I didn't even know I had an aunt until I was going through her things."

Her expression changed abruptly. "Oh, you poor dear. I'm very sorry for your loss."

I swallowed hard and pressed my lips together, looking down once more. I'd seen Kara get this way when she talked about her mother a couple of times, and as long as she kept looking down, she usually didn't cry.

"I guess I just wanted to meet someone who knew her. Tamara, I mean." I paused, thinking. "Did you ever meet her?" I asked, looking up.

"Just the once, when Rebecca was moving into that awful apartment in Brooklyn." Awful? Well, comparatively, I supposed. It was no Buckingham

Palace. And Tamara had been murdered there. I guessed it was awful enough.

"What was she like?" I asked.

Her eyes got that faraway look that people get when they are trying to remember something. "She was small, and dark-haired. Cheerful. I remember her eyes were a striking color—more gold than brown." That explained the looks she'd given me. Small, dark-haired aunt, with a tall, blond niece. I thought quickly. Should I say I resembled my father? "She and my mom looked a lot alike in the pictures I saw. I look more like my dad." I gave her half a smile.

"Is your father . . . ?"

"Alive? Oh, yes." Borrowing from Kara again, I said, "He's in construction. In New Jersey."

"Did you come here today all the way from New Jersey?" She made it sound like Timbuktu.

"Train into Penn Station," I said. "Just an hour or so." As far as I knew, I'd never been to Jersey. Once again Kara's background came to the rescue.

"Ah, that's not too bad then, is it?" she asked. I said that it wasn't. She seemed to be weighing something, trying to make a decision, and then sighed. "Well, I suppose it was a long time ago. I don't know what Rebecca would remember about Tamara. She has good days and bad days. As a result, I can't promise you anything, but I can set up a visitor's pass for you this weekend if you'd like."

"That would be . . . I'd be very grateful," I said. "Thank you."

"Not at all," she said. "How shall I let you know?"

"Let me know?"

"The time. The visitor's hours are a bit strict, I'm afraid."

"Oh," I said, thinking. "Um, my dad doesn't know that I'm doing this, so . . . do you have email?"

She hesitated, then said she did. I gave her my email address and she said she'd be in touch. I got up to leave. "Your father does know that you're in New York City today, doesn't he?" she asked.

"Oh, yes. I'm . . . heading over to the Met next," I said. "He's meeting me there later." *One lie stacked on top of the other.* Maybe that was in my favor. She might think I was lying about meeting my father, but probably not about who I was, or why I wanted to talk to her daughter. Was I actually getting good at this? And should I feel good about that?

On my way into work, it began to rain. I pulled my umbrella from my trusty backpack. The rest of the night passed. Work was boring. Not many people came in because of the rain, which grew heavier with intermittent thunderstorms. On the subway home, I skimmed through the ghost book again. I remembered seeing something about what to do to make ghosts leave you alone and thought that now might be the time to try it out.

Of the various pieces of advice given, there were three suggestions that sounded like things I could do. The first was "smudging": burning a bundle of dried sage leaves to "purify" your home. The problem was I had no idea where to get dried sage leaves. I could always buy fresh ones and dry them out myself, but how long would that take?

The next one, making lines of sea salt in doorways to keep ghosts out of specific rooms, sounded pretty easy too, though they recommended getting the salt blessed by a priest. That seemed unlikely at 1a.m. on a weeknight. I thought we had some sea salt in the kitchen cabinet. Maybe a non-holy salting would work just as well.

The third suggestion was speaking to the ghost and telling it "firmly in an unemotional voice" to leave me alone. "Some ghosts are unaware that they are dead," the text read, "and thus must be told that they are interfering with the business of the living and should desist from such activities." Great. I was supposed to tell a pissed-off ghost that it was dead? I didn't think so. But I *could* tell it to leave me alone. Theresa had said the guy who lived there before had done something like that too.

There were more suggestions, from putting up mirrors or scattering rice or some other small grain across the floor in every room, to painting the doors of the house red, among others. I didn't think Mr. Delgado would go for a red door after all of his complaining about changing the locks.

Shaking the rain from my umbrella in the hallway, I

flipped the entryway light on. The tall floor lamp that had been lying on the floor when I brought Derek over was lying on its side again when I walked inside.

Thunder rattled the windows ominously and I jumped. I walked slowly into the apartment, heading toward the kitchen. And then I heard it: a sweet, musical tinkling sound coming from Kara's room that made the hair on my arms stand up.

The lights in the room were off, but the tinkling continued. I took a deep breath and switched on the light. It was the jewelry box on Kara's bureau, the one she said didn't work anymore. Yet there was the tiny porcelain ballerina, turning slowly in a circle accompanied by the slow, out-of-tune notes of what might have been "Swan Lake." It was the creepiest thing I'd ever experienced.

I closed the top and the music stopped. I let out a breath I hadn't realized I'd been holding and then heard a *tick* to my right. I stood frozen, not sure what to do. I heard another *tick*, then another. I had that odd sense you get when you feel like someone is watching you.

Out of the corner of my eye, I could see the heavy antique mirror on the wall to my right, hanging at an odd angle. I couldn't bring myself to look into it. Instead I backed out of the room and closed the door. I flinched as lightning flashed, making the living room windows go white for a moment. The crack of thunder was louder and seemed much closer than before.

I stood in the hall facing the living room and heard a repetitive, skipping sort of noise coming from the other side of the room.

It was the remote control for the TV, spinning in place. Just spinning on its own.

Then it flew across the coffee table and into the air.

I shrieked and ducked, and the remote hit the wall just inches above my head.

I tried to remember what I'd read in the book. *Talk to the ghost firmly in an unemotional voice.* I spoke loudly into the living room. "Excuse me, please? Tamara? You need to stop messing with our stuff." My voice came out higher and squeakier than I wanted, so I made a conscious effort to lower it as I continued.

"I don't know who you think I am, or who you think the other women living here are, but we don't know you, and you don't know us. You need to leave us alone." I pulled the cord on the light in the kitchen and it flickered on. I felt ridiculous. Then the light flickered again.

There is something comforting about speaking aloud to someone, anyone, when you're nervous or scared, even if it's just yourself, someone who isn't there, or something you don't want to believe in. Opening kitchen cabinets, looking for sea salt, I kept talking.

"I don't know what happened to you, or why you're doing what you're doing, but you need to stop. Scaring people isn't helping anyone."

Inside the cabinet, I began moving boxes and canisters around. On the bottom shelf was pasta, flour, sugar, pancake mix, a bag of rice. The middle shelf held lots of canned soup and vegetables, jars of pasta sauce and peanut butter. The top shelf had spices and seasoning. *Bingo!*

"Listen," I said to the empty air, "I'm just going to go to my room. Please leave our things alone." I paused a moment. "I'm going to try to help you. I hope you believe and understand that. But I need you to be patient. And peaceful. Can you do that?"

I listened a moment, with another weird feeling like someone was watching me. I shivered and heard the familiar *creak* of one of the cabinet doors opening behind me and all of the hair on the back of my neck raised. Again, I couldn't bring myself to look and just stood stock-still for a moment, scared half to death.

Eerily, the kitchen light flickered, dim, then bright, and back to normal again, as if the ghost was responding. That was enough for me. I grabbed the sea salt and fled to my room.

To say that I slept that night wouldn't be inaccurate, though the sleep wasn't particularly restful. In the morning, the thick line of salt I'd poured across my doorway was undisturbed. Other than the floor lamp, the remote, and two open kitchen cabinets, nothing seemed to be out of place.

The line of salt across the bathroom's threshold

was also undisturbed. I didn't even know what I was looking for. Ghostly footprints?

After my shower, I checked my email. There was one new message from Elizabeth Black-Pitt. I had an appointment to see Rebecca at Holmwood Hospital the next day at noon. Perfect, especially considering that I had the day off.

I put on a green button-up shirt with my jeans and Converse sneakers. I really liked pairing those jeans with those sneakers. Those two items, aside from the sweater, tank top, and underthings I'd been wearing when I "came to" on Madison Avenue, were the only clothes I had from my former life. They felt like they were "mine" in a way that clothes I'd gotten since didn't. Unfortunately, nothing about the clothes were clues to my identity. The tags were all from generic clothing stores you'd find at any mall in North America.

If anything, the only noticeable thing about them was that the jeans and sneakers were actually vintage, as opposed to the fake retro gear that plenty of hipsters were wearing these days. I tried to tell myself that I should be reassured. Apparently, I was not only fashionable, but also no stranger to wearing other people's old clothes. It was a "real" me detail. The real me, whoever I was, liked secondhand clothing and shoes.

Maybe I was really into recycling?

I brushed my hair, put on my key necklace and left the house early with my backpack slung across one shoulder.

It was time to pay another visit to Derek.

"Hey!" Derek said, looking up from the newspaper he was reading. He was in his characteristic perched pose on the stool behind the counter, in jeans and a plain white t-shirt.

"Hi," I said. "I was wondering if you had plans after work tonight."

"As a matter of fact, I do not."

Was he always free? "Do you even *have* friends?" I asked.

He seemed insulted. "Friends? *I*? Why, yes, I do have friends. Loads of them."

"Yeah, right. I haven't seen evidence of them. Should I make a flyer to add to your wall here?"

I took a look at the bulletin board of occult want ads. One read "Team of Parapsychologists Seeks Volunteers" across the top. The fine print below mentioned a haunted estate in Sleepy Hollow. Someone had taken a red marker and written SATURDAY diagonally across it. I checked the date. It was this weekend.

"Do you think I should sign up for one of these things? Do they pay?" I asked.

I turned back to Derek. He was standing in profile with his arms crossed, frowning. "What?" I asked.

"Do you really think I don't have friends?" he asked in a dramatic voice, with one eyebrow raised. It was almost a Superman pose. I could practically see the cape hanging off his back.

"I . . . don't know," I said with a laugh. "*Do* you have friends?"

"Of course I have friends," he intoned. "I am a bowler." He made it sound like a sacred trust.

"A bowler?" I asked. "I'd have thought basketball with your height."

He cracked a grin and dropped the pose. "I used to play. Even got a scholarship on it. Then I tore my ACL. No more basketball after that. Now I bowl every Sunday as part of a league. Got my own ball and everything."

"Really?"

"Really. My team is called the Hand Cannons."

"Are you any good?"

"They don't call me Captain Hook for nothing," he said, holding his hand in front of him and then flexing his arm and going through the motion of throwing an imaginary bowling ball with a twist of his wrist.

"Captain Hook? Like from Peter Pan?"

"No. For the bowling move." He made the same flourishing motion with his wrist again. "Like that. On average I roll about a 180." He looked at me expectantly.

"I take it 180 is good?"

"It's above average," he said, raising his chin.

"Do I detect some false modesty there, Captain Hook?"

"You might, Tinkerbell," he said.

I laughed. "So, what do you want to do tonight?"

he asked.

"We have a movie date, if I'm not mistaken," I said.

"We do," he agreed.

I told him when I got off and he said he'd see me then, and off to work I went. Along the way, I stopped at a kiosk to look up the number for the hospital where Kara was being treated. I called and the operator connected me to her room. She picked up immediately.

"Hey, how are you feeling?" I asked. "It's Madison."

"Hey! I'm pretty good," she said.

"What do the doctors say?"

"Bean's heartbeat was a little irregular," she said, "but everything else seems fine. Just some breakthrough bleeding. It was all me, no fetal cells, nothing to worry about there."

"That's good news," I said. "Do you need anything from the apartment?"

"No, that's okay. My sister brought me some magazines and books to keep me occupied. Serge also brought some clean clothes I keep over at his place. That should last until they let me out in a couple of days. They have a few more tests they want to run."

A couple of days. That meant I had to solve our paranormal problem before then. I couldn't let Kara come home to a haunted apartment. For the baby's sake.

"Okay—well, I'll call and check in with you

tomorrow, or the next day then?" I asked.

"You don't have to," she said. No, I didn't have to, but I wanted to. It was important to me that she was safe.

"Has Serge been there a lot?"

"Every day. He's pampering the crap out of me. I'm seeing a whole new side of that man due to this pregnancy and now being in the hospital. Have you spoken to Julie, at all, by the way?"

"No! You haven't either?"

A jittery guy in an old military jacket approached me and said, "I need the phone."

"There's another one on 7th Ave. Just around the corner," I said to the guy, and to Kara, "Sorry, some guy wants the phone."

The guy gave me a look of disgust and shuffled off towards 7th.

"Oh, Maddy, get your own phone already," Kara said.

"I will, I will, I swear. Soon." I said, crossing my fingers. "So you *haven't* talked to Julie?"

"Oh, no, I talked to her last night."

"Do you know when she's coming home?"

"Sunday night, I think? She said that Tad was taking her to a bed and breakfast in Connecticut for the weekend . . . must be nice. Hey, looks like you might have the whole place to yourself for a couple more days."

"Yeah, if it wasn't kind of creepy, that'd be great."

"Has anything happened?" she asked, concerned.

"No, it's been fine," I said. That was mostly true.

"Well, that's good. Just, um . . . don't have any parties while we're gone," she said, and laughed. "I mean, I know you wouldn't. It's funny—you look young, but you don't act at *all* like a teenager. I forget sometimes you aren't my age."

"That's nice to hear. But just to reassure you, I promise not to have any parties," I said. Not that I'd have anyone to invite anyway.

"I'll check in with you tomorrow or the next day, okay? Say hi to Little Bean for me." We exchanged goodbyes and hung up.

Whew.

No roommates for the weekend.

Baby steps. Or *no baby* steps.

It gave me time. I hoped it was enough.

It was a fairly busy night at Christopher Street, but customer traffic slowed down considerably when it started raining again. Around half an hour from closing we were all bored and practically nodding off. Mac had spent the night training the new guy, Trendon. I was behind the cash register and Celeste was working bag check, rocking a cute pink t-shirt that matched her hair, along with neon pink fishnet stockings, low pink boots, and a short pink and black plaid skirt. The t-shirt featured an iron-on image of a white kitten surrounded by sparkles. It read CUTIE PATOOTIE.

"How the hell do you have so many clothes that

you can match them to whatever color your hair is and not wear the same thing every day?" I finally asked. It had been bugging me for weeks.

"I borrow clothes from other girls on my floor or I pick things up at Village Vintage," she said. "Like, the skirt belongs to a girl down the hall, the t-shirt I got from ViVi, but the stockings and boots are mine."

"So there is at least *one* good thing about living in the dorms," I said. Celeste was not a fan of her living space.

"The *only* good thing," she replied, handing a customer's messenger bag back to him.

I rang up the customer's purchase and put his comics into a bag. "Enjoy," I told him brightly. He smiled and left.

"You're in a good mood," Celeste said.

"I am?"

"Seems like it," she said. "You working tomorrow?"

"Nope, day off."

"That's why you're in a good mood."

"No, it's not."

"Do you *want* to work?" she asked, tightening her pink ponytail.

"Why? Are you looking for someone to cover your shift?"

"Noon to six," she said.

"Ah, I can't," I said. "I have a thing at noon. An appointment. Otherwise I would."

"*MAC?*" Celeste yelled to the back of the store.

It was just us four, no customers left.

"*WHAT*?" he yelled back.

"Ugh, stop yelling and go back there and talk to him," I said.

Celeste went skipping back and conferred with Mac for a few minutes, then returned.

"If you'll come in from three to nine, Mac says it would be okay. Billy will be here to open, and Trendon will come in from noon to four."

"Okay for you," I said. "For me, that's working six days in a row without a day off."

"What's your Saturday schedule?" she asked. I told her and she offered to take my hours. "I'll even take your Sunday hours too, if you want a real weekend. That way you get time off, and I don't have to worry about tomorrow."

"What's tomorrow?" I asked.

"You're asking the wrong question," she said in a sing-song voice.

"What question should I be asking?" I asked.

"What's *tonight*?" she said with a grin. She waited for me to ask. When I didn't, she pouted. "Oh fine, I'll just tell you then. A bunch of my friends got some Mollie and we're going to Roseland to see Paul Perone."

I had no idea what most of those words meant, but I assumed they were important.

Catching movement out of the corner of my eye, I looked down the long counter of various comic book paraphernalia and saw Mac coming out of the back with the new hire.

"Everything okay up there?" Mac asked.

"Quiet as a mouse," I replied, looking through the window at the rain. "A very wet mouse."

"I'm showing Trendon the basement," he said.

"Good luck," Celeste said. "Don't let the bedbugs bite."

Trendon made an alarmed face. "Don't listen to her," Mac said, rolling up the sleeves of his immaculate dress shirt. He went down the steps to the basement, with Trendon following.

"Anyhow," Celeste began again, this time in a conspiratorial tone, "I'm a little worried about making it to work with the comedown and this way I don't have to."

"I have no idea what you're talking about," I said.

"You've never heard of Paul Perone?"

"Nope."

"I guess you don't like EDM or drum and bass, then."

"I guess not," I said. She might as well have been speaking Italian.

"No way," Celeste said, her eyes looking a bit like Trendon's had moments ago. "Tell me you know what Mollie is."

"I know what Mollie is?" I said, uncertainly.

"What are you, a Mormon or something?"

"Amish, actually," I said. Amish, amnesia, fugue. Whatever.

Her brow furrowed as she tried to determine if I was telling the truth. "You liar. You totally know," she said.

I let her think what she wanted.

I wished I knew what she was talking about. Her Friday plans sounded a lot more fun than mine.

CHAPTER SEVEN

CHARLIE THE NOT-TUNA WAS STILL IN RESIDENCE on Derek's living room wall. "Hey, Charlie," I said.

"I do that too," Derek said. "It's like, I can't help but talk to it like it's alive."

"I get it. I talk to all kinds of things that aren't alive."

"So, what do you want to watch? The pizza should be here soon." He'd placed the order while I was still taking my jacket off in his kitchen.

"I have no idea," I said. "I've never even heard of most of your movies."

"Right!" he said. "I've been thinking about that."

"What?"

"I don't know, really. I was just trying to come up with a system we could use."

"A system we could use for what, exactly?"

"I don't know, maybe help provide some clues about your memory loss? Maybe?"

"Well, how about you just throw some titles at me?"

"Alriiiiight," he said, scanning his shelf. "How about we start with something easy. *Jaws*?"

"Of course I've heard of *Jaws*."

"*Raiders of the Lost Ark*."

"Duh."

"*Star Wars*."

"Double duh."

"*E.T.*?" he asked.

"Are you messing with me?"

"Well, it looks like your classic sci-fi knowledge is up to specs. How about something more recent? Have you seen *Titanic*?"

"About the ship?" I asked.

"You've seen it?"

"No. Just a poster somewhere."

"I thought every girl had seen *Titanic*."

"Not me."

"Okay, now we're getting somewhere. What about *Jurassic Park*?" he asked.

"That's about . . . dinosaurs?" I asked, taking an educated guess. "Never heard of it."

He made a puzzled face at that. "Hmm. Interesting." From the small table next to the futon he picked up brick-sized paperback book with dogeared pages and began flipping through it.

"Why's that interesting?"

"I loved *Jurassic Park* when I was a kid," he said. "Couldn't get enough of it."

"Yeah," I shrugged. "I don't know. Nothing comes to mind."

"*Very* interesting. Okay, I'm just going to read you a long list of movies. If you hear anything you recognize, that you know you've seen, stop me."

I said okay, and he began.

"*Star Wars Episode Three*," he said.

"I know that one. With the little furry guys in the forest. Ewoks, right?"

"*Episode Three*?" he asked. "Or *Return of the Jedi*?"

"There's a difference?" I asked.

He shook his head and started again. I hadn't heard of the next one, or the one after it. He probably read off two dozen movies until he got to *Fatal Attraction*.

"Stop."

"You've seen *Fatal Attraction*?"

"Yes. Psycho mistress boils bunny. Yuck."

"You saw Fatal Attraction but you never saw *Roger Rabbit*? You're sure of that?" he asked.

"Yeah. Why?"

"That is *weird*."

"What's weird about it?"

He came and sat next to me with the book and turned pages for me to see. "First, I was just going by classics, of . . . popular culture, basically. Those you know, but only up to a point. Based on your age—you're a little younger than me, but only by a few years—we should have seen some of the same '90s movies. But you haven't seen *any* of them. And looking at this," he pointed to the dog-eared book and opened to one page, "your knowledge of movies seems to stop . . . there."

"Where?"

"Well, it's less a where and more a *when*. 1987."

"What?"

"You don't seem to know any movies that were made after 1987."

"That's ridiculous."

"Take a look for yourself," he said. I took the book from his hand as the intercom made an alarming squawk from the other room. "Pizza," he said, getting up. "I'll be right back."

As he left the room, I gazed at the list of movies on the page he'd handed me. "Top-grossing Films of 1988" read the top of the page. I hadn't heard of a single one of them.

I flipped through the pages. From 1988 to 2014 (the last year the book covered) while there were plenty of comic book movies I had seen for sale in the store, from *Batman* to *Spider-Man* and *X-Men*, none of them were movies I knew. Not the way I knew that *Jaws* was about a killer shark, or that *E.T.* was a little beanbag alien hiding in a kid's house, or how *Fatal Attraction* was about a crazy stalker lady.

Why hadn't it occurred to me before?

Had I just assumed that they were movies that other people saw, but not me? Or that my fugue state had wiped my memory of them?

The sound of the front door closing was accompanied by the smell of garlic and cheese as Derek entered the room. My stomach growled.

"Any luck?" Derek asked, pulling paper plates out of a plastic bag.

"No," I said, and pursed my lips. I didn't know what to make of it.

He opened the box and offered me a slice.

After we'd each burned our mouths with piping hot cheese and put our slices down to let them cool, Derek said, "The thing that really gets me? You weren't even born yet."

"What?"

"When the movies you saw came out. I mean, sure, they've all played on TV a million times, so that's not a big deal, but . . . it's just weird."

That was one way of putting it.

CHAPTER EIGHT

DEREK DECIDED IT WAS A CRIME AGAINST NATURE that I hadn't seen *Jurassic Park*, so that was what we watched. My favorite part was the roar of the T-Rex. It sounded like a subway train fighting an elephant. But every now and then during the movie I'd find myself distracted.

Why did I have this huge block in my mind? And why did it have such an arbitrary cut-off point?

By the end of the movie, the kids made it out without getting eaten somehow, and the jackass lawyer and jerk programmer had both died, which they maybe probably deserved. You'd think that with all of the assholes in movies always getting killed, less people in the world would be assholes, but I guess nobody watches and thinks, "Hey! That asshole is just like me!"

Everybody thinks they're the hero. Even the assholes.

As the credits rolled, Derek offered to let me stay at his place again. I'd hoped he would, since I wasn't too eager to go back to my apartment. For a moment, I hoped he'd say I could sleep with him, but the minute I thought it I regretted it and hoped he wouldn't. Had I jinxed myself? It was hard to tell.

He brought out the same pile of sheets for the futon and wished me an awkward goodnight without trying to kiss me again. I couldn't decide if I was relieved or disappointed.

The next morning, we both slept late, and he had to run downstairs to open the store. He wished me luck with my day.

I changed clothes from my backpack, the ones I'd thrown in hoping I could stay at Derek's, then let myself out and walked to the F train.

The main brick building of Holmwood Hospital had two wings off a domed central building. Like two arms waiting for a hug. Or a straightjacket waiting to grab you and never let you go.

The receiving room smelled of oranges and cedar. The tall windows on one side of the room faced Lighthouse Park in the north of Roosevelt Island, while the windows on the west wall showed a long lawn, shaded with trees, before glimpses of blue water and gray buildings from the East River and the Manhattan skyline. A man sat at a baby grand piano in the center of the room, playing Beethoven's "Für Elise."

More than a dozen small sitting areas in varying shades of royal blue and sea green were spread across the room, each arranged carefully to allow visitors to have private conversations. I sat down in one of two soft chairs that flanked a small side table. Every sitting area had its own skylight, potted plants, and area rug. Comparing Holmwood to Spring House was like comparing filet mignon to hamburger.

"Für Elise" stopped and started again. My fingers tapped out the notes of the opening on my jeans, each hand playing its part. *Wait, am I playing the actual song?* I watched the small man at the piano playing, watching his hands move across the keys while my fingers mimicked his motions. Yes, it went: *E-D-sharp-E-D-sharp-E-B-D-C-A* . . . My mouth fell open. *I know how to play piano!* I wanted to stand up and shout it to the entire room, then thought better of it. But I *knew*. Other songs came unbidden into my head: "Moonlight Sonata" and "Ave Maria." I knew classical music: Chopin, Bach, Debussy, and loads of others. Holy shit. Was my memory returning? I thought and thought but nothing else came to mind.

I wondered if the man playing piano would get up soon. Maybe I could give it a try?

The orderly who'd taken my name and directed me to this room now returned, this time accompanied by a pale, freckled woman with her curly red hair cut to chin-length. Rebecca. She was older than her pictures, of course, with lines around her eyes and a sort of fragility about her. She was thin, dressed in khaki pants and a long-sleeved t-shirt.

"Hi again," the orderly said brightly. "Rebecca,

this is Madison. She's your visitor."

I stood, reaching out to shake her hand. Rebecca ignored the gesture and rubbed one hand across her upper arm and reached into a pocket with the other, retrieving a pack of cigarettes. She didn't look at me.

"I want to go smoke," she said. Her voice was plaintive, like a kitten mewling.

"Then go out to the courtyard," the orderly said. "Madison can join you there instead."

Rebecca gave the barest of nods and shuffled toward a set of frosted glass double doors. "She's not having a great day," the orderly said to me, lowering her voice, "but you can try. You have one hour. If you need anything, if she disturbs you, or she gets disturbed, just come find me at the desk. Okay?"

I nodded and thanked her. I could have asked what Rebecca might do that would disturb me, or vice versa, but I'd been in Bellevue. I'd seen a gray-haired woman climb up onto a table, raise her hospital gown, and pee all over a checkers game. I'd seen a guy in his thirties who had to be buckled down to make him stop playing with his junk. In group therapy at Spring House, I'd watched a woman act out her father dashing a puppy's brains out against a wall, and a week later watched a boy about my age pluck his eyebrows out while he talked about the death of his little brother. I knew disturbed.

In the courtyard, the blue sky hung above an open-air patio, complete with potted flowers, Ficus trees, benches, and tables. Rebecca sat on a white stone bench at a white stone table, smoking a cigarette and rubbing her upper arm reflexively. She didn't look at me. I'd rehearsed what I was going to say to her, a version of the same story I'd told her mother, but what if Tamara never had a sister? I mean, it's one thing to lie to the roommate's mother, but to the roommate herself?

"You're here about Tamara," she said, suddenly.

"How did you——?"

"My mother," she said, dismissing the woman who'd raised her with a gust of smoke.

"Did she tell you——?"

"I hate being in there when he's playing," she interrupted, her voice bitter. "I used to play, but then the meds . . ." Rebecca held up one freckled hand. It seemed to vibrate with tremors. "The shakes. That's the price of mental health. An unsteady hand and a nicotine addiction. I never smoked before they committed me. Now I can't stop."

She was quiet a moment. I squirmed, unsure of what to say.

"Tamara was an only child," she said, eyeing me.

Shit. Busted.

"I'm sorry," I said, "I——"

"Don't be," she responded, looking away again. "I don't get many visitors. Except my mother. But I'm pretty sick of her. She doesn't understand why I won't just 'get well' and be her prize-winning *show-daughter* again. Like that goddamn Pomeranian."

Most of this speech was delivered with a sneer, while "get well" came out in falsetto British. "She still have it?"

"I'm sorry?" I asked.

"The dog. The annoying fluffy lapdog. She said you came by the apartment."

"Oh. Um, I didn't see a dog—"

"Or hear one? You would have—the fucking thing was constantly yipping the last time I was there, it must have been three years ago? I guess she got rid of it. Or maybe it died. It's not like living with her was doing *me* any favors. That was why I moved in with Tamara in the first place. To get away from her." Her cigarette had burned down to an ashy nub while she spoke, but she tried taking a drag from it anyway. Near the filter it glowed red and she inhaled and let out a small puff of smoke, then stubbed the butt out on the patio beneath her feet. "I was away when *it* happened, you know," she said. "I was in Niagara Falls. He told me to go, so I went."

"Who told you?" I asked.

"He was beautiful. Handsome. He brought the piano in for me. For me! And Tamara was jealous. She went crazy, threatened me with a knife, ripped up a bunch of my clothes. He said he needed some time with Tamara to try to fix things. See, he was her boyfriend. But I was his secret. He had other secrets. Another woman. A blonde. Maybe she was his wife. That was why he told me to go. Just for the weekend. And then I came back, and Tamara was dead."

A glassy look came into her eyes, like she was under a spell. I didn't say a word, in case my voice might break it.

"They kept asking me if she had any enemies. Anyone who would want her dead. And there wasn't! And no one knew who he was, or where to find him, except me. Because of the piano. And I didn't tell. They didn't believe me, anyway. No one had ever seen him. The apartment wasn't in his name. It was in Tamara's. Nothing she told me was true. Maybe he wasn't even her boyfriend. Maybe, he was just . . ." she said, taking on a nasty nasal tone, "*a projection of my disease*. But then if that were true, how did I know about the piano?" The nasty tone became playful and she smiled at me.

I couldn't tell if the smile was sincere or not. She was angry one second and sweet the next.

"The piano in there?" I asked, gesturing toward the reception room.

"No! Not that one. *That* one my mother donated. I mean the one *they* brought."

"*They* who?"

"The movers," she said smugly.

"Movers?"

"The piano movers, the delivery men. When they delivered it to the apartment, they told me to sign. One Steinway Model M Grand Piano. The left corner of the fall was chipped—you know, the part that covers the keys? I played for hours on that thing. I even gave lessons to our downstairs neighbors on it. And when they came back later to take it back, they told me to sign again. So I signed. And there the address was at the top: Adderly House, Tarrytown, New York."

Adderly House? Tarrytown? Why did that sound familiar?

"What's that?" I asked, wondering if it was another mental institution or resident house.

"Noah's Ark."

"What?"

"Noah's Ark. In case of flood. I once thought I was Joan of Arc, you know."

Okay, now we might be heading into disturbed territory. "You did?" I asked.

"As if that weren't grandiose enough, I also thought I might have been touched by an angel. An archangel. Michael. Isn't it a beautiful name? I wanted to be called Sable but no one would call me that. What's your name again?"

"Madison."

"That's not your name."

"What? How could you know—"

"I know your name."

"You do?" A strange warmth fluttered in my chest.

"Yes, yes, I do, I do. *'I know your name,' the young queen cried, 'It's Rumpelstiltskin!'*"

I sagged. She had no answers. She was just crazy.

"The archangel used to sing to me. So beautifully. But the evil witch scared him away. And now I remain in this dungeon where he cannot find me," she said in a sing-song voice. "Spinning straw, spinning straw. Counting matchsticks." She pulled a cigarette from the pack with a shaky hand and lit it. "One match left," she said and blew smoke upwards.

She was silent a few moments, smoking. I stared at the closest Ficus tree, wondering whether I should leave. "Are you going to see my mother again?" she asked suddenly.

"I hadn't planned on it," I said.

"Don't. She'll mother you to death."

On the subway heading back into the city, I kept running Rebecca's disjointed conversation back through my head. Tamara had destroyed Rebecca's clothes and threatened her with a knife. Was the ghost just acting out the same events that led up to her death? Was Tamara's mysterious boyfriend the one who'd killed her? And why did Adderly House sound familiar? *And then it came to me*: Tarrytown. Tarrytown was also known as Sleepy Hollow, where the legend of the Headless Horseman came from. Tarrytown was also where that ghost hunt I'd seen advertised in Derek's store was happening. I was almost positive that ad had mentioned "Adderly House" on the flyer. It had to be a coincidence.

Didn't it?

There was one way to be sure.

CHAPTER NINE

"I REALLY DON'T THINK YOU SHOULD BE GOING alone," Derek said, leaning over the counter. Explaining why I wanted to sign up for the ghost hunt at Adderly House had taken almost an hour. During that time two tourists had come in, each actually buying a couple of books. I thought it might have been the first time I'd seen paying customers in his store.

"Are you offering to come with me?" I asked. "I thought you hated this stuff."

"Look, not only do I *not* believe in ghosts, but I also don't believe in the *business* of ghosts. It's all a scam and the people who perpetuate it are crazy at best, con artists at worst. Do you really think they'll be thinking about your safety? More likely they'll just be trying to film something scary they can upload to YouTube. Or wait, are these the guys who are trying to start another crappy reality show?" He took the flyer from my hands and gave it a quick scan. "Hm. Looks like they're actually associated with SUNY Mount Vernon. Well, I can at least drive you. How else do you plan to get to Sleepy Hollow?"

"Don't the trains go there?"

"Madison, seriously. I'll take you. It'll be much faster."

"I don't even know if they'll . . . Oh shit, what time is it?"

"It's 3:05."

"Gah, I'm late! I'll call you when I'm on my break."

I ran the three blocks to work. Billy was running the register and bag check by himself, while Trendon was restocking comics. A few customers were browsing the racks. Mac was in the back office with the timeclock. He made an exaggerated point of looking at his watch when I clocked in. "Sorry," I said, panting for breath.

"Just don't make it a habit."

"I won't," I said. "Am I on register or bag check?"

"Take over for Billy on bag check."

"Got it, boss," I said.

I went behind the counter, opposite the cash register, where Billy was standing, pale as always. With his full lips and sizable beak-like nose even his neutral expression always seemed snide, like he was sneering inwardly at the world. He was wearing his usual uniform of black pants, black comic book t-shirt, and combat boots, with his shoulder-length black hair pulled back in a ponytail. Today's t-shirt was a big green face with the word "Hulk" under it. About my height, Billy usually made eye contact when we were talking. Sometimes those eyes had

121

bags under them, especially when he'd been out drinking the night before. Today was one of those days.

"That's a rarity," he said.

"What is?" I asked.

"You being late. I think you're the only person who always gets here early."

"Yeah, Mac seemed kinda pissed or something."

"I doubt it. Nothing to worry about. Mac likes you. You're honest and friendly and you come in on time, plus you're a hot chick who likes and knows comics. You're lucky he's already married, or he'd have asked you."

"Ugh," I said, dismayed by the mental picture of Mac on one knee, holding out a small velvet box.

Billy laughed, clearly pleased that he'd gotten the reaction he wanted. "Speaking of your love life, how's the Sasquatch?"

"Oh, he's fine, as long as he has lots of shaving cream," I said.

Billy raised a pierced eyebrow. "What, can't he get electrolysis?"

"Too expensive. And painful. Bigfoot's kind of a wimp, didn't you know?"

"Aw, I'm sorry."

"For what?"

"Your date turned into a douche."

"He's not a douche!" I said, even though I wasn't exactly sure what it meant when referring to a person.

"He's not?"

"No. I mean, I don't think so." I stopped and thought about it while Billy rang up a customer.

When the guy was done paying, he handed me his bag check ticket, and I gave him his bag. He thanked me and went out. "So, how do you define a douche, exactly?" I asked.

"Well, he probably wouldn't thank you for giving you his bag from the bag check, for instance. That guy's okay. It's more like a dude who just does what his friends do, what other people do, just because he thinks it will be cool. He's obsessed with coolness and dressing well and what other people think and is probably a bit of a jackknob as well."

"A jackknob?"

"A dick."

"Did you make all of this up?"

"Some of it."

"Oh, good."

"Why is that good?"

"Because," I began, but then realized I didn't feel like finishing the sentence, and simply said, "Just because."

I'm really bad at slang, so I make up my own. It was good to know that Billy made up his own too. Slang was just another thing I didn't know about. It would have opened the conversation up to questions about what *else* I didn't know about, and why. And I didn't want to answer those questions right now. The only person at the store who knew my background was Mac, and he'd assured me he'd keep it confidential. It just never seemed like the right time to spill my deep dark secret to my co-workers.

Now that I thought about it, it seemed weird how I'd told Derek, who I barely knew, but hadn't told the people who I worked with and saw multiple times a week. But then I'd been considering dating him when I told him. *Had* been. Why did my brain phrase it that way? Was I no longer considering it? Maybe he was a douche after all.

Then again, he was a douche with a car who had offered to drive me to a ghost hunt he didn't even believe in. So maybe he wasn't a douche. He didn't dress well enough. And that reminded me: I had a phone call to make.

"Hey, Billy, you mind if I take a short break in about an hour?"

"Nah, that's fine. You going to get food?"

"Nope. Need to make a phone call."

"Why don't you just use my phone?"

"I don't want to put a bunch of charges on your phone. Plus, Mac."

"Where are you calling? China?"

"No, just, um, Tarrytown. In Westchester, I think?"

"That's fine."

"Um, it's weird."

"What's weird?"

"The call."

"Need to call Bigfoot?"

"No . . ."

"Gynecologist?"

"No!"

"Is it—"

"Okay, okay. It's a ghost hunt, all right? I'm signing up for a ghost hunt."

"Seriously?"

"Yes, seriously."

"That's awesome!"

"It is?"

"Duh. Is it one of the reality TV ones?"

"I have no idea. I don't really watch much TV."

"How'd you find out about it?"

"I saw this flyer," I said, unfolding it from my back pocket.

He scanned the page and handed it back to me. "Upstate, huh? How are you getting there?"

I folded the paper again and stuck it in my back pocket. "Sasquatch—whose name is Derek by the way—is driving me."

"I've always wanted to do something like that."

"Do you want to go?"

"I wouldn't want to cut in on your supernatural date, Maddy."

"It's not a date."

"Does Sas—I mean—Derek, know that?"

"I think so. He doesn't think I should go. He doesn't believe in ghosts."

"That's pretty narrow-minded."

While Mac was out getting himself some coffee, Billy gave me his phone and I called the number on the flyer. The phone rang. And rang.

"You have reached the voicemail of Professor Eric Gannon," said a recording. "If you are calling about volunteering, please—" BEEP BEEP interrupted the voice on the phone "—your name, age, gender, and your rating—" BEEP BEEP the phone went again. I pulled it away from my ear. The screen read "Incoming call." The same number I'd just called appeared below it.

"What is it?" Billy asked.

"I got the machine, but I think he's calling me back."

"So pick it up!" Billy said.

"How?" I asked.

"What are you, Amish?" Billy grabbed the phone, pushed a button, and put the phone back to my ear. "Hello?" I said.

"Hi," said the voice from the recording. "I just missed a call from this number."

"I was calling about volunteering," I said. "For the . . . ghost hunt . . . thing." Billy made devil horns with one hand and mouthed, "Yeeeeah," while headbanging.

"Ah! Excellent," the man on the phone said. "There are a few questions we have for potential volunteers. Do you have a few minutes?"

"Are you the person in charge?" I asked.

"Yes, I'm Professor Eric Gannon. I'm in the psychology department at SUNY Mount Vernon. I specialize in parapsychology, specifically ghosts. Are you a student at the university?"

"No, I'm—"

"That's fine. We try to get volunteers from different walks of life. I have a few other questions I'll need you to answer."

"Okay," I said. "What do you need to know?"

"Would you hold on a moment?" he asked. A lot of rustling happened on the other end. "My apologies. I needed to get pen and paper."

I must have had an odd look on my face, because Billy asked what was going on. I shrugged and rolled my eyes.

"Okay," Prof. Gannon continued. "Name?"

"Madison Roberts."

"Age?"

"Eighteen."

"Gender?"

"Uh, female."

"Of course. Sorry, it's just a formality."

"On a scale of 1 – 5, with one being no belief and five being absolute belief, where would you say your belief in the supernatural and ghosts falls?"

I thought for a moment, and said. "Four."

"Answering *only* yes or no, have you ever had any experiences that you have perceived to be paranormal?" he asked.

I paused before answering, "Yes."

"Answering only yes or no, do you have a heart condition, epilepsy, or any other condition of which we should be aware? If yes, please explain."

"No." Every time I answered yes or no, Billy happily nodded and mouthed "Yes" then shook his head and sadly mouthed "No."

"Stop!" I whispered, covering the phone. He cracked up.

"Last question. Answering only yes or no, do you have any physical disabilities in mobility, sight, or hearing that could prevent you from fully taking part in this field experiment?"

"No." I answered, holding a finger up at Billy, who—gearing up to make some ridiculous face again—deflated.

"Excellent," the professor said. "Let's see now. Age, good. Gender, also good. Belief four, okay, and then yes, no, no. Hmmm." I heard the sound of pages turning, as he murmured to himself. "Yes, right," he said. More pages turned. There was silence on the line a moment. Then, "Yes. We can use you. I don't suppose you happen to know a complete skeptic, do you? Someone who would rate a one for his or her belief?"

"Actually, yeah, I do."

"Could you convince that person to come with you? In addition to participants of different backgrounds, we also like to present a control group of non-believers in order to combat confirmation bias."

"Since he was going to give me a ride there anyway, that won't be too difficult."

"Excellent. Would you have him call me, then?"

"I'll ask him to," I said. I had no idea if Derek would.

"What about me?" Billy asked.

"Do you need any other volunteers?" I asked Prof. Gannon. "Another friend of mine is right here and he wants to know."

"Certainly," he said. "Put him on the line."

Billy threw up devil horns as I handed him the phone.

CHAPTER TEN

"SO THIS IS A DECENT CAR," BILLY SAID conversationally, his voice right in my ear. We were in Derek's Karmann Ghia, and Billy was sitting in the center of the small backseat, leaning forward to be heard over the sound of the engine.

"Glad you approve," Derek said.

It was about 5:30 in the evening as we sped up the Westside Highway. The sun was just beginning to set over the Hudson River, shining between the buildings on the opposite shore in New Jersey. The sky was orange sherbet with lilac petal clouds. I made observations about the water and the sky while Billy quizzed Derek on the particulars of the car, engaging in some male conversational ritual that led to a discussion of the college basketball playoffs of the previous month. I didn't even try to keep up.

Soon we were past the Bronx and heading into Westchester. Trees became more plentiful and the buildings became a lot shorter. We got off the highway at the Tarrytown exit, then followed the GPS directions from Derek's phone turn by turn for a several miles. The houses grew farther and farther apart, and the trees became thicker, taller, and more numerous.

Our last turn took us onto a winding dirt road without markers or any houses we could see. Derek's car bumped along slowly on the unpaved road which began to twist uphill in a series of spirals and S-curves. The setting sun spattered the woods in dappled shadows.

"Ugh, I'd hate to get stuck up here in the winter," Derek said. "Is there a house number?"

"No," I said, peering at the flyer.

"Oh, that's helpful," Billy said.

"Hey, you're the one who was all 'I can print the directions out' and then didn't bring them," I said. "If we get lost, it's your fault."

"Relax," Derek said, pointing to the comforting blue line on his phone screen. "Unlike you amateur ghostbusters, I have faith in science."

"I just didn't realize how far away it is from the main road," said Billy. "It's so isolated. Come on, we're going on a ghost hunt in the middle of nowhere. This is going to be awesome!"

I could practically feel Derek rolling his eyes. "Awesomely anti-climactic," he muttered, straining to see through the trees. "Ah, I think we might be getting close." He pointed ahead to a spot where pavement took over from the dirt. Everything smoothed out. The incline leveled out and our ride suddenly became smoother and quieter as the tires hit asphalt once more. The road widened and the woods opened up into a huge divided driveway, lined with pine trees on either side and a long rectangular reflecting pool filled with dark, leaf-littered water down the center. At the end was the house.

It was tall and white. A barn-like portion with several windows faced the driveway. "Dutch Colonial," Derek observed with some authority. Now it was Billy's turn to roll his eyes.

"How do you know that?" I asked.

"Well, from that arched roof, first of all, but mainly because my mother's a real estate agent."

As we pulled around a circular driveway, we were presented with four large Greek columns across the front of the house, framing its front door and wide front porch or patio. It contrasted bizarrely with the rest of the three-story building, which also had the same arched-roof appearance that Derek had said was Dutch. A white balcony with additional Greek styling loomed above the front door. It was like two architectural styles had gone to war and the house had lost.

"Dutch Colonial with . . . Greek columns?" Derek mused.

"Is that weird?" Billy asked.

"Definitely weird," Derek replied.

Two other cars were parked on the opposite side of the circular driveway: a black SUV, and a new-looking small silver sedan.

Derek pulled around where the other cars were and parked. Two people were on the porch, beyond the columns, standing next to a stack of cardboard boxes and black cases.

"There they are on the porch," I said.

"It's a portico," Derek said.

"Really?"

"Really," he replied with a hint of a smile. "But that's just a specific kind of porch."

I was worried that Billy's eyes might roll into the back of his head.

A man with glasses and sandy hair waved towards us. "Prof. Gannon, I presume," I said.

"He looks familiar . . . I think I might have seen him on YouTube," Billy said.

"I knew it," Derek said.

"Knew what?" Billy asked.

"Nothing. I shouldn't judge. I'm going to be objective."

"Riiight," I said, grabbing my backpack and opening the car door.

"What's that supposed to mean?"

I was going to ask him why he'd even come when Billy said, "Mom and Dad, I hate it when you fight," and got out of the car after me.

Out here in the country, Billy looked out of place. He wore his usual military-goth look with baggy black cargo pants and combat boots, along with a weathered black leather motorcycle jacket with three orange stripes around each bicep.

"How do you like my Wolverine jacket?" he'd asked me the first time he'd worn it to the store.

"That's Wolverine's jacket?" I'd asked.

"You're such a dork, Madison," he'd replied.

Derek and I were both in jeans and t-shirts. He wore a gray hooded sweatshirt over his while I wore a navy pea coat that got itchy when worn over short sleeves.

I took a quick survey of the house and grounds. It sounded as isolated as it looked. The only noises were a light breeze moving through the trees and crickets chirping nearby. The air was crisp and fresh. I didn't realize how used to street noise and air pollution I was.

The lawn area on the left side of the house featured a group of weathered white statues surrounding a stagnant fountain filled with green water. The statues seemed to be dancing nymphs or goddesses.

"What the hell is *up* with this place?" Billy whispered, as though someone important might hear him. He sounded fascinated.

The sandy-haired man in glasses approached, carrying a clipboard. He wore faded jeans and an untucked dress shirt with bright yellow and blue sneakers. He was probably in his mid-thirties and about my height. "I'm Prof. Gannon," he said, glancing at the clipboard. "You must be Madison, Derek, and Billy?"

We agreed that we were. He peeled a yellow sticky note off the top of the clipboard. "I have some release forms here for all of you to sign. It should only take a minute." He handed me the clipboard and pen, and I scanned the form. It listed all the info I'd given the professor over the phone, plus a check box where I agreed the info was correct and that I had no prior knowledge of Adderley House. It also granted him permission to film me without financial recompense. I checked, signed, and peeked at the form beneath mine. Billy's name was on it, so I handed the clipboard to him. He signed and handed the clipboard to Derek, who took an extra minute looking over the form before he signed with a sigh and handed it back to the professor.

He flipped through the forms and nodded. "Now if I could just see some identification to confirm your ages and identities."

Derek glanced at me, concern crossing his face. I shrugged and opened my wallet, taking out the only ID I had: my Spring House resident pass. Billy and Derek handed him their driver's licenses and he checked them over and handed them back. He examined them each carefully, but mine he gave special attention.

"You don't have anything else? Something with your date of birth, perhaps?" he asked.

I was prepared for this. I reached into one of the zipper pockets of my backpack and pulled out a certified letter from my social worker, Linda, that she had given me as some sort of official documentation of my ID-less situation.

Prof. Gannon's eyes scanned over the page, comparing it to my resident pass before holding the paper up to the fading evening light and squinting at it from beneath his glasses.

Billy watched all of this with some confusion. I could see the question forming on his face as he glanced at me.

"Ah," Prof. Gannon said, as if he'd found what he was looking for. He folded the letter back into its envelope and handed it back to me. "Very interesting. I suppose that's all in order. Follow me."

"What was that about?" Billy whispered as the professor led us toward the door.

"Later," I said.

We went up three steps on the side of the house between two white columns. Ahead of us, two dirty latticed glass doors—the kind that are called French doors—were closed. Up close, the paint on the house was chipped and cracked, though the columns and the stone porch—excuse me, *portico*—seemed in decent shape. A woman stood there among the black cases and cardboard. She held an electronic device of some kind and appeared to be taking readings of something.

"This is my colleague, Dr. Nina Hernandez," Prof. Gannon said. She was a medium height woman in her early-thirties. Her black hair was worn in a bun, and she wore a gray business suit with sensible shoes and thick black-framed glasses.

"Thank you for coming," she said with a smile. The smile transformed her from a foreboding professor into a raven-haired beauty. I wondered if she wore the glasses to put the focus on her brain and not her looks.

The sound of a car's engine and tires on asphalt

reached us as a white Saab pulled up to the parking area.

"That will be Katie Davis," said Prof. Gannon. "She's a student at the university, and also a volunteer participant." As she got out of the car, I estimated that Katie was probably nineteen or twenty, with highlighted brown hair that went past her shoulders. She wore tight jeans with tall brown high heel boots and a brown leather jacket. Something about her clothing and style said *money*. Maybe it was the way it all fit her perfectly.

"Hello, Professor," Katie said as she joined us. "I'm not late, am I?"

"Not at all," Prof. Gannon said. "I am grateful to you all for taking part in this experiment. Before we go into the house, I'd like to acquaint you all with a bit of its hist—"

"Wait, are we it?" Billy interrupted. "You don't have any other volunteers?"

"We did, until three days ago," Dr. Hernandez said, brightly, as though trying to put a good spin on it.

"And then we had three cancellations," Prof. Gannon said, "and another one this afternoon. This means that my usual assistants won't be here, though I do have one more person who should arrive any time now. Under the circumstances, and also due to our criteria, we were very lucky to have heard from you three."

"We lucky few," Derek muttered, low enough that probably only I heard him.

"As I was saying," Prof. Gannon said, "the house has an interesting history. Did you note the gambrel roof?"

"Yes," Derek said. "It's Dutch, isn't it?"

"Indeed," said the professor.

"What's a gambrel roof?" asked Katie, taking notes on a small pad like a reporter.

The professor made an arch with his fingers that resembled the roof of a barn. "Shaped like this," he said. "The style, while not exclusively Dutch, was brought over by early settlers from the Netherlands."

Katie nodded vigorously and jotted something down.

"Teacher's pet," muttered Billy.

The professor continued his lecture. "Originally built in the late 1600s by a wealthy Dutch merchant making a home for his family, one Klaus Van Horn, the house passed through generations of the family and was added on to as needed throughout the 1700s. Just before the turn of the century—in 1796, that is—the house was inherited by a distant relative, a widow who reverted to her maiden name, Irina Van Horn. Irina, who with her mother had traveled extensively in Europe and the Mediterranean, had the house renovated to include the Greek Revival stylings you see here."

Just then, we heard the arrival of another car. A battered 1970's station wagon with wood paneling on the sides came chugging up the driveway. A young woman with dark hair and dark eyes got out and walked toward us. She wore a long skirt and a shapeless long-sleeved sweater with a wide neck over it.

"Ah. Last but not least," Prof. Gannon said, "this is Zoe Brooks. She is our paranormal expert."

Zoe tucked her chin into her chest with a slight frown when the professor said "expert." I thought she might have been in her mid-twenties, but her shy demeanor and slouchy clothes left me guessing.

"Anyway," said the professor, "what's interesting about the architecture is that no one else in the country was building in the Greek style at the time. The Greek Revival period didn't come until later, in 1803 or so."

Was that interesting? I mean, I guess it could be interesting for an architecture nerd, but what did it have to do with a ghost hunt?

"Irina Van Horn and her mother appear to have only lived in the newly renovated house for two years before departing for Europe once more. It seems that small-town life did not suit them—or perhaps they left to avoid the outbreak of Yellow Fever that had ravaged the village.

"Over the years, other members of the family moved in and out, through to 1906, when the last living member of that branch of the family, Mary Van Horn, died. Then the Van Horn Homestead, as it was then known, stood empty for thirty-two years, until in 1938 a distant member of the family deeded the house and land to a young man named Michael Adderly, a popular singer—what they called a crooner back then—who had the house renovated in the Art Deco style with all the then-modern conveniences, including electricity, and moved in with his young wife."

Out of the corner of my eye, I saw movement. Zoe was looking at the ceiling above us, but then she caught me watching her and looked at her feet. What had she seen?

"The carriage house—which you'll see around the back—was converted to a two-car garage. The landscaping was added, including a tennis court, pools, fountains, and statuary, at that time. However, Michael Adderly experienced much tragedy here. He became a complete recluse. He retained ownership through the early 1990s, when he mysteriously vanished.

"His earthly estate, including the house—which by then was known as Adderly House—was to go to his nephew, a young man seen around town a handful of times in the three to four years before Adderly's disappearance. However, no one was able to find the nephew. As a result, the estate was left in trust with a management company that has attempted to rent the house out several times over the years. Unfortunately, they have managed only to maintain it due to—well, that's why we're here. Questions?"

The whole time the professor lectured, Katie furiously scribbled into her notepad. Dr. Hernandez, in the meantime, alternately checked the device she was holding and watched the rest of us. Zoe didn't look up from her feet again until Gannon stopped talking.

Billy slowly raised his hand. Prof. Gannon nodded at him, and Billy asked, "Exactly why *are* we here? Is the place haunted, or what?"

Prof. Gannon exchanged glances with Dr. Hernandez, who shrugged and smiled brightly at him. He sighed, and said, "For the purposes of this field experiment, my colleague has requested that I not inform participants about the nature or background of any suspected paranormal activities here in order to avoid bias or expectation on your part. We don't want your perceptions tainted by prior awareness."

"Why did you tell us the history of the house then?" Derek asked.

Dr. Hernandez smiled. She seemed to approve of the question. "The history meets exemption criteria for the research we're doing today," she said.

"Huh," Derek said. "Interesting."

I took this to mean that knowing the house's history wouldn't affect whatever we found or saw. Why she couldn't just say it that way, I had no idea.

"I have another question," Billy said. When the professor nodded again, Billy continued, "Does the house have anything to do with the Headless Horseman?"

Derek snorted. Katie's pencil stopped. Dr. Hernandez seemed amused. Zoe flushed.

Billy looked chagrined. "Well, we *are* in Sleepy Hollow."

Prof. Gannon's eyebrows drew together a moment and then he took a deep breath. "I'm afraid I can't answer that question as it might bias your experience as a participant."

Billy's mouth opened for a second and then closed. It seemed like he was about to ask another question, but then decided not to.

"Any other questions?" the professor asked, looking around. When there weren't any, Prof. Gannon rubbed his hands together. "Excellent. Let's head inside and get set up."

Billy took his phone out of his pocket, presumably to check the time—something he normally did several times per hour. "What the—? I don't have any signal," he complained.

Derek checked his phone. "Neither do I."

"Me either," Katie said, checking a device with a hot pink cover.

"You might as well turn them off," Prof. Gannon said. "I don't know if we're just too far from the nearest cell tower, or if there's some kind of electrical interference, but you'll never get a signal until you get back to the main road."

"Creepy," Billy whispered. He seemed to be enjoying this.

"No reception in the boonies," Derek said, and shrugged. "Not that surprising."

"Miles away from the nearest phone," Billy replied with a grin. "Can't call for help."

"Not true, actually. There's a working phone in the caretaker's cottage, which is only half a mile out past the carriage house," Prof. Gannon said, hefting a large cardboard box. "Shall we head in?"

CHAPTER ELEVEN

THE FOYER WAS LARGE, WITH A DUSTY GLASS chandelier hanging in the center of the room. Its crystals hung in cascading rows like sequined fringe. Behind it, a stylized wrought iron banister with geometric shapes curved upwards along black and white marble steps. Arched doorways led to other rooms both up and downstairs.

Prof. Gannon led us through the right arch into the huge living room. The walls were elaborately paneled, while most of the furniture was covered in white sheets. The room's focus was a large ornate fireplace covered in white and blue tiles. All of the other furniture surrounded it: two couches, two coffee tables, two chairs. Even the lighting flanked the fireplace, two lamps built into the walls with gold-tinted glass shades facing upwards like tulips. Was that a piano in the corner of the room? Was it *the* piano? The one Rebecca had mentioned?

I impulsively walked toward it before seeing something move in the corner of my eye. I glanced to my left, toward the tiled fireplace. Nothing was there. I shook my head and found Zoe's eyes on me.

She tilted her head meaningfully at the fireplace, then raised her eyebrows with an expectant look.

Was she asking me what I'd seen? I shrugged. I hadn't seen anything, really. Just a shadow, probably. It could have even been my own. Even so, I got a creepy feeling and wondered if I should try to avoid being around Zoe. What did the professor mean that she was a "paranormal expert" anyway?

Just as I was wondering this, the professor brought in some clamp lights that he attached to the tulip lamps.

"The electricity isn't on. It was supposed to be," he said. "I'll have to check the fuse box after we set up."

Zoe was looking at the fireplace again, her face scrunched in confusion as she examined the white tiles with their blue illustrations.

"The Delft tiles in that fireplace are original to the house," the professor commented. "Everything else was renovated. So what do you think, Zoe?"

She tucked a strand of hair behind her ear and grimaced, her eyes scanning the ceiling before coming to rest on the professor. "It's . . . um . . . going to be interesting, I can say that."

He leaned in closer and, in a low voice, asked, "How many?" I guess he thought I wouldn't be able to hear.

"How many what?" Billy asked, carrying in a cardboard box full of cables.

"Three," Zoe said, ignoring him.

The professor seemed somewhat taken aback,

his eyes going wide for a moment. "Already?"

"They're curious."

"You see ghosts," I said to Zoe, not asking.

"Yeeeah," she said, somewhat reluctantly.

Billy dropped the box. "Really? In here? Where?"

"Careful with that!" the professor shouted, rushing over to check the contents.

"There was one in here. Over there," Zoe said, pointing toward the fireplace, "but he's gone now."

"Really? No shit?" Billy said. "Did you see it, Maddy?"

"Um, no," I said.

Zoe gave me a look like she thought I was lying.

"See what?" Derek asked, carefully setting down a heavy box marked CAMERA EQUIPMENT.

"Nothing," I said, and went to see if there was still more gear outside.

There wasn't. Billy and Derek had wasted no time moving all of the equipment inside. The crystals in the chandelier tinkled as Derek's head brushed against the lowest row as he planted the last of the boxes beneath it. I peeked through the archway behind the stairs to see a kitchen done in green tiles. I also noticed a door that might have led to the basement. I ducked my head back into the living room, where Katie, Dr. Hernandez, and Prof. Gannon were setting up lights. Despite their efforts, the shadows in the room deepened in the twilight.

I went over to the fireplace to see what I could see. It was immaculately clean. No ashes, no logs, not even a bit of kindling to get a fire going.

The white tiles with the blue drawings seemed to depict biblical stories. There was an image of a whale on one tile, and another with a man versus a giant. Yet another had a large boat with animals. Weird. I wondered why I was just wandering the room, and then realized that my wandering was purposeful, that what I was actually doing was avoiding the one thing in the room that had brought me there: the piano.

Summoning up my courage, I walked over to it and peeked beneath the sheet. There it was, the logo *Steinway & Sons* etched in gold. But what about the fall? Julie had said it was chipped. I sat down and ran my fingers along the bottom edge. The left corner had indeed been chipped off. Bingo. It had to be the same piano. And now, here I was, sitting on a piano bench, knowing that I knew how to play. I doubted it was in tune, but I longed to run my fingers over the keys. I assumed what I knew was the correct posture.

"Do you play?" asked Zoe. I hadn't realized that she'd walked up beside me.

"I . . . think so," I said. *What a weird answer. You're going to have to do better than that.*

Zoe's raised an eyebrow. "Well, let's hear a few notes."

I raised the fall and tentatively touched an ivory key. A rich C, bell-like in tone and perfectly pitched, sounded in the room. Prof. Gannon stuck his head in. "Uh, don't do that, please."

147

I jumped up, my legs pushing the bench back a few inches. "Oh! Sorry," I said, letting the white sheet fall back across the piano.

"Zoe," Prof. Gannon said, holding up a finger and moving it from side to side, as if he were reprimanding her.

"What?" she said, incredulously. "They like it."

"Who likes it?" I asked. But Prof. Gannon just held his finger up again and make a "tut" sound, then curled his finger in a come-hither motion and gestured for Zoe to come. She went, like a child reluctantly reporting to a parent for punishment.

She was definitely young, I thought. Older than me, maybe even older than Derek, but probably around his age or not much more. The large sweater she wore over her skirt made her seem shapeless. I could just see Kara trying to give her a makeover like she had me. I was still most comfortable in jeans and t-shirts, but she'd taught me to show off my figure—such as it was. I didn't think much of my appearance but others said I was pretty.

I was a little warm, so I took off my coat and backpack and hung them on the coat rack near the front door, where everyone else's things were. I found myself looking at my reflection in a mirror there while everyone else bustled back and forth. Light eyebrows, a dusting of freckles across my nose. High cheekbones. I poked at one. Who was I? What was my background? Was I French? German? I couldn't speak a lick of it. Irish? I wished for the thousandth time that I had some hint to my identity other than an old matchbook and a key hanging on a chain. I pulled on the key through the material of my shirt and the chain went taut around my neck.

"All right," Prof. Gannon said, calling my attention back to where I was and what I was supposed to be doing. "You'll be going through the first floor in teams of two. We were supposed to have electricity, but it's not working. I'm going to have to go check on that. For now, every team member gets a flashlight with a red filter to keep you from ruining your night vision. This is just our first pass. After full dark, we'll keep flashlights off and pass out walkie talkies. I will be stationed here with the equipment."

Dr. Hernandez began messing with the walkie talkies while Prof. Gannon loaded new batteries into flashlights, flicking them on to test them once before handing them out. "Madison and Billy, you will have thirty minutes to explore the kitchen and connecting hallway. Derek and Katie, you will have the same amount of time to explore the dining room. Dr. Hernandez and Zoe, the living room is yours."

"Professor?" Katie asked, her hand in the air. "What are we looking for, exactly?"

"Anything that strikes you as strange, out of the ordinary. I don't mean strange items, though there are plenty of those in this house, but rather odd noises, smells, feelings. Inexplicable phenomena. That kind of thing. Changes in temperature. If you see something, *say* something, as they say on the subways." He gazed at us all for a moment and asked, "Good enough?" Billy shrugged and nodded, and I saw Katie and Derek do the same. I nodded too. "Very good," the professor said, checking his watch. "And . . . go. Meet back here in thirty minutes."

"Here we go," Billy said, clicking on the flashlight, headed toward the kitchen. Derek nodded at me and went in the opposite direction with Katie. I was a little bummed that he and I weren't together. I followed Billy into the hallway that led to the kitchen. Behind an open door, there was a little bathroom, just a half-bath, probably for guests to use, done up in black and—were they red? No, that was the flashlight—white checkerboard tiles with a black toilet and black sink. The room was small and the water ran when Billy tried the tap. "Good thing to know if you need to go," he said.

There was a door on the right, farther down the hallway. "What do you think this is?" Billy asked.

"No idea. You open or me?"

"I'll open," he said, and did. I held my breath a moment and then let it out. It was an empty closet.

Billy sighed and closed the door. "Kitchen next?"

"Sure," I said, and we made our way back to it.

Some light was still coming through the windows so we turned off our flashlights to save power. There wasn't much of note aside from the color scheme, a round white table, white chairs, white counters, and lime green cabinets with glass doors that revealed empty shelves. One door led to a porch on the back of the house, another was a pantry that was almost completely empty except for a few prehistoric cans of food. The ancient refrigerator—resembling a coffin in size—was empty, luckily, though it smelled of mildew. Billy searched through a few drawers while I checked to see if the water was running in the sink. It was. I almost expected it to be brown—or possibly even red—but the water came out clear and boring.

"Hey," Billy said, holding up a corkscrew he'd found. "Check this out!"

"You found a corkscrew. Congratulations," I said.

"No, no, not the corkscrew itself, but what the corkscrew *implies*."

"Which is?"

"Wine. Corkscrews are for opening bottles. *Wine bottles*. Therefore, where there's a corkscrew, there's wine. I bet this place has some kind of awesome wine cellar or something. We should find it."

"I think we're just supposed to do the first floor, the kitchen and hallway over there."

"Boring," Billy intoned. "Come on. The basement is bound to be spookier than this."

"I don't know if I want to go to the spooky basement," I said, looking through the cabinets beneath the counter tops. Pots and pans and mixing bowls lined most of the shelves. Some were empty.

"Why did you come here then?" Billy asked. "And what was up with your ID? Don't you have a license or state ID?"

Ugh. I did not want to get into that discussion. Not one part of it. I pointed at the one door we hadn't tried. "Think that's the way down?" I asked him.

"Oh, hey, it just might be," he said, forgetting his question. He opened it, and the hinges creaked loudly. "Confirmed," he whispered. "We have stairs going down."

A vaguely musty, damp smell emanated from the doorway now—a basementy smell, I thought, kind of like the basement at work.

"Do you really want to do this?" I asked.

"Totally," Billy said. "I'll go first." He stepped tentatively onto the first step, which beneath his weight creaked with a little *eep* sound at first, as though the step was protesting.

I hesitated at the top of the stairs, watching the red beam from Billy's flashlight bob in the darkness. I wasn't sure if we'd get in trouble for going down to the basement when we were supposed to be exploring the hallway and kitchen, but I wasn't sure what else there was to investigate besides the dishes and glasses. Billy was right, it was boring. For the first time since coming to the Adderly House, I felt some doubt. I felt foolish. What the hell was I doing there, and why had I dragged Billy and Derek into it?

Maybe I did owe Billy an explanation. I directed my flashlight into the stairwell and grasped the handrail and went down into the red-lit dark.

The musty smell was stronger as I reached the bottom of the stairs, and the air felt colder and damper. "So, Billy, about why I came here . . ." I began, only to realize I couldn't see the light of his flashlight anymore.

"Billy?" I said, and waited for a response. Nothing.

It was too quiet and too dark. "Billy?" I said again, lifting my flashlight to scan the area around me.

"HA! Gotcha!" Billy said suddenly, clicking on his flashlight beneath his chin. He was just a foot away from me, provoking both a brief, hysterical scream and a punch as I whirled on him. "Owww," he said. "I'm just fucking around."

"Well, don't. You scared me half to death."

He rubbed his upper arm. "Damn, girl, you can punch."

"Remember that," I said, pleased with myself. I could punch a guy and make it count. That had to be a worthwhile skill. Maybe I'd taken self-defense classes. Or boxing. Or maybe I'd had an older brother. No way of knowing.

"Did you find the wine?" I asked, shining my flashlight around the room. There were arched ceilings that were over seven feet high. Shelves had been built into the walls, with small boxes and barrels piled on them. Wooden crates had been stacked on the floor against the walls where there were no shelves.

"Not yet," Billy said, scanning with his own

flashlight. "Bingo," he said when the light landed on a rack filled with dark, dusty bottles. "Man, some of these aren't even labeled. Whoa! This one is from 1939," and picking up another, said, "1926. That must have been a good year. There are five bottles of that one alone."

"What do you think is in all of these boxes?" I asked.

"Hm, good question," he said. He pulled down a small wooden box and I came closer to take a look.

The top of the box was engraved with the word HABANA, and the latch, while firmly closed, was not locked. A partially torn sticker on the side read, "For cigars imported from H—" with a bunch of Spanish words I couldn't read.

"A cigar box," I said.

"Wow, old Cubans, huh? Too bad they're probably dried out." Billy handed me the box and I gave it a little shake. Something rustled inside.

"Should we open it?" I asked. I felt strange. Like I was invading someone's privacy.

"Duh, yes," Billy replied. "Go ahead."

Billy held his flashlight over the top while I opened it. Inside were photographs. Small black and white pictures with thin white borders. The one on top showed a man and woman posed together, smiling, their clothes probably from the 1920s or '30s.

"Precious memories, huh?" Billy observed. "I guess that's probably all there is in this place. Didn't the doc say that the owner disappeared?"

"Something like that," I said. I wasn't sure. I skipped a few photos and studied another. It also featured a man and woman posed together, smiling. That was weird. I scanned the next one. Another photo of a man and woman posed. Were they all the same photo? I went back to the top. No, the clothing was different from image to image. And the backgrounds varied. But most of them were snapshots, some square, some rectangular. All were black and white and had white borders around the edges.

"What's up?" Billy asked.

I propped the box on stack of crates and showed him what I'd noticed. Billy unscrewed the red filter from his flashlight to get a better view. We paged through the stack together. In every picture, a couple stood, smiling. "Wait, are they the same people every time?" Billy asked.

I took a closer look. "Maybe?—no," I quickly amended. From photo to photo, the girls varied from tall to short and chubby to skinny. Some had glasses, some had short hair, some long. In every photo, though, it was the same man. Sometimes in a suit, other times a short-sleeved shirt, sometimes wearing a hat, but always the same jaw-length dark hair that framed his face, the same crooked smile. "The guy is. It's always the same guy. The girls are different."

"Serial killer much?"

"Yikes," I said. Then, looking closely at one image, I realized the girl was wearing one of those long skirts they call "poodle" skirts from the 1950s. I went back to the first photo and showed it to Billy. "When do you think this was taken?" I asked.

"I dunno. Maybe the 1940s or so? I'm not great with history."

"And what about this one?" I asked, showing him the one with the poodle skirt.

"That one's definitely the '50s. The skirt's a dead giveaway."

"Why did this guy keep so many pictures of himself posed with so many girls?"

"Maybe it was his trophy collection. Doc said the guy was some kind of singer back then, right? Maybe he was just getting a lot of tail and wanted to record it."

"Tail? Really?" I said, turning the flashlight on Billy.

"What word do you want me to use?" he asked. "Nookie?"

"I think this is important," I said. "I'm going to bring it upstairs." I put the photos back in the box and closed it.

"Yeah, I think our thirty minutes are about up anyway," Billy said. "Can you fit this bottle of wine in your backpack?"

"Billy!" I stage-whisper-shouted at him. "Put it back!"

"But Mom!" he whined. "I promise not to drink and drive!"

"No way. Besides, I left my backpack upstairs." It was one thing to snoop around in the basement, but stealing a bottle of wine just seemed wrong.

"Fine," he said, and pouted. The bottle made a solid *clink* as Billy placed it back on the rack, and we made our way back upstairs. Light poured in the doorway to the kitchen from the other side of the house.

The foyer seemed bigger now that it was fully lit, and Zoe was walking back in the front door, carrying a large toolbox. She went through the archway opposite the living room. Dr. Hernandez sat in a folding chair, making notes on a clipboard. Her glasses had slid down her nose and she seemed deep in thought, utterly uninterested in the machines and monitors that surrounded her.

"Dr. Hernandez?" I asked. She regarded us inquisitively. "We found this box of photos. I don't know if you'd be interested in looking at them?"

She frowned minutely, and without even looking at the box, gestured to a card table set up with a monitor on it. "Just set it down there and we'll take a look later."

I was disappointed, but I put the box down as I'd been told. I could hear Derek's voice in the next room, the one where Zoe had gone with the toolbox. "Where's everyone else?" I asked.

"They're in the dining room," she said, gesturing toward the left room, "except for Eric—Prof. Gannon—and Katie. They've gone up to the caretaker's cottage and should be back soon." She resumed her note-taking. I turned around to ask Billy if he wanted to check out the dining room only to realize that I could hear his voice coming from it.

"Bottles and bottles of wine," he was saying as I entered the room.

"Stop acting like a criminal," I said, then stopped in my tracks. The room was dominated by a long black table with low-back black chairs. The light-colored wooden floor had been inlaid with concentric rectangles of black wood, starting at the edges of the room and getting smaller until the last one surrounded the table and chairs. Two red crystal chandeliers hung suspended over the table's center. Long black drapes hung in the tall windows facing the front of the house, and an archway led down a hallway somewhere.

"Wow," I said.

"Impressive, isn't it?" Derek said.

"Actually, if anyone here is acting like a criminal, it's me," Zoe said. She was standing next to a set of French doors and unpacking several screwdrivers from a tool kit. Next to her was one of those Japanese screens, the kind that act as room dividers. It was black and decorated with three peacocks in different poses, each one on a different panel.

"What are you guys doing?" I asked.

"I'm preparing to do a little amateur burglary," she said, gesturing at the door.

"Wait, doesn't that just lead outside?" I asked.

"It looks like it," Derek said, "but it doesn't."

"He's the one who noticed it," Zoe said. "If you go outside, you can tell there's another room right here. This screen was actually attached to the wall in front of the doors. Unless you pulled it down to see behind it, you'd never even know it was here. You should have seen Prof. Gannon's face when— Derek, right? When Derek told him."

"Nice going," I said to Derek. "When did the lights come on?"

"About five minutes ago," Derek said. "He was about to leave for the caretaker's cottage to call the management company when I found this. He said he'd ask the caretaker for the keys."

"Then if there are keys, then you won't need to pick the lock, right?" I said to Zoe.

"Oh, I can't pick a lock," she said. "But here's a lifehack for you: if a door is locked, and you don't have a key, if the hinges are on your side, you're in business."

"Handy," I said.

"You're so cool," Billy said. He was clearly in awe of Zoe.

Zoe smiled shyly in return. "Not really," she said.

"But you see ghosts," I said.

Derek took on a wary look while Billy's face lit up.

"I don't like to talk about it," Zoe said.

"Why not?" Billy asked incredulously. "If I had a superpower, I'd never shut up about it."

"Because people think you're crazy when you say you see ghosts," Zoe said.

"But you're *not* crazy, right?" Billy said.

"Sometimes I wonder."

"What do you mean?" Derek asked.

"It's one thing to be four years old and have what your mother thinks is an imaginary friend. It's another thing entirely to be woken up in the middle of the night by the spirit of a woman who has just died in a car crash who wants you to tell her husband that she doesn't blame him for her death."

"Whoa," Billy said. Everyone was quiet a moment.

"Sorry for bringing the mood down," Zoe said with a sigh. "What about you, Madison?"

"What about me?"

"Yeah, what about you?" Billy echoed.

"What?"

"Can you see them?" Zoe asked.

I bit my lip. "I don't think so. Not as far as I know, anyway," I said. "But . . ."

"But?" Zoe asked.

"But I'm pretty sure my apartment is haunted."

"What, seriously? And you didn't even tell me?" Billy snapped.

"It's not the kind of thing you go around telling people!" I said.

"Did you know?" Billy asked Derek.

"Yeah," Derek said.

Billy raised his eyebrows and glared at me.

"That was how we met," Derek continued. "I work at Thirteen Books. She came in for research."

"I *knew* you looked familiar," Zoe said.

"Been there?" Derek asked.

"A couple of times," she said. She turned to me. "So what's the deal with your ghost?"

"I'm really not sure. There's kind of a lot."

"I can't believe you didn't tell me about this," Billy said.

"Billy, come on—I didn't even know you were into ghostly stuff until yesterday."

"You couldn't have guessed?" he asked, gesturing at his all-black wardrobe.

"Wait, are all of you Fives on the belief scale?" Derek asked.

"I'm a Four," I said.

"Five," Zoe said.

"Three," Billy said. "I kind of want to believe, but I don't really. If that makes any sense."

"You're a One?" Zoe asked Derek.

He snorted. "When the professor asked what my belief was on a scale of one to five, I asked, 'Isn't there a Zero?'"

"Wow, I'm kind of surprised," Zoe said.

"Why's that?" Derek asked.

"With you working at Thirteen Books, I mean," she said.

Derek explained about his uncle owning the bookstore as well as the building, and a conversation followed about the rates of rent in New York City. Zoe lived by herself in Queens. Billy had grown up in the Bronx, and still lived there now, with three roommates. "The apartment sucks, but the rent is cheap," he said.

As this discussion wound down, Prof. Gannon returned with faithful Katie at his heels. I couldn't help noticing how hard she was trying to impress him with her good student routine. I wondered if she was a two on the belief scale. It would mean he had one observer for every measurement on the scale. I wondered if that was on purpose.

"Well, I'm glad to see everything all lit up now. The master fuse just needed to be reset," the professor said. "No luck with any extra keys, though Mr. Kong—that is, the fellow I spoke with on the 24-hour help line for the management company— gave us express permission to enter any room on the grounds as a part of our investigation."

"What does a real estate management company need a 24-hour help line for?" Derek asked.

"Yeah, seriously. I wish I could get 24-hour help from . . . did you say 'Kong'?" said Billy. "I tried calling my slumlord when my ceiling started leaking right over my bed. No answer. Didn't return my calls for three days."

No wonder Billy slept on park benches. I felt a little bad for him and a lot grateful toward Mr. Delgado for being there when we needed him.

Prof. Gannon said, "However, that is entirely beside the point, as we have permission, and a locked room to enter. I am impressed with your observational skills, Derek. None of the other groups we've had in the house ever noticed it."

"Hanging a room divider on the wall just seemed odd to me—like someone was trying to hide something," Derek said.

"How many other groups have you had in here?" asked Billy.

"Three," the professor said. Katie carefully scrawled the number down in her notebook.

"Did each group have five observers that each had different measurements on your belief scale?" I asked.

The professor raised his eyebrows. Katie glanced back and forth between the two of us, waiting for him to answer.

"I'm afraid I can't answer that at present," Prof. Gannon said.

"Did any of the other groups have any supernatural encounters?" Billy asked.

"I'm afraid I can't—"

Billy cut him off. "Right, bias and all that. I almost forgot," he said.

"So about these doors . . ." the professor said.

"Not a problem," Zoe said, picking up a slim screwdriver. She held the business end beneath the top hinge of the right door and tapped it once with the hammer. A skinny metal bolt popped out of the top of it. Then she did the same with the other two hinges.

"Now we just pull out the pins, lift, and voila!" she said. She put down the tools, grasped the doorknob and one of the hinges, and gave the door a lift.

"Well done," the professor said as the door slid out of the hinges. Then, when it almost toppled over onto Zoe, he and Billy both sprang forward and helped her set it down. A dark gray curtain hanging from the other side of the door let out a puff of dust in Katie's direction, making her cough.

The room beyond was dark. Red shag carpet appeared in the slice of light from the dining room chandeliers, but other than that, it was hard to tell what was in there.

I clicked on my flashlight and stepped through the doorway, shining the red light into the darkness. Motes of dust spun through the air as the beam revealed shelves filled with books on the opposite wall.

"Library," said Zoe.

I could make out a desk and some kind of low couch as the main furniture of the room, along with a desk lamp and a floor lamp in one corner. "I see some light fixtures," I said.

"I'd better get some more clamp lights," the professor said.

"I can get them, Professor," Katie said, a bit too eagerly.

"No need," he said and stepped out of the room.

"Should we go on in?" Billy asked in a low voice. "Dark library hidden away in a haunted house? Who knows how long since anyone's been in there. This could be epic."

"I think we should wait," Katie said doubtfully, casting her glance toward the doorway.

"We should at least wait for the lights," Derek said.

I felt along the wall of the library for a switch and was pleasantly surprised to feel my fingers brush against a hard button. I pressed it, and the floor lamp in the corner lit up.

"Let there be light," I said with a smile, and stepped into the room.

Chapter Twelve

MY FIRST IMPRESSION WAS JUST ONE WORD: WOOD. The room had dark-reddish brown wood (was it mahogany?) bookshelves on every wall all the way up to the ceiling, which had been painted a rich burgundy. A lacquered black desk, covered in scattered papers, dominated the left side of the room. The other side of the room featured a low red couch and a round arm chair upholstered with leopard print. The floor lamp stood behind the couch, its copper shade reminiscent of the wide end of a bugle.

The room smelled like dried rose petals—like the potpourri Julie kept a dish of in her bedroom.

"What's that smell?" I asked.

"What smell?" Billy asked.

"Like dried roses," I said.

"It's the books," Derek said from the dining room. "Old books smell like that. It's the paper rotting."

Zoe and Billy crowded in behind me. The red shag rug beneath our feet was thick, muffling the sound of their footsteps. I continued to take in the room, paying attention to the odd details. The shelves were filled with books and oddments: small statues, ornamental boxes, a bottle, a bell. Derek and Katie were still standing in the dining room.

Billy whistled a low whistle and said, "Pretty swank."

The right wall next to the light switch had a few floor cabinets and an old-timey record player sitting on top. Was that a phonograph? A golden statue of an Egyptian woman with her arms held out, almost a foot high, stood next to it. Above that hung a framed oil painting of the sun hanging low over the ocean. I couldn't tell if it was rising or setting. There was no way to tell without knowing which ocean it was.

There were no windows, but there was a single latticed door centered in the far-right wall, surrounded by bookshelves, and partially obscured from view by the couch.

Billy walked up to the desk, stepping around some papers that had fallen to the floor. A *thud* sound came from behind the desk, like something falling over, and Billy froze. "Um, what was that?" he asked.

My heart just about stopped in my chest. "You mean that wasn't you?" I asked.

"No." He stood completely still.

"Zoe, are there any—?"

"Not that I see," she said.

All three of us stood very still, listening.

There was another *thump* and then Billy let out a

screech as a small dark shape, low to the floor, bolted past him toward the couch.

Everyone began asking questions at once, with Derek ducking beneath the door frame to get into the room and Katie running toward the foyer, while Billy clutched his chest and Zoe and I began laughing.

"What's wrong?" Derek was asking.

"Professor!" Katie was shouting.

"Is that a—?" Zoe began.

"A fucking cat? Are you shitting me?" Billy exclaimed.

"Quiet!" I yelled, and then when everyone shut up, I bent down to look under the couch. Two yellow eyes stared back at me and hissed. Well, the eyes didn't hiss, but that was all I could really see.

"Psst," I said. "Here, Kitty." I rubbed my fingers together in the cat's direction.

A small black nose edged out of the darkness and sniffed my fingers. Derek bent down to see, startling the cat. It hissed again and the nose and eyes disappeared. There was a scrambling sound, and I peeked beneath the couch just in time to see black legs and a tail vanish through a missing pane in the latticed door.

"It's gone," I said, turning to face the group.

"Everyone all right?" asked Prof. Gannon, entering the room.

"Yeah," I said. "We just scared a cat."

"I'll leave you three to it then. Zoe, come with me. I have an abnormal reading on one of the UV monitors that I think will interest you. Katie, you should come too if you want to include it in your report." Prof. Gannon headed towards the foyer. Zoe and Katie followed him.

"Damn thing almost gave me a heart attack," Billy muttered. He began looking through the books on the shelves.

"I wonder what it was doing in here," Derek said.

"Sleeping, maybe?" I offered.

"Maybe it was hunting mice," he suggested. "We get them in the store. They love to chew paper."

I picked up a piece of paper on the desk. It was sheet music.

"You were pretty good with that cat, by the way, Madison," Derek said.

"Yeah, right. So good it ran out of the room."

"No, I'm being serious. You were like, natural with it. Maybe you used to be a cat person."

"Hm. Maybe," I said. I hadn't really thought about it.

Billy glanced up from the book he was holding. "What are you two talking about?" he asked.

"He doesn't know?" Derek asked, surprised.

I sighed. "No."

"What? What don't I know?" Billy asked, putting the book back on the shelf.

"I really don't want to talk about this now," I said. "Can't it wait?"

"That depends," Billy said.

"On what?"

"On how juicy your secret is."

"It's about my past. My . . . family . . . and stuff," I said. It was sort of true. I leafed through the desk papers, finding more sheet music and plenty of blank pages.

"Oh," Billy said, seeming relieved. "Whatever then. Tell me whenever you want." Billy didn't like his own family at all. He'd once remarked that the only surviving members of his family that weren't in jail just hadn't gotten caught yet. I hadn't asked for more detail.

"Thank you," I said, lifting another piece of sheet music. Beneath it was a golden locket. Inside was a tiny, inch-tall portrait of a woman with piles of white hair like Marie Antoinette. On the opposite side, an engraving: "Myne Always, Irina." I read it aloud.

"Hey, let me see that." I put the locket in Billy's outstretched hand.

"Irina?" said Billy. "That was the name of one of the owners. She was the one who added the Greek stuff to the house, wasn't she?"

"But wasn't that before the renovation and Adderly?" I asked.

"Yeah, I don't know. Maybe he just found it in the house and kept it," Billy mused.

"We should show it to Prof. Gannon when he gets back," I said as the locket came back to me. I put it down and continued to leaf through the papers.

There was a stack of magazines on the opposite side of the desk. The word *Look* was emblazoned in big red letters across the cover of the top one. In the lower right corner, *10¢* appeared in a red rectangle, with the date May 17, 1938 below it in smaller print. The man on the cover had jaw-length dark hair and held a large square microphone. He smiled a crooked smile.

"Hey, it's the guy!" I said to Billy.

"What guy?" Derek asked, coming over to look.

Across the bottom of the cover the text read MICHAEL ADDERLY, and beneath that, VOICE OF AN ANGEL.

"Michael Adderly. The singer," I said. "Billy and I found a box of pictures down in the basement with this guy in all of them. He's why it's called Adderly House."

I studied the image. His lopsided smile was somehow both cocky and warm. It went all the way to his vivid blue eyes, which crinkled at the corners beneath thick eyebrows that complemented his high cheekbones and strong chin. The bridge of his nose was somewhat crooked, as if it'd been broken once or twice. Along with his slightly disheveled dark hair, it made him seem both disreputable and boyish.

"Holy shit, check this out," Billy said, holding out a record in a paper sleeve. " 'The Kiss. Michael Adderly with Les Elliott and His Orchestra.' Should I put it on?" he asked, gesturing with his elbow at the old record player.

"Sure, why not?" Derek said.

"What are you guys up to?" asked Zoe as she

came back into the room.

"We're trying to play a record of Adderly singing," Billy said. "As soon as I can figure out how to work this thing, that is."

"Have you ever seen a picture of him?" I asked Zoe.

"Who, Adderly?"

I nodded and held up the magazine cover. "Oh, hotness," she said. "Can I see it?"

"Sure," I said, handing it to her.

The next issue of *Look* had a blonde woman with very red lips on the cover. A black and white picture of Michael Adderly and a pretty, laughing bride appeared along the right side in a column of photos advertising the other contents of the magazine. ADDERLY WEDDING, it read. The magazine was dated July 26, 1938. "And here's his wedding," I said. Zoe held out a hand and I passed the magazine to her.

The next magazine in the pile had a picture of a baby on the cover, and Michael Adderly appeared in the column of photos again. The baby's skin was orangey, an unnatural crayon flesh-tone, and I suddenly realized that the photo was probably black and white that had been tinted. All of the covers probably were. In the side column photo, Michael Adderly was looking downward. The caption read ADDERLY TRAGEDY. The date on that one was December 13, 1938.

"Adderly Tragedy," I read aloud.

"Tragedy?" Derek said. "What's that about?"

"Dunno," I replied.

"His wife died. Am I the only one who listened to the history of the house?" Billy asked.

"I don't remember the professor saying anything about the wife dying," I said.

Billy continued tinkering with the record player. "Well, no, but the professor did say *tragedy*, and when Adderly disappeared, the house was supposed to go to the nephew, right? So Adderly obviously didn't have any kids. You said he got married. I figured the wife must have died."

"Actually," Derek spoke up, his eyes scanning a magazine article, "It looks like he had three wives total. And all three died. One from a chronic illness, another fell out of a window at home—here, I guess—and the other was hit by a car in the driveway. Also here."

"I told you he was a serial killer," Billy said.

"He was born in 1910," Zoe said, reading from the magazine with Adderly on the cover. "I guess he's about . . . twenty-eight in these pictures. Signed by Romeo Records in 1937. He had a number one hit the next year."

"He'd be over a hundred years old if he was still alive," Billy said, still fiddling with the record player. "But nobody knows what happened to him, right? Prof said he disappeared in the early 1990s? So he'd have been eighty-something by then. I'm actually a little disappointed that we didn't find his corpse in here."

"The night's not over yet," said Derek.

"Gross, you guys," I said.

The magazine Derek had been reading showed Michael Adderly on the cover, sitting on the steps in front of Adderly House. The headline read: AT HOME WITH MICHAEL ADDERLY. The magazine was dated September 26, 1944.

"Got it," Billy said, and then the room filled with the sound of a needle drop, that repetitive white noise of an empty recording just before the music starts. Then the music started, an orchestral piece of jaunty melody. Billy made an exaggeratedly-excited face, opening his mouth and snapping his fingers in time with the music.

And then there was the voice.

It lanced through me, pierced my solar plexus and took up residence in my chest. I could feel the words in my lungs, the notes in my ear, loneliness and wanting bundled together in a rich tenor that ranged into baritone on the low notes.

It hurt, this voice. It hurt not to have it close by, near me. I knew the song. I didn't know the song, I knew the voice, even though there was no way I *could* know the voice. I could feel myself pressed against a chest I'd never been held against. I longed for the feeling of his lips on my brow. His voice swelled within me, stirring ghosts of memory, insubstantial as smoke, leaving me aching. My chest ached for feelings I'd never felt, dreams I'd never dreamed, a love I'd never known.

I couldn't think. I could feel, only feel, truly feel, and it felt like life, this feeling, like desire, like being set on fire on the inside with wanting, wanting this voice, this singer.

I was lost in a maze of emotion. Was this how other people felt? Lost in a hazy dream-world of need? The fire burned, warming me from the center of my chest and expanding outward through my torso.

Too soon, the song ended.

I felt hollow. Bereft.

My breath came shallowly. I took a deeper breath and blinked. My eyes were wet. All at once, I came back to reality. Billy and Derek and Zoe were all looking at me. Katie and the two professors were at the doorway.

I blinked, and everyone looked at me expectantly. I realized that I'd been asked a question. That a conversation had been going on and, while I'd been aware of it on some level, I hadn't actually heard the words being spoken.

I felt like I had been to the moon and back.

A polite response would be expected in this type of situation. I reached for something to say.

I glanced from person to person, not sure who had spoken. "I'm sorry," I said. "What did you say?"

"Are you okay?" Billy asked.

I blinked a few more times and took a deep breath. "Yeah, sorry. Just spaced out," I said.

Billy said, "I was just telling Prof. Gannon about the locket—" *CRASH.*

The loud noise had come from somewhere on the second floor. Everyone shrieked or jumped or screamed. A confusion of voices followed, with everyone talking at once.

"Was that a ghost?"

"What the hell was that?"

"Probably the cat again."

"Everyone quiet down!" This last statement came from Dr. Hernandez. There was silence for a second. Then the lights went out.

Katie and I both gasped. Billy said, "Ohhhhh, shit."

Zoe, who was standing near me, muttered, "Really?" while Prof. Gannon sighed heavily.

Dr. Hernandez's voice once again took command. "Everyone stay calm and don't move. Those of you who still have your flashlights, please point them at the floor and turn them on." I pulled mine from my back pocket and six other beams of red light clicked on within a matter of seconds. The room had deep shadows but the light from the different flashlights was enough to see one another and the furniture by. "Prof. Gannon, what's the plan?" Dr. Hernandez asked.

"Well, the equipment can run on battery for another half hour or so," said Prof. Gannon. "I'm going to check the breakers and the main switch."

"Should I come with you again?" Katie asked. The beam from her flashlight bounced along the floor in his direction.

"No, Katie, you stay here so you don't miss anything else. I'll be back in a few minutes," he said. "Dr. Hernandez, I leave you in charge."

"On it," she said. The room grew just slightly dimmer as Prof. Gannon left and took his flashlight with him.

"Dr. Hernandez, you're good to have around in an emergency," Derek commented.

"USMC," she responded.

"You were in the Marines?" Billy asked.

"Why's that surprising?"

"Well, you're a doctor. That's not how most people think of Marines."

"The G.I. Bill paid for my doctorate."

She seemed unconcerned with how Marines are perceived.

Several of us started as something went *THUNK* upstairs. "Oh, man, we have *got* to check that out," Billy said.

"It's probably the cat again," Derek said.

I glanced at Zoe. Even in the dim light, I could see that she had her lips pressed together tightly.

"I'm game," I said. Anything to distract myself from the uneasy feeling that the song had brought on.

"I'll accompany you," Dr. Hernandez said.

"I should probably come too," Zoe said, sounding resigned.

"Can I stay here?" Katie asked nervously.

"All by yourself?" Billy said.

"I'll stay with her," Derek said.

"That's settled then," Dr. Hernandez said. "We'll take the stairs in the foyer, while you two supervise the equipment."

"Do you want to take one of the night-sight cameras?" Katie asked as we filed out through the dining room and into the foyer.

"Hell, yeah," Billy said with a grin. "All the better to see the ghosts with."

CHAPTER THIRTEEN

WE MOUNTED THE CURVING BLACK STAIRS IN THE darkness with our flashlights bobbing. Dr. Hernandez was in the front, I was in the middle, and Zoe and Billy were behind me. I heard Billy ask Zoe about the ghosts she'd seen.

"I'm not supposed to talk about it with anyone else here," she said in a low voice.

"Why not? The bias thing?" he asked.

"Pretty much," she said. "Prof. Gannon doesn't want me to influence any of your testimonies."

"So how long have you been able to see ghosts?" he asked.

"My whole life, pretty much."

"Wow."

I grinned, listening. He seemed interested in her. I was glad. I'd never been able to tell if Billy was flirting with me or if he was just naturally friendly. Sometimes it seemed like he was just joking around and other times it seemed like more. Kara had lectured me about the dangers of dating co-workers, so I never tried to pursue it. I didn't see him that way anyway.

At the top of the stairs a short hallway and banister connected an archway on either side. Dr. Hernandez pointed her flashlight through the right arch and then the left.

"What's the weirdest thing you've ever seen?" Billy asked Zoe.

"Like what?"

"I don't know. Anything supernatural."

"I see dead people *all the time*. That's just a regular day. But did you notice the fireplace downstairs? The art on the tiles tells Bible stories—like Noah's Ark—*that* seems weird to me," Zoe replied.

Noah's Ark. Someone else had mentioned that recently. I thought back and an image of a white stone table and bench came to me. Right. Rebecca. Rebecca had mentioned Noah's Ark when I asked her about Adderly House. *It couldn't be. Had she been to the house?*

I thought back to what she'd said. Something about an archangel that used to sing to her? She said he was named Michael—could it be? Michael Adderly with the "voice of an angel"? And she said he "was beautiful . . . handsome." I thought of the image of Michael Adderly, gorgeous on the cover of *Look* magazine. It must have been him—but that was in 1938. Tamara had died in 1992. It was around the same time Adderly had disappeared. Maybe due to a guilty conscience.

But it didn't make sense. He'd have been eighty-something by then. How could an old man have been "so beautiful" and handsome to a couple of college students and been two-timing them both? Could it have been the nephew the professor mentioned?

And then I remembered the pictures. The box of pictures. Every picture posed with a different girl. Lots of girls.

But Michael Adderly was always the same. Different years, different decades. Same hair, same smile. As if he didn't age at all. I swallowed uncomfortably.

My mind jumped back to what I'd read about Tamara. Her body was found in the apartment but they thought she'd been killed elsewhere. Why? Because there was hardly any blood at the crime scene. No blood, because none was left in her body.

Where did it go?

What if someone took it out?

No. No way, I thought.

Then: *Michael Adderly is a vampire.* I suddenly felt sick.

Had he posed as his own nephew so he could inherit his own wealth and start over? But then, where was he? If he had truly disappeared, it would explain why no one could find the nephew either.

I had to laugh at myself. It couldn't be true. I was being silly. There was no such thing as vampires. *Just like there's no such thing as ghosts?* a voice in my mind queried.

I didn't dignify it with a reply.

At the end of the upstairs hallway we found a smashed vase in front of a window. Dr. Hernandez blamed the cat, while Zoe scanned the walls and ceiling. Billy kept futzing with the camera, trying to get it to work. Ornately carved double doors stood to the left of the window.

"What's in there?" I asked.

"Master bedroom," Dr. Hernandez said.

"Should we check it out?"

"After you," she said, waving her flashlight in a blur of red.

"What color is that?" I asked. The whole room seemed sort of brownish-mauve colored.

Dr. Hernandez unscrewed the filter at the end of her flashlight. "It's blue," she said, shining light on the walls and across the bed.

"Is it okay if I take the filter off mine too?"

"You can do whatever makes you feel comfortable," she said.

Blue wasn't enough of a description. It was not unlike entering a dark blue cave—passing through the double doors, our flashlights picked up walls upholstered in blue-green silk, and a round king-size bed with a blue-green coverlet. Once again, my feet sunk into thick shag carpeting, though in this room it was dark blue. Heavy damask curtains—also blue—obscured the windows entirely.

"Holy fuck. This bedroom is almost as big as my entire apartment," Billy said.

"Anything look disturbed?" Dr. Hernandez asked.

"Since I don't know what it's supposed to look like, I really can't say. There aren't any smashed vases as far as I can tell."

I resumed looking around, using Zoe's method of scanning from floor to walls and ceiling. It was just a huge dark bedroom. Matching night tables stood on either side of the bed. There was a blue velvet chaise longue and small round table next to it. A vanity set with a mirror and a low cushioned chair. A crystal chandelier hung centered over the bed. Double doors against the far wall revealed a very large bathroom finished in green glass tile with a long tub and double sinks. Beyond, two more double doors opened to an empty walk-in closet that was bigger than my room.

"Man, the battery on this thing is totally kicked," Billy complained from the bathroom doorway, holding the camera aloft. "I'm going back downstairs to see if they have another. Don't find any ghosts without me." His footsteps retreated down the hall, then echoed faintly as his combat boots clunked down the stairs.

I closed the closet doors and made my way back through the bathroom. The tub was huge. Man, Michael Adderly sure knew how to live. Two sinks, perfect for the married couple brushing their teeth side by side.

Or fangs.

"What's next?" I asked, coming back into the bedroom once more.

"Well, there's—" Dr. Hernandez began, but then stopped suddenly, looking at Zoe.

"There's wha—?" I asked, only to be interrupted

by a terse shushing from Zoe, who was holding her hand up.

I listened. There were footsteps. Footsteps that sounded as though they were ascending stairs. At first, I thought it was just Billy, but then I realized that the sound was coming from the wrong direction. Not from outside the room behind us, but *inside* the room, ahead of us, getting closer.

I inhaled sharply and stared at Zoe. She shrugged her shoulders.

Even in the dim partial light, I could see that Dr. Hernandez looked as if she'd swallowed something nasty.

The footsteps sounded different too. Not Billy's chunky combat boot sounds, but the *click-clack-click-clack* of a woman's high heels on wood. I swallowed, scanning with my flashlight, when the steps stopped.

All was silent. Then I flinched as a hollow metallic *click* sounded. This was followed by the high-pitched squeak of hinges protesting as part of the upholstered wall slowly opened.

We were all frozen to the spot. Motes of dust hung in the beam from my flashlight. And then, from the darkness beyond the hidden door, there was movement as a figure glided through the beam of light. I was so unnerved I couldn't even take a breath, and then I realized that the figure was wearing a brown leather jacket and tight jeans. I inhaled loudly and sighed with relief.

"Jesus, Katie," I said, or began to say, intending

to bitch her out for scaring us to death, when a string of unintelligible words left her mouth and she swung at me.

There was no time to duck, or get out of the way. I instinctively curled my body in toward the punch, relaxing my muscles with its impact instead of hardening them against it. Rather than making myself a wooden block the punch could smash, I became rubber to absorb it.

Her fist hit my shoulder instead of my face. Pain radiated like heat from where the blow connected. "*Puta!*" she shouted and her nails came toward my face. That time I was able to step back out of the way and then Dr. Hernandez tackled her.

Zoe was yelling something about it not being Katie's fault, and Katie was continuing to yell in Spanish, and in a few short moves Dr. Hernandez had Katie on her knees, both her hands held behind her back and her face pressed into the bed.

In the midst of all this, I wondered how it was that I knew how to take a punch like that.

"Are you okay?" Dr. Hernandez asked.

"Yeah," I said, and rubbed the spot where I'd been hit. "She connected but it wasn't bad."

"No!" Katie cried, the first English word I'd heard come from her since she'd entered the room. She began raising and smashing her head against the bedclothes without effect, growling and muttering to herself.

"Is she speaking Spanish?" I asked.

"No Spanish I ever heard," Dr. Hernandez said.

"I mean, it's Spanish, but it's different. I can barely make it out."

"Be still. *Detenerlo*," Dr. Hernandez warned, raising Katie's hands at an unnatural angle that must have been very uncomfortable. The head smashing ceased.

"She's possessed," Zoe said softly.

"What?" Dr. Hernandez and I exclaimed in the same incredulous tone.

"How do you know?" I asked.

"I just do. Have you got her?" Zoe asked Dr. Hernandez.

"Oh yeah, she's not going anywhere."

"I'm going to try something," Zoe said. She moved closer to the bed and knelt down at eye level with Katie.

"Hey," she said.

"Are you sure this is a good idea?" I asked Dr. Hernandez.

She shrugged. "*She's* the supernatural expert."

Zoe tried again. "Hey!"

Katie—or whatever was inside Katie—growled something unintelligible.

"Take me," Zoe said. "I won't fight you. She's fighting you now, but I won't."

"Um, Zoe?" I said.

She ignored me. "Come on, just leave her and take me. I'll let you in. You can say what you have to say, but if you attack any one of us again, I *will* make things *very* unpleasant for you. Understood?"

The figure stopped struggling and Katie

slumped like an abandoned rag doll.

"Why you are in my house?" came the voice from Zoe's lips, in heavily accented English.

She stood.

She was looking directly at me. Her face seemed odd, somehow less Zoe-ish than before. Her lips were pursed, and her eyes narrowed. Her stance was different too, the way she tilted her head and held her hands on her hips was confident, aggressive, not at all like the girl in the shapeless skirt and sweater. Now they hung elegantly on her, her posture straight, shoulders back. Zoe, I realized, slouched.

I stared at Dr. Hernandez, hoping for a clue of what I should or shouldn't say, but she was busy checking Katie's pulse with one hand while continuing to restrain her with the other.

Cripes. What the hell are you supposed to say to a ghost? What did the ghost book say? *Don't be emotional. Speak calmly and with authority.*

"I have a right to be here," I said. "I have permission. You had no business attacking us."

"Did you come here to steal him away from me?" she asked, her fists curling at her sides.

"What? No. Wait, who?"

My response seemed to mollify her and the fists uncurled. "Michael, *mi corazón*, my husband," she purred.

"Michael . . . Adderly?"

"You see, you know him," she said smugly. "He is very famous."

"You were . . . you're his wife?"

187

"*Sí,*" she said.

"What's your name?"

"Rosalita DeJesus Rosario Adderly."

"What do you want?"

"I want . . . I want you to know."

"To know what?"

"He kill me. He marry me and bring me here to die. If I don't come, then I don't die that way. You see? He kill me with his love. Just like the other."

"The other . . . his other wife?"

"*Sí,*" she said. Then she blinked several times and pinched the bridge of her nose. Had her shoulders slumped?

"Is there anything else you wanted to say?" I asked.

"She's gone," Zoe said, in her regular voice.

Katie moaned, no longer face down and on her knees, but now lying on the bed on her back. "She's coming around," Dr. Hernandez said. "Katie, talk to me. Tell me your last name."

"Huh? My last name? It's Davis," she mumbled.

"Good. And what time of year is it?"

"Spring."

"Also good. Where do you go to school?"

"SUNY Mount V."

"Excellent. And can you count backwards from ten for me?"

"I guess," Katie said. She counted down from ten and seemed much calmer afterward.

"What am I doing in here? How did I get here?" she moaned.

Zoe stepped up. "What do you remember last?"

"Going to use the bathroom. Rinsing my hands. Putting lip gloss on."

"And then?"

"Nothing. Then I was here. Did I fall? My head is pounding. And my wrists feel sore."

"You, um, you required a little—" I broke off as Zoe coughed and shot me a look. "—caretaking."

Dr. Hernandez asked Katie if she felt well enough to sit up, and Katie said she'd try. I leaned closer to Zoe and whispered, "What's up?"

"She could still have connection to the ghost. Better not to call her attention to it."

"Hey, so what'd I miss?" said Billy from the doorway, holding the camera on his shoulder.

Zoe and I gave one another a look. First I giggled and then she did.

Chapter Fourteen

THE DARKNESS OF THE SECRET HALLWAY SEEMED to swallow the shaky beam coming from my flashlight. A dusty, disused scent assailed my nostrils as I took a step inside. I ducked to avoid a cobweb, and a floorboard creaked beneath my feet. Ahead, some thirty feet down the narrow passage, my flashlight caught a folding ladder extending from the floor to a trapdoor in the ceiling, probably leading to the attic.

The rest of the crew was standing in the doorway of the master bedroom, peering into the dark and awaiting my report, when I heard a soft sound farther down the hall. I froze. Was it another ghost? Someone else a ghost had possessed? The soft sounds continued, getting closer. Something small, down on the floor. I swung my flashlight around and screeched. The small black cat stopped in its tracks, its glowing eyes reflecting the flashlight beam back at me.

"Are you okay?" Zoe yelled, while Billy muttered something or other.

"I'm fine," I yelled back. "It's the cat again."

"Fucking cat!" I heard Billy say.

The cat was still standing in the same spot. It was purring. I bent down and rubbed my fingers together in the cat's direction. It stared at me a moment and continued purring, then slowly padded over to me and dropped something on my shoe. I swung the flashlight down, revealing a dead mouse.

"Uck," I said. Did the cat want to share its dinner with me? Did it want me to praise it for catching a mouse? "Good kitty," I said, and rubbed my fingers together again. The cat stood on its hind legs and bumped my hand with its head and purred even louder, then placed its front paws against the leg of my jeans and rubbed its head on my hand. Its black fur was soft and sleek.

"Are you done messing with that cat?" Billy asked, coming down the hall with the night sight camera on his shoulder. The cat flattened its ears and took off in the other direction.

"I am now," I said.

"Hey, what's this? Up the ladder to the spooky attic? We going?" Billy had spotted the trapdoor and ladder.

"I thought maybe we should wait for the others?"

"Where's the fun in that?"

"This isn't all about fun, you know. They're actually trying to do an experiment of some kind."

"Who cares? I came here to see ghosts. I haven't seen one yet," Billy said. "The scariest thing in this place is that cat. Hey, do you think this hallway meets back up with the library? There was a door in there, right? And that's where the cat ran?"

"Maybe," I said. "And this old attic ladder is probably what made that loud thud."

"Yeah, maybe," Billy said, "but did it come loose, or what? Maybe it's been like that for years."

I shone my flashlight around the floor at our feet and around the feet of the ladder. There were marks in the dust on the floor as if it had recently been disturbed. Some looked like paw tracks, but others were clearly shoe prints. The dead mouse appeared to be gone, which I was happy about. I didn't want to hurt the cat's feelings by rejecting its gift, and I also didn't want to step on it and have it go squish.

"Zoe, is anyone else coming?" I called.

"Yes, I hear them coming now," she called back.

"That's what she said," Billy snickered. When I didn't respond, he continued, "So let's go up-up-up before they get here!"

"I'm not going up there without backup," I said. "And neither are you."

"Fine," he sulked. "At least turn off your flashlight or put the filter back on, will you? You're killing my night vision."

"Fine," I said, switching it off.

"So what's up with your ID anyway?"

"Can we *not* talk about that now?"

"Come on, Maddy, it's me. Spill. You on the run? Hiding from the mob? What?"

"Why do you want to know?"

"I dunno. I just do."

"You won't believe me."

"Try me."

I opened my mouth to speak and heard several voices in the distance.

"Okay, later," I said, "but not now. I don't want to explain it to a whole group of people."

"Fair enough," Billy said. "But you owe me the truth and I'm gonna get it."

A powerful beam of light shone down the hall into our eyes.

"Ah, yes," the professor said, coming toward us, "the old servants' passageways. Of course. And an entry to the attic. Well done, group! You haven't been upstairs yet, have you?"

"No, sir," I said quickly.

Derek and Zoe followed him.

"It's getting a little crowded in here," I said.

"Alley-oop then," said Billy, removing the night-sight camera from his shoulder and handing it to the professor so he could climb the ladder with both hands.

"Don't touch anything!" the professor called, pushing his glasses back against his face from where they'd slipped down his nose.

"Hand him back the camera," I suggested. "Then his hands will be occupied."

"Good call," he said. "You give it to him."

"Ummm," said Zoe, catching my eye with a worried glance up toward the attic.

I gazed up but didn't see much in the dark. Was that a darker shadow within the shadows? That had to be Billy, didn't it?

But no, it couldn't be. We heard Billy yammering to himself up there. His voice was muffled by distance. He was nowhere near the doorway.

Zoe gave me another look again and I signaled her by raising my eyebrows and index finger at the same time. She nodded.

What the hell? Why did she think I could see ghosts? I'd never seen the ghost at my apartment, had I? I shivered just thinking about it. It made me feel really sorry for Zoe.

"Madison, will you go up next?" said the professor. "Then Zoe, then Derek, then myself?"

I stuffed my mini flashlight in my pocket, nodded and grabbed onto the rungs, and climbed. Halfway up, the professor handed me the camera. Billy reached down from the top and I handed it to him.

The attic was something else. Huge, stretching from one end of the large house to the other, dusty and letting in dim moonlight from unseen seams. Dust cloths covered a majority of items. The uncovered ones stood out. Over there was a tall oval mirror, and in that corner a rocking chair, and right next to it a rocking horse. Most of the stuff seemed to be made of wood and quite old.

The professor made it up the stairs and regarded our discovery. "This must be some of the original furniture. I've seen these shapes in some of the restored houses in the area. Pretty fantastic stuff."

"Is it worth a lot?" Billy asked.

"Depends on its condition," Derek said, climbing up. "It's really too bad they haven't been able to sell this place off. Some people would pay a fortune for the antique furnishings alone."

Prof. Gannon spoke up. "Ah, but it's not for sale, you see. It's being held in a trust of some kind. Every few years, they attempt to rent the place out, but it never lasts long. Because of . . . well, you know, of course."

"Of course," I said. Derek rolled his eyes.

"So what do we need to do now that we're up here?" Billy returned from his foray to the back of the house.

"The same as before. Look for anything unusual."

I glanced over at Zoe who seemed to be entranced by a painting she'd located. "What'd you find?" I asked, taking out my flashlight.

It was a portrait of a young lady. The image appeared somewhat dark around the edges but the subject was luminous. Her light blond hair framed her face in carefully placed spiral curls, and two hooded blue eyes stared down a long, regal nose. She was fairly young, probably in her early twenties. A hint of a smile played around her red lips. A white underdress peeked from beneath a claret-colored gown that revealed her creamy skin from collar bones to décolletage, exposing one breast with a pale pink nipple.

"Wow," I said. "That's daring."

"You like my girlfriend?" Billy asked from across

the room, waving toward the painting. "She's a hottie, huh?"

"Catharina Van Horn, 1677," Zoe said, pointing at the corner of the painting where this information had been painted into the oils. "Or . . ." She held a hand over the *Cath* part. "Arina . . . Irina?"

" 'Myne Always, Irina,' the locket said. But she was a white-haired old lady, wasn't she?" I asked. "Or was that a wig?"

"It was very common in those times for mothers and fathers to give their children their own names," Prof. Gannon mused. "Klaus van Horn—the original builder of the house—I think Catharina was his daughter. That is very probably her."

"She reminds me of a girl who went to my school," Zoe said. "Spoiled thing, and all the boys fell over themselves trying to impress her. She made fun of my clothes. Then one day I just snapped and asked Jimmy to make her stop—Jimmy's an Irish ghost who helps me out from time to time—and he splattered ink all over her pinafore—dress, I mean. *Pinafore* was his word. Anyway, she left me alone after that."

Before any of us could respond to that crazy story, Billy called out, "Hey, what's this?" He was standing in front of a window, examining the edges of the sill.

"What's what?" I asked.

"The wood is dented. On both sides," he said, gesturing.

Sure enough, there was a large area where the

window frame was scarred and the paint was cracked.

"That's weird."

"It's like something was thrown into it, isn't it? Something big?" Billy said.

"But it would have broken the window," I said.

Derek, who'd been nearby and listening, came over to us. "It probably did break the window. Look at the glass on this window compared to that one over there." He was right. The glass on the other window looked odd, almost wavy. "That's the old original glass," Derek explained. "This is new. Or new-ish, anyway."

"Maybe somebody was locked up here. You know, mad aunt in the attic or something like that," Billy said.

"A mad aunt threw a chair out a window or something? So what?" I asked.

"Maybe it wasn't a chair," Zoe said quietly. "Maybe it was a person."

"Oh my God. That's right," I said. "Didn't one of Michael Adderly's wives fall out of a window in the house?"

"To fall out a window might be considered an accident, but to be thrown out would be murder," Derek said, as if he were quoting something.

"Murder by defenestration," Billy concurred.

Prof. Gannon returned from the other end of the attic and asked what we were discussing. Billy and Derek explained, and the professor examined the window. "An interesting discovery," he said.

"But how strong would someone have to be to throw a person out a window?" I asked.

"Pretty strong," Prof. Gannon said.

"Hella strong," Billy said.

Vampires are hella strong, some part of my mind suggested.

I unlocked the window and opened it. There was no screen.

"Hey," Billy said. "Before sticking my head out, I'd check to make sure the window's gonna stay up. Unless you feel like playing guillotine," he added with a sinister grin.

"Thanks, Billy," I said, rolling my eyes, but checking anyway. The window seemed stable enough. I glanced at Zoe. "All clear?" She nodded. The last thing I needed was some mad aunt's ghost pushing me out the window.

I stuck my head out, trying to see down to the ground. A roof to a lower floor slanted beneath me. I started to pull my head in when I noticed something pale among the dark shingles on the roof close to the house. I pulled my flashlight through the open window to get a better view. Several shingles were cracked and damaged, one of them cut in half, and the pale wood beneath it was what had caught my eye. I ran the flashlight from one side of the window to the other, and the cracked shingles continued in a narrow path alongside the attic to the right, disappearing at the edge of the house, as if they went around the corner. "Huh," I said aloud.

"Huh, what?" "What'd you see?" "What is it?" came the chorus of voices from inside. "Check it out," I said, pulling my head back in.

Derek and the professor both peered downwards out the window, using their flashlights to see what I'd seen.

"How very odd," the professor said, pulling his head back in.

"What do you think did that?" I asked.

"Maybe a tornado tore up the tiles," Derek offered.

"Where does it go? I mean, how far does it go?" I asked.

"Let's take a look," Prof. Gannon suggested.

With each of us peering through various windows on the attic level, we could see that some shingles on the other side of the second-floor roof were damaged and formed a path, too, which led off the next edge.

"Where does that roof go?" I asked him. "I mean, what's on that side of the house?"

Billy's eyes were huge and excited. "Let's find out!" he exclaimed.

Chapter Fifteen

The trail of damaged shingles seemed to end at the edge of the roof overhanging the hallway window where we'd noted the broken vase on our way upstairs.

"And look out there," Billy said.

A small single-story building stood twenty feet from the house. "It's a building," I said.

"No shit. Did you notice the window?" Billy said.

I stepped back to get a better view of the window.

"Not that window, dummy. The one on the building. Up near the roof. Use your flashlight."

The beam disappeared into the darkness without reaching the building. "I don't see anything," I said.

"Here," Billy said, taking my flashlight and twisting the top of it clockwise several times. "Now try."

The beam went much farther this time, I maneuvered it upwards along the slanted roof to the apex, and then back down the other side. There was a circular window there, and its glass was broken.

"You don't think . . ." I said, as the professor, Zoe, and Derek joined us.

"I don't know," Billy said. "It's a hell of a long jump, but it's not impossible."

"Prof. Gannon, what's that building over there?" I asked.

"It was once the carriage house. It was modified into a garage by Michael Adderly, I believe."

"Can we check it out?" Billy asked. "We think whatever did that damage to the roof might have also damaged one of those windows."

He thought a moment and shrugged. "Sure, I don't see why not," he said, jingling the set of keys in his pocket.

We tromped downstairs and said hello to Dr. Hernandez and Katie, who were sitting with the monitors and other equipment, chatting quietly. Billy set down the night vision camera on one of the two tables. "Battery's dead again," he said. Dr. Hernandez smiled politely and took it from him.

Prof. Gannon explained what we were up to and Dr. Hernandez said, "Katie and I will stay in the house while the rest of you investigate." I sort of got the feeling that she was keeping an eye on Katie, trying to make sure she didn't go crazy again. It wasn't what she said but the way she said it, with a curt air of command that indicated she was making the choice *for* Katie, and didn't give a damn what Katie wanted to do.

Just as we were grabbing our coats from the coat rack before heading outside, the lights in the house came on in the foyer and the living room and dining room. "Hooray," "All right," and "*Opa!*" were some of the cheers that various members of the team uttered.

Zoe muttered, "Sure, give us the lights back just as we're going outside. Nice one," out of the corner of her mouth. Was she talking to a ghost?

Everyone put on their coats except Billy, who left his leather jacket hanging. "It's not far. I don't need it," he said. I suspected he was showing off again, probably for Zoe.

The professor went out first, followed by Derek, Billy, Zoe, and me.

The night air was crisp and hundreds of stars speckled the sky like pinpricks of light shining through a dark piece of cloth. "You okay?" I asked Zoe quietly.

"Sure," she said with a sigh. "I just get a little tired of ghosts and their games from time to time."

"They play games?"

"Oh, sure. Not all of them, but some. Turning lights on and off, breaking objects, opening and closing doors."

"They do that for fun?" I asked, thinking of my apartment ghost.

"Not exactly. Maybe some of them. Others do it to try to communicate or because they're angry. But it all feels like games after a while."

"The ghost in my apartment does some of that stuff," I said.

Zoe's eyebrows rose. "Do you know what he or

she wants?"

"I'm pretty sure it's a she. In fact, I think I know her name. And that she was murdered," I whispered.

"Oh, you should—" Zoe began but abruptly stopped. "I'll tell you later," she whispered back.

We'd arrived at the garage.

Prof. Gannon opened the side door to the building and turned a light on inside. The room had thick wooden beams and tall ceilings, and everything seemed to be coated with a fine layer of dust. Cobwebs lurked in the corners and clung to some of the beams. The room had plenty of space, enough to maneuver around. It could keep two cars side-by-side, though there was only one now, covered by a dusty gray tarp on the far side.

Billy was checking the floor. "Well, there's no broken glass," he said. The round window was on the same side of the garage as the side door where we'd come in. There wasn't anywhere glass could hide over on this side.

"Somebody must have cleaned it up at some point," I said. Billy shrugged and walked over to a narrow table against the wall—a work bench, with dusty bottles and tools on it. Zoe joined him.

Derek was lifting the gray tarp slowly, revealing a vintage silver coupe. He gave a low whistle. The car had a convertible top and a long hood flanked by low fenders over whitewall tires that were most definitely flat. It was a Lincoln-Zephyr. I didn't know how I knew that it was a Lincoln-Zephyr. I just knew that I knew. Why did I know? And why so much detail? I knew that it had a V-12 engine, and that they had been luxury cars in their time—this one was from the early 1940s—and most of them had problems with oil pressure, oil sludge, or build-up.

Sure enough, there were old oil stains on the concrete floor on the empty side of the garage where I was standing. I imagined that there were more stains beneath the car itself, even if it was sitting on a large protective floor mat of some kind.

I knelt down to look underneath the car and my skeleton key slipped out of my shirt on its chain. I tucked it back and put my face closer to the ground, but couldn't see any stains on the mat.

"Madison?" Prof. Gannon asked. The unspoken question was *What do you see?* or *What have you found?*

I shrugged. "Just looking for oil stains."

"Why?"

I gestured at the old stains on the opposite side. "Just thought there might be some." I pulled the flashlight from my back pocket and used it to scan the mat. Not a drop of oil. That I could see, anyway. Maybe the oil stains on the other side had been from a different car.

Kneeling next to me, Prof. Gannon also scanned beneath the car, and lifted the mat next to the tire to peer beneath it. "Now that's odd," he said, pointing. "What do you make of those?"

There were marks on the concrete floor from the tires. That didn't seem strange. What did seem strange was that the marks went from side-to-side with a bit of an upward curve. Almost like a Nike swoosh.

"Someone moved the car," I said.

"Sideways?" Prof. Gannon asked.

"Well, diagonally, maybe," I said. "But it would have to be someone strong. Someone *really* strong."

"Yeah, like a werewolf," Billy said. "Or a mutant." He was holding a pair of dirty goggles in front of his eyes.

I rolled my eyes at his comment. "Can ghosts . . . ?" I let the question trail off.

"Not usually," replied Zoe. "Although there are always stories—"

I interrupted, "But *why* move a car sideways? Why not just pull it out and put it back in?"

"That's what *she* said," Billy said with a snicker.

I pointedly ignored him.

"Hmm, I would like to get a better look at those tire marks," the professor said.

"Can we do that, Prof. Gannon? We could back the car out, if you have keys to it," I said.

"I do not, I'm afraid. But we can release the parking brake if it's engaged, and with one person steering and the others pushing, it should only take a few of us to roll it outside. Provided it's unlocked, of course."

"Of course," I repeated.

Derek, who'd been scrutinizing the car from hood to trunk, said, "That probably wouldn't be a good idea with the flat tires. You might damage the wheels, and this car is definitely worth something."

"Not a problem," Zoe said, holding an old bicycle pump from the table she and Billy had been checking out. "We can just pump them up with this."

Each tire took a lot of effort to even partially fill with air. I offered to assist but was shooed away. Three sweaty men and thirty minutes later, we'd pushed the car out into the driveway. The mat seemed pristine. "Well, let's check out those tire marks," Prof. Gannon said, and began to roll the vinyl mat into a long cylinder, soon revealing not only the tire marks—which went a few feet sideways—but a slightly recessed three-foot square of metal set into the floor.

"Whoa," I said.

"Nice!" Billy exclaimed.

"Huh," said Derek.

Zoe didn't say anything. Prof. Gannon said, "Well done, everyone. None of the other groups ever thought to check the carriage house."

The metal square had an inset handle as well as a keyhole. The professor peered at it closely and said, "Fishy. Hmmm," and began looking through his keyring.

"Did you just say 'fishy'?" Billy asked.

"I said Fish-ay," Prof. Gannon replied.

I stood very still. It couldn't be.

I swallowed. He'd said *Fishay*, but I knew that

wasn't how it was spelled. The French don't pronounce -*chet* at the end of a word the way we do. It's pronounced -*shay*. It was just too weird of a coincidence. I hadn't seen any Fichet locks anywhere in the past several months—and I'd read how it was very rare to see that brand outside of Europe.

"Do you mean *Fichet?*" I asked, even though I knew the answer. I clasped the double-headed *sans souci* key through the fabric of my shirt.

Everyone who'd been looking at the professor expectantly while he flipped through the keys now looked at me.

"Yes, I said *Fichet*," the professor said. "Unfortunately, there doesn't seem to be a matching key here . . ." he trailed off. "Are you all right, Madison? You seem a little . . . off."

"You don't look too good, Maddy," Billy said.

I didn't feel too good. I imagined my face had gone white.

Derek grabbed a tall metal-backed chair and sat it down behind me. "Sit," he ordered.

I sat, staring at the keyhole in the metal square on the floor, rubbing my thumb against the edges of the double-headed key through the cotton of my t-shirt.

"Hey," Zoe said.

I looked up at her. "This isn't a ghost thing, is it?" she asked. I shook my head.

"No. No, I'm sorry. I just . . . I have this old key. I've had it . . . well, ever since I can remember." I glanced at Derek and he nodded, like he was telling me to keep going. "And the key actually says *Fichet* right on it. It just seemed strange to me. I've never seen a Fichet lock anywhere."

"That cool one you wear? Man, too bad you don't have it with you," said Billy.

I curled my fingers around it through my shirt. "But I do, actually."

"The odds of your key going to this lock have probably got to be in the tens if not hundreds of thousands," Prof. Gannon said.

"I agree," Derek said. "But would it hurt to check?"

"No, not at all. Or at least I can't imagine how it would. Seems a bit silly, but why not."

I took a deep breath and pulled the chain from around my neck and handed it to Prof. Gannon. My hands were shaking a little.

As he took the key, he tilted his head to the side. "This is important to you, isn't it? This key, I mean."

"Yes." I swallowed.

"I'll bring it right back," he said. He knelt by the metal square and inserted the key. "It fits," he said, surprised. "But there's really very little chance that it will—"

"Geez, will you try turning it already?" Billy snapped.

"Very well," intoned the professor, and turned the key with an echoed metallic *clink*.

"Holy shit," Billy whispered.

Zoe's mouth was open. Derek looked worried.

Prof. Gannon got up and came over to me. "Where did you get that key, Miss Roberts?"

"I . . . I told you. It's mine."

"You didn't find it here, on the grounds?"

"No. I've had it as long as I can remember. I told you."

"And how long is that? Since you were a child?" he prompted.

"Well, sort of . . . maybe? I'm not really sure."

"When do you remember first seeing it?"

"I . . ."

Prof. Gannon grabbed my shoulders and shook me. "Where did you get that key, Miss Roberts?"

"Hey, ease off! I've seen her wearing that key at work. She definitely had it already," Billy said.

The professor released my shoulders and whirled to face Billy, looking at each of us in turn, ending with me. "But where did it come from? Do any of you have any idea of the statistical improbability that a key you just happened to have just happened to work on a hidden trapdoor you just happened to find on an estate where you just happened to show up for a research study?"

"No?" I said, timidly.

"One in a million! One in ten million! Maybe a hundred million!" the professor shouted.

I flinched. He was right. It was almost impossible.

"Hey, come on now, Doc," Billy said.

"Prof. Gannon?" Zoe said, trying to get his attention. He ignored her, staring at me.

Derek had been watching me, and now took a step closer to me. "I think maybe you should tell them, Madison."

"Now?" I asked.

"Yes. Now."

"Tell them what?" Billy asked.

"About just how long her memory is," Derek said.

I sighed. The expectant faces in the room were all pointed at me. "What's the date again?" I asked Derek.

He told me and I sighed again, mentally counting from October. "Just over six months," I said. "Six months and two weeks, give or take a few days."

"Of what?" Billy asked, confused.

"Of memory. That's all I have. That's why I don't have a proper ID. That's why I don't know where the key came from. I have amnesia."

"And you didn't think that would be something you should mention when I interviewed you over the phone?" the professor asked through gritted teeth.

"I didn't think it would matter!" I said.

"*Tabula rasa*," Derek muttered.

"But she's not a blank slate, are you, Madison? You believe in ghosts. Why?"

"Because I think my apartment is haunted."

"How did that bring you here?"

"Um, guys?" Billy said. "Can we just go check out what's in the trapdoor and explain all of this other stuff later?"

"You aren't mad?" I asked Billy.

"Honestly? It's not really my business. I'm not sure I believe you, but if it's true, it does explain why you can be such a dork," he said.

It wasn't like he was the first person who didn't believe me. Julie still didn't. Even the doctors at Bellevue had been skeptical at first.

"I don't . . . This is very complicated," Prof. Gannon said.

"What's complicated about it?" Derek asked.

"While we have permission to enter any room on the grounds . . . the fact that Madison—which I presume is not your actual name?" He paused and looked at me and I shrugged, "—had the key to that room—I presume it's a room down there—may invalidate any material gathered from our entry into that room, or any of the data in the rest of the house. If so, it will make all the data we collect during this study invalid. All of it!"

"Bummer," Billy said.

"But why?" I asked.

"Because every discovery and observation that any of you have made is now suspect. It's likely that you were acting on previous information and directing the actions of the group either consciously or subconsciously." He sighed deeply. "Damn. Damn. Damn damn damn damn!"

Double-quadruple damn. "But I . . ."

"But nothing, Maddy," Billy said. "Listen, Doc, I read all about this place online before we even came up here. I read about Adderly and his dead wives, how his body had never been found. I read about how a repairman working in the attic a few years back had a heart attack and died, and how a caretaker died on the same night three years later in a tragic accident that involved a beheading. And speaking of beheadings, some people believe that the Headless Horseman *was* seen here a couple of times like twenty years ago. I also read that Adderly was a survival nut and had locked himself up in an old root cellar. It's why I wanted to check the basement first thing. So if anyone has ruined your study by having previous information, it's me."

Now it was my turn to sit there with my mouth open. Zoe was looking at Billy with a mixture of dismay and admiration. Derek gave a nod of respect.

"Google exists, Doc," said Billy. "You can't stop progress."

Prof. Gannon looked defeated. "But you signed the release stating you had no former knowledge of the premises," he said.

"Yeah, well, before I signed up for this thing, I didn't. I figured that counted."

"I knew . . . that is, I *thought* I knew there was a piano," I said. "But that was it. I swear."

"What . . . how did you know there'd be a piano?" Zoe asked.

"According to . . . an unreliable source, the Steinway was loaned out in the early 1990s to two girls who lived in Brooklyn."

"Looks like your unreliable source wasn't as

unreliable as you thought," she said.

"I guess not."

Prof. Gannon sighed heavily. "Well, that's it, then. There's no point in going on."

"Are you fucking kidding me?" Billy asked. "What about the trapdoor? Don't you want to know if Adderly is down there?"

"If he is, don't you think we should let him rest in peace?" the professor responded.

"That's not a good reason not to check. I haven't seen his ghost at all," Zoe said. "You'd think I would have if he died under suspicious circumstances. Though I will say that the ghosts of Adderly House are oddly shy, with the exception of Rosalita, of course."

"Zoe!" the professor reprimanded.

"I thought it didn't matter now," Zoe said. She winked at me and Billy when the professor turned away. She was on our side.

Billy spoke up again, "Plus, if I help find him, it might get my name in the paper or something. This is probably my only chance for fifteen seconds of fame. It's not like I'm going to do anything else exciting with my life."

"I'm for checking out the trapdoor," Derek said, "but not to look for Adderly. I'm curious about what Madison's key leads to, and I'm pretty sure she is too."

"Well, Maddy, how about it?" Billy asked.

Everyone turned to look at me.

"I . . . well, I mean, we've come this far. I've spent

all this time trying to convince myself that my memories don't matter. But I can't leave here without knowing. Maybe there's a clue to my identity down there. Maybe I'm related to the old caretaker or someone who built the thing. I don't know. But not going down there isn't an option. It just isn't."

The professor was shaking his head and looking at the floor.

I got up from the chair where I'd been sitting since Derek put me there and went to the professor. "Please, Prof. Gannon? They say it's a dissociative fugue—you know what that is, don't you? Maybe my memory needs a jump-start. If there's some clue to my past down there, I need to see it. Please. I'm begging you."

I could feel the tears welling in my eyes as the professor looked up at me and sighed again.

"It's not like we need your permission anyway, Doc," said Billy.

"Fine, we'll go," he said.

"Thank you," I said. "I feel good about this."

CHAPTER SIXTEEN

IT TOOK BOTH DEREK AND BILLY TO OPEN THE trapdoor, which made a strange popping and then sucking sound when it was opened, complete with a *whoosh* of stale air. The door was extraordinarily heavy, three inches thick of reinforced steel and concrete, and the lock mechanism went all the way through it, with a hole on the back where the *sans souci* key could be used to lock it from the inside. When shut, the door locked no matter what, and had to be opened with the key either way. I found myself wondering whether it was a safe room or a jail cell.

A set of very steep concrete stairs led down into the earth and darkness.

"Who's going first?" Billy asked, clicking on his flashlight.

"Professor?" I asked.

"It's your key, Madison. You ought to be the first one," Prof. Gannon said. There was something about his tone that made him sound less than sincere.

I took a shaky breath. I didn't really want to be

the first person to go down there, but he was right. It was my key. That made it my responsibility. "Sure," I said, trying to sound confident. I switched on my flashlight and began my descent.

The stairs were very steep, steep enough that I felt as if I'd fall if I didn't brace myself against the wall as I descended. At first, the circle of light from my flashlight was very bright and very small from when Billy had last adjusted it, so I twisted the top until the beam was wider, illuminating more of my path. At the bottom of the stairs, there was a wall and a doorway on the left. "There's a door," I called back. As I turned, my flashlight caught a smear of something dark along the doorjamb—a brownish-red handprint. Like old blood.

Keeping my flashlight trained on the handprint, I stepped through the doorway to make room for Billy, who was coming down the steps next. "Whew, these steps are steep—oh, shit! Is that blood?" he asked, catching sight of the stain.

"Best guess? Yeah."

"God, I love this place," he said, with a huge grin.

I scanned the area with the flashlight. The room we were in was large and rectangular, with a billiards table in the center, and a white couch, a bar, and empty bookshelves along the walls. Compared to the basement in the house, the air felt curiously dry, and the mildew smell was completely absent. I'd expected cobwebs. There were none.

The professor came down next, followed by

Zoe. Derek brought up the rear, awkwardly crouching in the tight space. Billy excitedly pointed out the handprint to each of them.

"Ew," Zoe said.

Derek held his hand over the print, dwarfing it. "Small hand. A woman's?"

"Told you he was a serial killer," Billy said.

"I wonder if we shouldn't contact the authorities," Prof. Gannon mused.

"And tell them what? We found an old handprint? Hell, that could be paint for all we know," Billy said.

I walked over to take a look at the pool table. "Um, guys?" I said.

"What is it, Madison?" Derek asked.

"I don't think the handprint is paint."

"Why not?"

"Take a look." I shined my flashlight over the table.

"How the hell did they even get that thing down here?" Billy asked from the doorway. All four joined me and Billy whistled low. "Damn."

An amorphous black stain took up a third of the surface and one of the rails was smashed in. Half a broken pool stick lay on the green felt nearby.

"Is that blood?" Zoe asked.

"I think so," I said.

"I don't feel good," Zoe said. Her face seemed almost greenish in the dim lighting.

"Are you going to be sick?" the professor asked. Zoe's eyes were closed and her lips were pressed tightly together. She was breathing deeply through her nose like she was trying not to hyperventilate. "I can handle it," she said after a few moments, and opened her eyes.

"Let's carry on then," said Prof. Gannon. "Madison, where would *you* like to go next?" He was *definitely* being sarcastic.

A rack of pool cues with one empty slot hung on a nearby wall, and two entryways led from the room, one to our immediate left, the other to the right toward the back of the room, near the bookshelves, past the couch and the bar. "The bar," I said.

The long white couch was immaculate, as if it had never been used. The oak bar stood beyond it, holding a bottle of scotch, an empty glass, and a chessboard with the white and black pieces already set up to play. The shelves behind the bar were empty.

Derek held his flashlight on the board. "One of the white knights is missing," he said. "So's the black queen—oh, wait. There's the knight." He pulled a horse-headed chunk of white from among the other white pieces. "It's broken."

"Is that marble?" the professor asked, looking over the set.

"Seems like," Derek said, fitting the two chunks together.

"Here's the queen," Billy said, picking up the black piece from the bar near the bottle of scotch. Of *course* Billy was checking out the scotch. "Huh, that's weird," he said.

"What is?" Zoe asked.

"Well, the queen was just sitting there, right?"
Zoe nodded.

"But the knight was in pieces on the board. All
mixed in with the others, not by itself?" Billy said.

"Yeah," Derek answered.

"Well, if you dropped a chess piece and it broke,
wouldn't you throw it out? Or if you wanted to glue
it, maybe you'd set it aside, right? But you wouldn't
just toss it back in with the others. And it probably
didn't fall apart on its own. Somebody must have
broken it on purpose," Billy finished.

"But if that's marble . . ." the professor
mumbled, clearly troubled.

"Well, maybe someone dropped it and didn't
want anyone to notice it was missing at first?" I
offered.

"I had a marble chess set when I was a child. The
pieces were a bit smaller than these, but it was very
sturdy," the professor said. "I dropped a few pieces
over the years, and they occasionally chipped, but
they didn't break."

"I found some books," Zoe said, standing by a
built-in bookshelf near the empty doorway. "And
that looks like a bedroom," she added, indicating
the room beyond.

"On it," said Billy, striding through the doorway,
brandishing his flashlight.

"What books did you find?" the professor asked.

Zoe shined her flashlight along a shelf that was

second from the bottom. "*Collected Shakespeare, Crime and Punishment, War and Peace, Complete Works of Poe*, the *Complete Poems of E.E. Cummings*, a . . . fifteen book set of Dickens, *Alice in Wonderland,* and *The Maltese Falcon,*" she read.

"Nothing like a little desert island reading," Derek quipped.

"Hey, did you find anything in there?" I yelled to Billy.

"Nah, nothin'," Billy said, emerging from the doorway. "Just a bed, some sheets and blankets, an empty night table. Nothing under the bed or the mattress. Hell, I even checked under the drawer in the nightstand in case somebody taped something under it. Nothing. What'd you guys find?"

"The classics of Western literature," Derek said.

"Oh—yeah, duh, of course! This was Adderly's bunker, guys. I told you: I read that he was some kind of survival nut. He must have planned to stay down here for years!"

"Yeah, just one problem with that," Derek said, shining his flashlight along the ceiling from the bar to the entryway that led to the stairs. "No vents. No vents, no air. No air, no survival," Derek said.

Unless you're a vampire.

"Well, maybe the air vents are elsewhere," I said.

"Or maybe they hadn't been installed yet," Billy suggested. "I mean, the place wasn't done—he hadn't even filled the bookshelves."

The professor was opening books, turning a few pages, and closing them, while Zoe held both their flashlights so he could read.

"Anything interesting?" I asked.

"The newest book here was printed in 1989," the professor said. "The oldest in 1904. It's curious. Very curious."

"Are we ready to move on?" I asked.

"Lead the way."

I moved towards the entryway and peeked inside. It was a small empty room with a door in the far wall. Summoning my courage, I walked up to it and turned the knob.

A faint scent of sawdust wafted through the air as I opened the door. "Hey, check it out," Billy said, standing in the empty room behind me. His flashlight pointed at the floor, following a trail of dark spots that led to the doorway where I was standing.

Zoe stood behind Billy. Between our three flashlights bouncing off the light gray floor and white walls and ceiling of the small room, I could see fairly well. Zoe had that same sickly look on her face that she'd had before as she took in what were probably old blood stains.

"Um . . . I think . . . maybe I should stay back here," she said.

"Why? I thought you saw ghosts all the time," Billy said.

"I do, and that's exactly why I don't want to go in there," Zoe replied, "and neither would you if you'd seen some of the things that I've seen."

"What have you seen?" Billy asked eagerly.

"Really, Billy?" I asked. "Can you try to focus on the task at hand?"

Derek entered the room with a crooked grin on his face, I think because I was giving Billy a hard time. The professor was behind Derek, looking apprehensive. "We should contact the police," he murmured. "The blood . . ."

"No body, no crime, Doc," Billy said. He nudged me with his elbow. "Go on, Maddy."

I looked at each of their faces. The professor seemed concerned and Derek still amused. Zoe looked better than she had. "You okay, Zoe?"

"Yeah. I'll survive," she said with a bit of an embarrassed smile. "I really don't like the sight of blood. At all."

Billy was bursting at the seams. "You want to go first?" I asked.

"I thought you'd never ask," he said, and led the way.

There were unfinished and partially finished wooden frames for walls throughout the room, with exposed wires inside the frames at the edges of the room and hanging down from the ceiling. Several pieces of drywall were stacked in one corner. It seemed as though the long rectangular room would have been segmented into two. Billy used his flashlight to follow the dark spots on the floor for a few feet, but stopped suddenly. "They just stop here," he said.

"That's a little weird," I said.

"What's that?" he asked, his flashlight catching

a thin, dark object on the floor. It appeared to be the other half of the pool stick we'd found on the billiards table, one end stained a deep brown.

"Uck," I said. "Zoe, don't look."

Our group moved through the first partial room to the second, through the skeleton of a doorway, and there, in the corner, in a sitting position on the floor, was the man himself.

Or what was left of him.

Grayish hair hung in wispy swirls on top of leathery skin stretched over the skull. The nose and eyes were sunken, with the eyes thankfully closed over protuberant cheekbones. The lips and gums had receded from the teeth in a hideous grin. An over-sized black suit jacket and white shirt, open at the collar, with white cuffs at the wrists, ended in claw-like hands. The shriveled skin covering them was like old parchment paper. The suit had probably fit once, before he wasted away. Skinny legs in black pants ended in shiny black shoes.

Everyone was silent a moment, possibly in shock.

I found myself looking at the teeth, scanning for fangs. There were none. I sighed in relief—it *had* been a silly thought after all. Practically hysterical. But not the funny kind of hysterical. The crazy kind.

Then I heard Zoe say, "Oh" behind me, then there was an intake of breath, and a flurry of movement as Derek caught her.

She seemed to have fainted.

"Shit," he said, struggling to hold her upright. "Zoe?"

She didn't respond.

"Zoe?" Prof. Gannon asked. Her head lolled against Derek's chest. Prof. Gannon checked her pulse quickly and didn't seem to like what he found. "We need to bring her back upstairs. *Now*. Derek, can you manage?"

"I can get her to the stairs, but I'll probably need help getting her up them," Derek said, and scooped Zoe up in his arms, one hand beneath her back, the other behind her knees.

They were leaving the room when Prof. Gannon stopped and looked back at me and Billy. Neither of us had moved.

"Well, that's it, then," he said with an impatient gesture. "Come on."

I was frozen to the spot.

"We'll be along in a sec, Doc," Billy said.

The professor stood there staring at us a moment and then a shout from Derek tore him away with a curse.

"You okay, Maddy?" Billy asked.

Sure, I wanted to say. I wanted to say I was fine. But something, somewhere inside me, was not fine. Something awful had happened, some part of me seemed to say. My stomach hurt. I felt a light sweat breakout on my forehead. My vision seemed oddly clear, but a little fuzzy around the edges. Was I going to faint too? No. I closed my eyes a moment and bit the insides of my cheeks. The pain sharpened me up.

I took a deep breath and opened my eyes. I had to know.

Billy was regarding me steadily.

"Is that him?" I asked. My voice sounded strange in my ears.

"You want me to check his wallet?" Billy said. "You know, it's not a bad idea, actually. Not sure if we should touch the body though. Police hate it when you do that."

"You know a lot about what police hate?"

"I've watched my fair share of procedurals."

"Why didn't you leave with the others?" I asked.

"Why didn't you?" he shot back.

"I don't know," I said. I couldn't explain it, but I couldn't leave without knowing.

"I just want to know if it's him," Billy said.

"Me too," I said. "It looks like one of those mummies at the Met," I said.

"Looks like he was thrown there," Billy said, shining his flashlight above the seated figure to a spot on the unfinished wall where the wooden frame was broken. Behind, one slat appeared to have pierced the body, impaling it through the torso.

"That's a pretty terrible way to go," said Billy.

I shined my flashlight on the desiccated corpse again and caught a sparkle of something metallic inside the collar. "What's that?" I asked. I knelt in front of the body to get a better look, and Billy knelt alongside me. "Shine your flashlight here," I said, pointing to the collar. It was an awkward position to kneel in—I almost lost my balance, and rather than touching the body, I gripped the wood frame above it to steady myself. The piece of wood shifted under my weight.

Suddenly, the body slumped forward, detaching from the slat on which it had been pinned.

Its face was only a few inches from mine when its eyes opened—clear light blue eyes that seemed so wrong in that wretched face.

The clawed hands moved and gripped my shoulders, digging painfully into my skin. My eyes met the corpse's for a moment, a moment that seemed to stretch and lengthen as those eyes widened. Then the corpse shouted, "No!" in a guttural voice like sandpaper. It threw me to the side with inhuman strength, where I hit the wall hard, and then nothing.

My head ached, pounding, and I heard a wet slurping sound before I opened my eyes. The room was dim, but my flashlight was still lit and lying on the floor next to my hand. The body, or mummy, held Billy in its grip, face buried in Billy's neck, and the wet sounds it was making were unmistakable: it was drinking.

This is some nightmare, I thought. *Some fantasy my mind dreamed up when I thought Michael Adderly was a vampire. It can't be real.*

I tried to stand and failed. The flesh of the vampire's face was slowly filling in, the hands coming back to life, almost inflating, the nose emerging, the skin losing its leathery appearance, the hair darkening. It was Michael Adderly. Thinner, slightly older, perhaps, than he'd appeared in the magazines, but that crooked nose, those eyes that stared right through me, that was him. And he was eating my friend.

"Get off of him!" I shouted, throwing my ragdoll body at the two of them, trying to tear Billy away. Adderly pushed me away with one hand and I fell back to the floor.

When I looked again, Adderly was no longer in the corner. He was now standing in the doorway, Billy's limp body folded over one arm. He looked back at me.

"Chris?" he said, as if he were uncertain.

And then he was gone. Gone from the room, gone with Billy, just gone.

CHAPTER SEVENTEEN

"WHAT DO YOU MEAN YOU WON'T CALL THE cops?" I shouted at Prof. Gannon. "All you wanted to do was call them, but now that Billy is missing, you won't?"

"You want to call the police? What do you plan to tell them? Maybe I should be the one calling them and pressing charges!" he yelled back.

"What?"

"That's right! Against the two of you for trespassing!"

"Trespassing? What are you talking about? You invited us here!"

"You lied on your release forms!" the professor shouted back. "Legally, you have no right to be here!"

"So that's it? You just use people to do your stupid studies and don't care about what happens to them? You're a jerk!" I shouted.

"Madison, calm down," Derek said, placing his hands on my shoulders.

I whirled on Derek, knocking his hands away. "I don't want to calm down! A fucking vampire just stole my friend! Where did he go?"

"That way," Zoe rasped from her position on the floor, pointing to the left of the old Zephyr, still sitting in the driveway.

I rushed out, leaving Derek's "Madison, wait . . ." in my wake.

The pine woods were dark and deep and I stood in their midst, listening, listening for sounds of a large creature crashing through underbrush, breaking branches. I heard nothing but what seemed to be the usual night forest sound of crickets and frogs in a symphonic trill.

"Michael!" I shouted. "Michael Adderly!"

There was no response.

"I know what you are!" I shouted. "I've seen Rebecca. I know you murdered Tamara! She's a restless spirit because of you, Michael! She haunts her old apartment because you killed her! They trusted you! They trusted you like Rosalita trusted you, and she died too!"

My throat was starting to hurt. The crickets paused in their melody for a moment and then continued.

"Give me my friend back. Give me Billy back, and I will leave you alone. I won't tell anyone about you. I swear. Just, please, give him back," I said, my voice breaking into a sob.

He had to give Billy back. He just had to. If he didn't give Billy back, then . . . then I'd gotten Billy killed, as good as I'd murdered him myself.

"Billy," I sobbed.

If the vampire was out there, listening, he was unmoved by my pleas. But then, why would he be? A vampire. A murderer who'd killed his own wives and a girl in my apartment and God only knew who else. And now he was probably murdering my friend.

I knew his secret. And he knew I knew I knew it. Was I stupid? Was I trying to get myself killed?

The dark woods suddenly seemed oppressive and dangerous, as if the trees themselves were closing in. The darkness pressed all around me.

I was an idiot.

I took a few steps backward slowly, scanning the shadows for movement, and then I ran.

When I arrived back at the garage, I was out of breath, covered in small scratches and welts from running through branches, but otherwise unharmed. If Adderly had heard me, he'd made no sign.

The rubber mat was back in place and the Zephyr had been rolled back in and covered with the drop cloth once more. Derek leaned against it, clearly waiting for me. "Are you okay?" he asked.

It was a hell of a question. Of course I wasn't okay. My friend had just been kidnapped by a serial killing vampire and I'd basically just told said vampire he should kill me next. Not to mention the little cuts and abrasions I'd gotten in the woods all stung.

I shook my head and put my hands on my knees.

I hung my head low, trying to catch my breath.

"Zoe and Prof. Gannon went back into the house to pack up," Derek said.

"Bully for them," I said.

"Where did you go?"

"I went to look for Billy."

"He ran out of there pretty fast," Derek said.

"What?"

"He ran out—"

"I heard what you said," I interrupted. "*Billy* didn't run anywhere."

"Madison," Derek said in an infuriatingly calm voice, "I don't know what you think you saw, but—"

"—But what? Are you going to tell me what I already know? Which is that vampires don't exist? I get that."

"If you call the cops and tell them that you saw a vampire kidnap your friend, they're going to lock you up. Billy is an adult. They'll just tell you that if he's still missing tomorrow to file a missing person report. There is nothing we can do at this point."

"I know your stance on this, Derek. That there's just nothing 'out there' that isn't explainable by science. But you tell me what happened to the body downstairs, then. You tell me why it's missing. You tell me where Billy went. Because I really want to know."

"I don't know what happened. But I know whatever was in the basement was not alive, Madison! The only explanation is that Billy took it with him. I mean, I went down and looked. It's gone. All that's left are some broken pieces of wood."

"I'm telling you, it came to life and attacked Billy and took him."

"Do you have any idea how insane you sound?"

"I don't care how I sound! I saw what I saw! Zoe saw it too! Why didn't you?"

Derek held his hands up in front of him, as if he were trying to placate someone dangerous by showing that his hands were empty. He spoke slowly and quietly. "Madison—I didn't see him. Neither did Prof. Gannon. We were both facing Zoe at the time. And she had just woken up, so who knows what she really saw, versus what she *thought* she saw."

"Really, Derek? Really? After everything else that's happened here, you're going to fall back that? On the . . . what did you call it, the fallibility of the senses?"

His hand, which he'd been about to place on my shoulder, fell to his side, and his voice took on a sad, distant quality. "Do you even recognize the difference between fact and fiction, Madison? I want to help you, but how can I? Your entire existence is fictional, starting with your name. Hell, for all I know, you might have lied about that too."

It was like a punch in the gut. I opened my mouth to reply, but there was nothing else to say so I shut it.

It didn't matter that he didn't believe me. Billy was still missing. That was the important thing.

"So that's it?" I said. "That's the end of the investigation? We're all just supposed to pack up and go home now and forget what happened here?"

"Look, don't take it out on me that your death-obsessed friend and co-worker just had a psychotic break. I mean, hell, Prof. Gannon thinks that all three of us were in it together."

"In *what* together?"

"I don't know, some conspiracy to sabotage his work on the Adderly House, planting a fake body here . . . your key . . . he even accused me of working for Dr. Hernandez. He said she's trying to disprove his data."

"*Are* you working for her?" I asked, not because I thought he was, but because I knew it would annoy him.

"Am I . . . ? Why are you asking me that?" he asked.

"Well, you hate the supernatural, don't you?"

"*Hate* is a pretty strong word. I don't think I care enough about it to *hate* it."

"But you don't believe."

"No. And apparently, neither does Dr. Hernandez. That's what they were doing here. Prof. Gannon was trying to collect data that proves the existence of the supernatural, while Dr. Hernandez was collecting data demonstrating that belief in the supernatural is passed along from person to person, kind of like mass hysteria."

"Mass hysteria?"

"Yeah, that's why they had that Zoe girl here."

"You mean she's an actress or something who was supposed to get us to believe in ghosts?"

"No, Prof. Gannon says she's for real. For him, she proves his theories, but for Dr. Hernandez, she's the catalyst that kickstarts other people's belief. That's why they were looking for people with different levels of belief. The 1 to 5 thing."

"So you're on Hernandez's side."

"I don't work for her, if that's what you're saying."

"I don't know what either one of us is saying anymore," I said. Talking about it was pointless. Billy was gone, Derek didn't believe me, and the professors were at war. There was no point in calling the police. Derek was right. Like Billy had said: *No body, no crime.*

Derek bowed his head and sighed heavily. He was quiet a moment and then said, "I'm going to go into the house to help everyone pack up. Are you coming?"

"I think I need a minute," I said.

He stalked off toward the house, leaving me and my flashlight alone in a small circle of light in front of the garage. It took me about five seconds of listening to the crickets to realize I probably ought to follow him.

The foyer was a bustle of activity between the two professors. No one really paid me any attention. In fact, they seemed to be ignoring me on purpose. I went to pick up my backpack from the coat rack where I'd hung it and stopped short when I noticed

Billy's leather jacket with the orange stripes on the sleeves still hanging there. Should I take it with me? Leave it there? What if Billy came back? There was a chill in the air and he'd need it. I left it.

When I turned around, the foyer was empty of people. There were still a few card tables set up, a monitor and two cardboard boxes filled with clamp lights, and the wooden cigar box that held the photographs of Michael Adderly and girl after girl after girl. His victims. I wondered if Tamara was in there, or Rebecca. Or hell, even me. Before I'd even really decided or thought about it, I opened my backpack, took two steps to the table, and slid the box inside it.

I picked up a box of clamp lights and turned to take it outside. "I'll take that, thank you," Prof. Gannon said coldly, taking it from me. Derek took out the monitor and Katie took out the other box of lights, and Dr. Hernandez began to break down the tables. I stood there with my hands in my pockets and began wondering where Zoe had gone to. She was the only one who had possibly seen what I'd seen.

I went outside, and there she was, sitting in the driver's seat of the old wood-paneled station wagon, leaning back against the headrest, her eyes closed.

"Zoe?"

"Yeah?" she replied groggily.

"Did you see what I saw?"

"I'm not sure. I saw a blur. Motion. Then?

Nothing." She pressed her fingertips to her temples and massaged in small circles.

"You okay?"

"Not really. I just feel tired, and my head's all fuzzy pain. Dust bunny massacre up there."

"Dust bunny massacre, huh? You need a broom? Or how about coffee? Maybe just some sleep?"

"Sleep. Yeah, that's all I really want to do right now. My head is killing me. I, uh . . . I don't suppose you can drive? I can give you a ride home later on when this passes."

I thought about it. "Well, Derek's my ride . . . but slide over," I said. She slid.

I opened the door and got into the driver's seat. This was the steering wheel, and the key to start the ignition would be on the right, kind of under . . . there. Yeah. I turned it. The car started. On the left side of the steering column somewhere below the dash, I felt around and found a button the size of a fat cigar stub. I pulled it. The headlights came on, and above the steering column, circles of numbers and a line of letters lit up. P was for *Park*, R for *Reverse*, D for *Drive*. One of the circles measured speed, the other measured RPMs. I knew this. I put my hand confidently on the lever for the transmission, pulling it toward my body and then smoothly moved the indicator to N for *Neutral* and then back to *Park*. "No problem," I said with a smirk.

Derek came out, awkwardly carrying a card table under each arm. He seemed astonished to see me behind the wheel. "What are you doing?" he asked.

"Zoe needs a ride home," I said.

"But you can't drive," Derek said.

"I can, actually."

"Can't she just catch a ride with us?"

"She can't," I said.

"I really don't want to leave the car here," Zoe mumbled, rubbing her temples again. "Plus, my mom needs it to get to work tomorrow."

"So you're just . . . leaving?" he asked.

"Well, I was gonna say goodbye first."

"Oh," Derek said. He seemed a bit crestfallen. What did he expect? What did I expect? It wasn't like it would be a pleasant ride back with him thinking I was crazy and me thinking he was a close-minded jerk. I didn't even know how we were supposed to get past that, but I knew it wasn't going to happen in the Adderly House driveway.

"I'll, um, call you," I said, throwing the transmission into reverse. "Bye!" I waved as I drove off, my wrist moving a bit too enthusiastically as he stood there with the two tables and an unhappy look on his face.

CHAPTER EIGHTEEN

ZOE'S APARTMENT WAS COVERED IN MYSTICAL symbols. Hand-painted designs wrapped around the walls beneath the ceiling and over and around every doorway and every window, probably hundreds of sigils, symbols, and patterns slapped on in thick black paint. Multiple wind chimes, made of wood, metal, clay and other materials hung suspended from the ceiling with different colored string, interspersed with sparkling crystals of every shade. The air felt different once I crossed the threshold. Was it warmer? Colder? Why was I getting goosebumps?

"Whoa," I said.

It was hoodoo. I didn't know why the word *hoodoo* seemed fitting to me—or why I would even know it—but I knew, and somehow I could tell that the stuff painted on Zoe's walls was real.

"Yeah, I don't bring too many people home," she said, shrugging out of her coat and hanging it on a hook near the door. It was a small apartment on the first floor, with the bedroom and living room separated by a hoodoo-covered archway and a couch facing a little TV in the corner. "Give me your coat. I'll hang it up for you," she said. We'd already discussed that I should crash on her couch that night and she'd drive me home in the morning. She seemed to be feeling better after napping in the car for most of the way back.

"So . . . all of this?" I asked, gesturing at the symbols and doohickeys hanging from the ceiling. "Does it keep ghosts out?"

"A girl's gotta sleep at night," she said.

"Huh. What about salt?" I asked.

"I hate all of those little grains under my feet," she said.

"But it works?" I asked.

"It can. For a while. Eventually it wears off, though."

"Sage?"

She gestured at a small ashtray with a partially burnt bundle of gray-green leaves in it.

"Wow," I said, taking it all in.

She indicated I should sit on the gray couch and went to get us both glasses of water. "I'd offer you something stronger, but I don't drink," she said.

"That's okay. Me either."

I studied the symbols over the doorway and window but didn't recognize any of them. Some seemed to repeat, while others did not.

"Did you do all of this yourself?" I asked when Zoe returned with the water.

"No, no. I found someone who specializes in this kind of thing. He did it for me."

"Maybe I should get him to come to my place," I said.

"Or I could just come over and find out what your ghost wants," she said. "It's the least I can do since you drove me home."

"You don't have to do that, but . . . well, I would appreciate it. The only problem is that it mostly comes out at night. You wouldn't see it tomorrow morning," I said.

"That won't be an issue," Zoe said.

I explained what the ghost had been up to, and Zoe periodically interrupted me ask questions: what I knew about the ghost's death, what I thought her name was, etc. Once I told her that Kara and Julie would be back Sunday night, she insisted on coming to see "my" ghost.

"Now, let's talk about the elephant," she said, after taking a drink of water.

"Elephant?" I asked, mystified.

"In the room. You know, what your real story is? Amnesia doesn't really happen to people, does it? That's just soap opera stuff."

I felt a cold, draining feeling from my head and hands I had come to recognize as a cocktail of dread, surprise, and shame. It was the same feeling I'd gotten when Derek had said my existence was fictional.

"It does happen, actually," I said. "I can show you my hospital paperwork, if you want."

Zoe seemed unconvinced.

"How do you feel when people say that you're

lying about seeing ghosts?" I asked.

She frowned. "It used to bother me. But now? Screw 'em."

"I was examined at Bellevue. Extensively. I took polygraphs. Passed. They tried truth serum, hypnosis, nothing. Either I'm super good at lying— guess what, I'm not—and fooled like twenty professionals, or I'm telling the truth. So should I say 'screw you'?"

"Alright," she said. "My apologies. You have to admit it sounds unlikely though."

"About as unlikely as ghosts . . . and vampires," I said.

"I didn't see anything, you know. When I came to in the garage, all I saw was a blur come up out of the trapdoor and disappear in the woods. What happened?"

"But the . . . you mean you don't remember the corpse?"

"Ugh, no. I definitely don't remember a corpse. I remember there were some old blood stains, and that's where it all goes blank for me."

I told her about everything up to when I was grabbed. "I wonder if I have bruises," I said, pulling the neck of my t-shirt aside to check my shoulder. Zoe leaned forward to check my back for me.

"It's definitely a little red back here," she said. "It might bruise by morning." She seemed very matter of fact. *Too* matter of fact.

"Aren't you going to freak out?" I asked. "I just told you that a corpse grabbed me."

"I hate to say it, but I've heard worse," she said.

"Ugh. Remind me not to ask."

Zoe knew things. Things no one should have to know.

"So what happened next?" she asked.

"Well, then it got . . . kinda crazy. It looked right at me and it yelled, 'No!' and threw me into the wall—"

"Wait, it yelled *no*?"

"Yeah."

"No . . . what? Like, leave me alone? Bad touch?"

"Well . . . I guess it was like it was saying no to *me*. It grabbed me, and was going to do . . . something . . . and then it looked at me. Like, really looked at me, and then it threw me aside, and I guess I hit my head and passed out."

"What happened when you woke up?"

"When I came to? It was . . . feeding. On Billy."

"Feeding?"

"Like, sucking his blood from his neck-shoulder area. Like Dracula."

An expression of incredulity passed over Zoe's face. So she did have limits to what she'd believe.

"We'll skip that for now. What happened next?" she asked.

I explained, all the way up to the part where Billy had been draped over his arm like an overcoat and Adderly had said *Chris*.

We were both quiet for a moment. Then Zoe said. "God, poor Billy."

I shook my head sadly. "I know. I feel

responsible. I don't know what I'm supposed to do."

"You can't do anything. Not for now, I mean. Damn, I wish we had some of those old magazines from the house."

"Why?" I asked.

"For research. I mean, we don't really know what we're up against."

"Well, we do have the Internet. And the library. As for what we're up against . . . Like I said, I think it's a vampire."

"Yeeeeaaaah, I know you *think* that."

"So the girl who can talk to ghosts doesn't believe in vampires, I take it?"

"It's just not something I've ever heard of. You'd think at least one of the ghosts I've talked to would have run into one."

"Well, I don't have any of the magazines, but I do have something. Billy found it in the basement." I fished the wooden cigar box out of my backpack.

"What's that?"

"This may support my idea about him being a vampire. Creepy photos."

"How creepy?"

"Not super creepy . . . Just pictures of Adderly posed with various girls. It's the way the hair and outfits change that's creepy."

"How did you get this?" she asked, looking inside the box.

"I swiped it when no one was looking."

"Wow, and I thought Billy was the criminal of

the group," she said with a smile. It turned to a frown as she paged through the black and white images. "Okay, let's just go with the vampire theory for a few minutes. Why would it push you away? Clearly, it was starving down there for who knows how long. Twenty or thirty years? And it has you in its clutches, looks at you, and says no, and goes for Billy instead. What's so special about you?"

She paused a moment, regarding one of the photos. "Hey, this one almost looks like you. She could be your older sister, maybe . . . or well, more likely your grandmother, or great-grandmother."

Zoe handed me the picture. It appeared to be from the 1920s or 1930s. An attractive woman in her early twenties with a nose and chin like mine stood cheek-to-cheek with Adderly, her eyes mostly obscured by her wavy dark hair and stylish bell-shaped hat. I could kind of see the resemblance.

"Do you think that's how I got the key?" I asked. "Do you think she's the Chris he meant?"

"Hell if I know," Zoe said, still paging through the pictures. "Whoa. I think this is Rosalita. Do you want to look?" she asked.

I was almost afraid to. But Zoe gestured with the box so I took it from her. The girl she said was maybe Rosalita was a vivacious, laughing girl with dark hair, dark eyes, and dark lipstick. Not exactly how I pictured her, but there was something in the set of her shoulders and the possessive way she clutched Michael Adderly's arm that held a hint of familiarity.

There were twenty-six pictures in all. Adderly through the years, posed with girls from the twenties through the sixties, as far as we could tell, and he never seemed much older than he did in the first one. "You want to tell me why you were at Adderly House in the first place?" Zoe asked.

I explained about Rebecca and Tamara and the piano. My unreliable source.

"Come on, you gotta admit that's weird," I said.

"Oh, I agree," Zoe said. "I just keep wondering if there's some rational explanation, you know? Like maybe he was part of some costume party where all the women came in outfits from different eras and he just posed with them in different spots."

"And just happened to have a million changes of clothes nearby so he wouldn't be wearing the same thing in every picture. And it least five different kinds of cameras and film stocks. And one of them was his wife. Was Rosalita his second wife? His third?"

"I forget," Zoe said, flipping each of the photos over in tandem. "Nothing written on the backs. It *is* really weird that you had that key."

"Tell me about it."

"And you're sure you're not lying?" She gave me a skeptical look.

"I'm not. Does it bother you?"

"I don't know. I mean, I deal with ghosts on an almost daily basis. But this is above my pay grade. Amnesia, vampires . . . are they connected? But if he was down there since the 1990s when he supposedly disappeared, how could that affect *your* memory? You can't be older than twenty or so."

"Beats me." I yawned.

"Tired?" Zoe asked sympathetically. "Let me grab you some bedding." She pulled a pillow and sheets from a closet and handed them to me.

"Thank you . . . for everything," I said.

"You're welcome." She paused a moment while I made up the couch. "Are you and Derek a thing?"

I finished tucking a sheet into the cushions. "I think we *were*. I don't know now. I mean, we had been hanging out. We kissed. He let me crash on his couch. But . . ."

"But he didn't believe you about Billy."

"He didn't believe me about anything."

"To be fair, he didn't *see* anything."

"I know, but it still hurts."

She frowned a moment and then said, "Well, there aren't a lot of people out there who can see what we see."

"What do you mean, 'we'?"

"I saw you in Adderly House."

"Saw me what?"

"You looked right at ghosts twice."

"I did what now?"

Zoe's brows drew together in a look of confusion. "Didn't you see them?"

"No. I swear to you, I did not see any ghosts."

"Did you see anything at all? Anything weird, I mean. Not like the walls or furniture."

I thought back to my experiences in Adderly

House. "Not really? I guess I maybe saw a shadow once or twice where I didn't think there should be one."

"By the fireplace, right? And in the attic?"

I thought again. "Yeah. How did you know? You saw ghosts both times?"

"Yes."

"That's weird."

"It just means you're sensitive to their presence but you haven't learned how to see them yet. Makes sense since you're the only roommate who noticed the ghost in your apartment."

Ugh. I didn't want to be sensitive to ghostly presences. The thought made my head hurt. I rubbed my temples and another yawn forced its way out of my mouth.

"We should get some sleep," Zoe said.

"Yeah, I guess so."

"I'm going to make some chamomile tea. It helps me sleep. You want some?" she asked.

"If it will help me sleep? Yes. Yes, please."

I couldn't sleep. Michael had said a name to me: *Chris.* We sometimes called the comic book store Chris Street. Is that what he meant? That seemed like a stretch. Did he know me? Had he known someone who looked like me? The woman from the picture that Zoe said looked like she could be my great-grandmother? That seemed more likely. I picked up the box and found the photograph. I wanted a better look at it.

Michael looked happy in the photo. Like he was trying to keep from laughing over some secret joke. It was all so odd. Could she be a clue to my past?

I put the picture back and took out another. It was the photo with the girl that Zoe had said was Rosalita. Michael still looked happy in this one, but maybe a little less so. Rosalita was looking more at him than she was at the camera.

I pulled out another photo, and then another, going through the pictures obsessively, poring over each of them for details, and in every one of them, I found myself captivated by Michael Adderly's face. As I arranged the photos in what seemed like chronological order, Michael Adderly's smile— genuine in the first four pictures or so—seemed to stiffen, stretch, and sag as the images went on. By the last few photos, he was still smiling, but his eyes looked sad. What did it mean? That he regretted killing all the girls that had come before his latest conquest?

I thought back to the moment in the library at Adderly House when Billy had played that record. Everything around me had seemed to fade. Reality slid away like a satin sheet falling to the floor. Then the voice. Even thinking of it made my chest feel tight with longing. I felt unfulfilled, like I was missing a vital part of myself. The man who sang like that, he was the man who smiled and looked sad in photographs.

The song. His face going from happy to sad.

What did it mean? Why had he hidden for twenty-plus years in that basement? And why did I have a key to it?

I boxed up the photos once more, and began to close the latch on the box, but I couldn't bring myself to close it. I was feeling so many things. Conflicted. Yearning. Afraid. I had no basis for this kind of emotion. I didn't know what I was supposed to do with it. I closed the box anyway and laid down.

I slept fitfully, waking from faceless dreams of joy and fear that faded on waking. That was nothing new. I often had weird dream hangovers that I couldn't really remember. But now instead of confusion I could shrug off, I was left with a palpable emptiness. Somehow, part of me now seemed to feel that my lack of memory meant I'd lost more than my identity and my history.

No. I'd lost all of the *feelings* that would accompany my memories: love, laughter, tears, anger, frustration. It was as if prior to hearing Michael Adderly's recorded voice on that record player, all the feelings I'd had were just like the secondhand clothes I wore, emotions I borrowed from other people, not *mine*. But now, now I could feel. I *felt* the loss of my memory.

And I wanted it back.

Zoe offered me coffee and cereal the next morning. We sat facing one another at a two-seater table at the edge of her kitchenette. Mystical symbols were scrawled along the ceiling and window. In between mouthfuls of crunchy cinnamon cereal, I gestured upwards and asked, "It's hoodoo, isn't it?"

Zoe gave me a surprised look. "It is. How'd you know?"

"I just did. Like, how do I know how to drive? Or play piano? Or speak French?"

Zoe covered her mouth before saying, "Ohmygod, you don't have a license."

"Um, oops? Sorry about that. But you really were in no condition to drive."

While we ate, I asked Zoe more questions about ghosts. She could see them at all times of day or night, when they were present and willing. Most were.

"You said something about the ghosts at the Adderly House being shy," I asked. "How many did you see there?"

"Total?"

"Yeah, total."

"I saw five."

"Five, really? Is that unusual? The amount, I mean."

"A little. Most places are only haunted by one or two ghosts. There are exceptions. Like cemeteries. Or places where a major tragedy has occurred. Adderly House was . . . different. The ghosts didn't want to be seen. As soon as we'd enter a room, they'd leave. Or they'd watch us until I looked directly at them, and then they'd disappear. I mean, I almost got the sense that they wanted to talk but couldn't. And that's weird. And then there was Rosalita—and that was odd too."

"Yeah, she was odd alright."

"That's not what I mean. I mean that all of the ghosts except Rosalita were avoiding us. And the way she came through what's-her-name . . ."

"Katie," I said. "What about it?"

"I think that Rosalita must have had a strong personality in life. She felt very willful, and angry too. I think that in some ways when a person dies mad it creates a spirit that's more powerful than your average ghost. I mean, I can let pretty much any ghost possess me whenever I want, but for a ghost to grab some random, non-sensitive and use her against her will—that shows power. I've never seen that before. Of course, she might have been feeding off of us, too."

"What do you mean?"

"Well, ghosts are kind of like, I don't know, like energy receivers. They can take energy and do something with it—sort of like a light bulb giving off light. Without any energy though, a light bulb is dark. But the more energy they get, the more they can do—the more light they can shine. But if no one notices them—the ghosts, I mean—then they don't get energy. In Adderly House, there were the two of us, noticing them, in one way or another. Maybe that was what let Rosalita possess Katie."

"The ghost in my apartment, Tamara—I think she possessed my roommate."

She took a breath. "That's rare. Two possessions in your presence? Unless your roommate's a medium, or the ghost is really powerful, I think they might be tapping into your energy. Which means you may have some kind of magical energy about you. It would explain why you were sensitive to their presence and maybe how you know what hoodoo looks like, even if you don't remember how you know."

I didn't know how to respond to that idea. But if I could believe in ghosts and vampires, why not? "Magical energy?"

"Practitioners exist. Like I said, I know a guy. He's the one who did all of this." She gestured at the symbols painted around her apartment.

I shook my head. It was all too much.

"I don't suppose you know what day and month Tamara died?" Zoe mused.

"April. Around the 12th."

"There's something weird that happens around death anniversaries. It's like a resonance of some kind allows spirits to reappear."

"Didn't Billy say something about how different people had died in Adderly House on the same day?"

"Yeah. The caretaker. And that poor headless ghost . . ."

"So there *was* a headless horseman?"

"Well, there wasn't a horse. And this guy was

wearing an old coverall like you see gardeners and handymen wearing. I'm no expert, but he didn't look like a Hessian mercenary to me."

"That must be the repairman that Billy mentioned."

"Probably. I wish I'd had a chance to talk with him. But how would that work? No head, no talk. Plus the whole running away from us thing."

"Do ghosts usually just walk right up and get all chatty with you?"

"Usually. They're kinda pushy, actually." I was quiet for a moment, thinking about what that would be like. The word *horrible* came to mind, followed by *disturbing*.

A couple of hours later, we entered my apartment. The lamp was still in its familiar position on its side on the floor, and the lines of salt I'd spread across my bedroom and the bathroom doorways were still there. The apartment was warm, too warm, and the air felt stale. I opened a window in the living room to let in some fresh air.

Zoe took off her sweater and hung it up. When she turned around, I noticed she was wearing a black t-shirt that read THERE IS NO SUCH THING AS A HAPPY MEDIUM. It took me a second, but then I chuckled appreciatively. She asked me to be silent to allow her to concentrate on making contact, so I shut up.

I pointed out the lamp and Zoe nodded at it and

stepped into the living room, moving toward the window. I could see into the kitchen from where I was standing. Several kitchen cabinet doors were ajar.

Zoe pressed her hands against the window frame where I'd watched Kara scream from the fire escape before passing out. Zoe stayed in that position for a moment, and then turned around and went directly toward Kara's bedroom.

I stayed in the living room, watching Zoe through the doorway.

"She's here," Zoe said, staring at something I couldn't see. Suddenly I was glad I couldn't see. I got goosebumps.

"Are you the spirit of Tamara Meadows?" Zoe asked. She seemed to wait for an answer and then nodded at me.

My palms were sweating. "Ask her why she attacked my roommates," I whispered.

Zoe made a puzzled face. "She wants to talk directly to you."

"Uh . . ." I said.

"Yes, I'll allow it," Zoe said, talking to empty space somewhere above Kara's dresser. Then the air seemed to leave her body all at once. She shrank in on herself, shoulders curled inward, head bowed, and then she seemed to unfurl herself with blazing eyes and a fierce expression.

"So what do you want to know?" she asked with a nasal Long Island accent.

"Tamara?" I asked.

"That's my name. Don't wear it out."

"Why did you attack us? Why did you shred Julie's lingerie and stab her pillow?"

"Who?"

"My roommate Julie."

Zoe's brow creased. "I don't know what you're talking about. I didn't attack you. You said Julie? Not Rebecca?"

"Not Rebecca. Her name is Julie. Julie Moon."

"I don't remember. Everything is different."

"What do you mean?"

"I can see now. I couldn't really see before. But then I saw you. You bitch. You wouldn't tell me where he is."

"Who? Michael?"

"Michael," she echoed, her voice softening sadly.

"I've seen him," I said. "He took my friend. I swear to you that I am going to stop him. I don't know how, but I will find a way. He should pay for what he did to you."

"Did to me?"

"He killed you—didn't he?"

Zoe's head shook from side to side, and the nasal voice said, "It wasn't Michael! You're crazy! He would never hurt me! He tried to protect me."

"From who?"

She sighed. "It'll be easier to just show you," she said, and touched my forehead.

The girl lies in bed, the back of her head to the doorway. Her head rests at an unnatural angle. Straight brown hair partially obscures her face, the rest of its length fanned across the white and black paisley pillow. Her skin is unnaturally pale. It's not a lovely alabaster or creamy ivory; instead there is a chalky, almost gray whiteness to her skin.

Her limp hand dangles off the bed, fingernails gone blue. This much is visible from the bedroom doorway. This is what the landlord sees when he enters the apartment in the morning to fix the leaky kitchen faucet, as he'd promised the day before. The landlord calls the police.

A closer look reveals her eyes are open. A petite brunette with golden brown eyes in her late teens or early twenties. The bedclothes are pulled up to just below her nose. Beneath it, where her mouth and neck should be, runs an angry red and gray ruin of veins and tubes and ligaments that were never, ever meant to see the light of day. It is as if her jaw has been torn off and her throat has been ripped open by some curious animal that then took the time to dissect it.

Beneath this desecration, there are no other wounds. She wears a tank top and shorts. The tank top is white and stained with red, contrasting with the gray of her skin.

But where is the rest of the blood? The paisley sheets, the mattress . . . they should be soaked through, sopping with red. There's not a drop on the bed. Hardly any in the girl. Hardly any at the scene. Her lower jaw is found beneath her head as soon as the coroner moves her. The sight is so disturbing to a rookie policeman on-scene, he bolts for the bathroom.

The coroner estimates—based on temperature and the progression of rigor mortis—that she has been dead only four hours.

Soon the detectives will determine she was killed

elsewhere, then brought to the bedroom. But not in the tub. Not a drop, not a smear there. There are three drops of her blood in the entryway. Just three tiny drops. No blood of any quantity elsewhere in the apartment, not in the drains, not in the toilet, not outside the windows to the fire escape. No fingerprints found at the scene other than those of the apartment's occupants.

Robbery is ruled out as a motive almost immediately. Her purse and wallet are in the kitchen, her jewelry in plain sight in the bedroom. There are no signs of forced entry, although a lamp in the entryway has been knocked to the floor, presumably as the killer carried her body into the apartment.

Who would want her dead? The roommate is out of the country. A rival at school has a rock-solid alibi. A boyfriend identified as a person of interest cannot be located. They don't even have his last name. There isn't a single lead. Not a single foreign hair or fiber on her body. The lack of evidence baffles forensic experts.

The sun sets, and rises again. Days pass. Weeks. Months.

The case is left unsolved. It goes into a cold case file, forgotten.

Such a violent, unthinkable murder.

Her spirit is left unsatisfied, malcontent, disturbed. Rooted to the spot. Unable to rest.

And when the veil between the worlds of the living and the dead thins . . .

She haunts.

Then, in reverse order, images in flashes, the police, the landlord, the girl in the bed, flashes of more movement in and out of the apartment, days passing, and then slowing, slowing.

I watched the events unfold as if they were happening to someone else, though I was seeing through Tamara's eyes, the eyes of her ghost, as she flashed through the last months of her life.

Her debut performance at Carnegie Hall. She has just come down the stairs off stage to a standing ovation. Michael Adderly approaches, wearing a suit and tie. He is handsome and young, holding a bouquet. This is their first meeting. Flashes of other meetings, dinners, always at night. The two of them singing together. He shows her the apartment and she moves in with Rebecca. The piano, a Steinway Model M Grand Piano, arrives.

Flashes of Michael drinking from her wrist. Michael kissing her forehead. Her attempt to kiss him, his refusal.

Then, a red-haired girl playing at the piano. It's Rebecca, young, maybe twenty. Michael Adderly sitting next to her, showing her something in his wallet. Michael laughing with Rebecca, playing a duet with Rebecca. Sitting next to Rebecca.

Too close.

Outrage. Jealousy. Ultimatums. Threats.

Michael stands between them, trying to calm Tamara. He leaves with Rebecca.

Tamara's hands shake as they shred Rebecca's clothes with a knife. She stabs the knife into the center of Rebecca's pillow.

Michael returns, entering from the fire escape. Tears. An argument. He takes out her suitcase and begins packing it for her. She doesn't want to go. They argue again. Michael gets a call and leaves. Tamara screams into the mirror in her room, then cries, taking her clothing out of the suitcase and putting it away.

Fast forward. Night becomes day becomes night. Sitting by the phone. Waiting.

A sound on the fire escape. A beautiful, haughty woman in her early twenties steps into the room through the open window. She wears a black dress, accessorized with black gloves and stiletto heels. She has light blond hair pulled back in a tight bun, topped with a stylish black-veiled hat. Her blue eyes blaze, ringed in dark eyeliner. Beneath them, her regal nose and dark red-lipsticked mouth sneer.

The woman's face is familiar, but I can't place it.

Tamara flees to the front door. The woman is impossibly fast. Standing before the door, the blond woman snarls, showing fangs. Her hand shoots out, catching Tamara by the throat and lifting her off her feet. Tamara kicks, knocking over a standing lamp in the entryway. The woman sinks her fangs into the girl's neck. The feeling is both painful and exquisite.

The woman pulls back and smiles a vicious red-tinged smile. "You see," she says in a Germanic accent, "He will always come back to me. He will always be mine."

The last thing Tamara sees before everything goes black is a drop of her red, red blood falling to the floor from the woman's red, red lips.

I staggered, the pain in my neck and the trauma of the experience feeling much too real.

"That woman," I said, my mind reeling. "Who was she?"

"Van Horn," came Tamara's voice from Zoe's mouth.

Now I recognized her. The woman I'd seen in Tamara's vision was the spitting image of the girl in the painting in the Adderly House attic. The clothes and hair had had a three-hundred-year makeover, but it was her.

"Catharina Van Horn?" I asked.

"Irina Van Horn," Tamara said, and then Zoe slumped to her knees.

I helped her up, and she was Zoe again. She slowly got to her feet. "I understand," she said to the empty air next to her. "I'll tell her."

Zoe's eyes softened and seemed to watch something move upwards in the air and then off through the window.

Then she turned to me and said, "She's gone. Like, *gone* gone. She won't be back."

"What do you mean, *gone-gone*? Where?"

"Wherever they go."

"You mean, like heaven? Or hell?"

"Could be either. But she's . . . at rest, now. She asked me to thank you."

"Thank me for what?"

"For allowing her to move on. It looked peaceful."

"But why was she a ghost?"

"You saw what happened to her, right? A lot of the time when there's a haunting, it's because the ghost has unfinished business. She couldn't let go until someone knew the name of her murderer."

"So you're saying she's gone for good?"

"I think so."

"Thank you," I said, spontaneously hugging her.

She laughed and hugged me back. "Sorry," I said. "I don't really hug people."

"It's okay. It seems to happen in these situations," she said with a smile. "I have to head out, though. Gotta get the car back to Queens. You'll be okay now." She gave me her number and I gave her my email. I took my usual teasing about not having a cell phone and saw her to the door.

I began cleaning. Turns out salt's a bitch to sweep up. No wonder it's bad luck to spill it.

Then I put the living room back the way it belonged and closed all of the kitchen cabinets, straightened the mirror in Kara's room, and closed her door. The whole time I kept thinking about everything that had happened: Adderly House, Michael Adderly, Billy, Catharina or Irina Van Horn, Tamara. I'd set out to clear my home of supernatural activity, and I had. But at what cost? What kind of can of worms had I opened?

I'd just finished when I heard keys jingle in the door. Kara came in, a bag of groceries cradled in one arm. Her hair was up in its signature ponytail and she wore stretchy pants under a floral print maternity shirt. While I helped her put the groceries away, she caught me up on her hospital tests (all fine), seeing her father and sister at the hospital (also fine), and the remainder of her weekend with Serge (better than fine). I kept stealing glances at her, looking for signs of lingering psychic trauma: bags under her eyes, pale skin, nervous twitches. She seemed okay to me. It looked like Tamara's brief possession hadn't done Kara any lasting damage. She seemed to have bounced right back, and for that I was thankful.

After the groceries were put away, she rummaged through the cabinets and pulled out a baking pan. "I'm making lasagna tonight," she said. "Wanna help?"

"Sure, but I have no idea what to do."

"I'll *teacha* you *everyting* you need to know," she said with an exaggerated Brooklyn-Italian accent, making me laugh because she sounded almost exactly like Mr. Delgado. We got to work. Lasagna's a process and a half, but with the two of us working on it, the time passed pleasantly enough.

It was dark by the time Julie finally arrived, entering the apartment wearily. She carried her small suitcase and a shopping bag. She took off her coat and scarf, revealing a black turtleneck and dark jeans that looked stylish on her petite frame. "Oh my God, that smells amazing!" she said, referring to the glorious scent of baking lasagna. "Can we eat now?"

Over dinner, Julie went on and on about the bed and breakfast where she and Tad had stayed over the weekend, from the king-sized bed to the fresh croissants every morning and the in-room jacuzzi and blah blah blah.

"What did you do all weekend, Madison?" Kara asked.

"Oh, I worked. Went to the library. That's pretty much it," I said.

"You really ought to go out more," Julie said. I think she was trying to be helpful.

"Whatever happened with what's-his-name? David? Daniel?" Kara asked.

"Derek," I said. "I don't know. I don't think it's going to work out."

"Damn, I miss everything," Julie said. "I demand details, woman!"

I shrugged and gave in, describing Derek, how we'd met, the movie dates, the kiss, and his dig regarding my lack of memory.

At that last detail, Julie pressed her lips together and inhaled deeply through her nose. "Yeah, about that. Madison, I'm sorry. I owe you an apology."

I blinked at her. "I . . . you do?"

Julie nodded. "Yeah, I do. I was freaking out about all of the weirdness going on here, and I said some things about you that I shouldn't have, and I don't know if you even heard me or not, but you didn't deserve that, and I'm sorry." Wow, talk about concessions—or is it confessions? I felt a little bubble of resentment towards her that I hadn't realized I'd been carrying around pop.

"Of course I forgive you," I said. "It was a stressful time. Forget it."

"We're all good here?" Kara asked.

"I feel good. No weirdness the rest of the weekend either," I lied.

"That's a relief. I checked my windows and everything and it seems okay in there too," Julie said.

"Me too," Kara said. "the mirror's right where it ought to be."

"We probably just imagined the whole thing. It could have happened to anyone," I said.

"Who wants dessert?" Julie asked. "I got cheesecake."

Between my full stomach and finally feeling safe in the apartment again, I fell asleep quickly, tucked beneath the sheets in an extra-large white t-shirt and my undies.

I awoke just as quickly.

There was nothing, just the sense of having been completely out, followed by the sense of being wide awake in the dark and not knowing what had woken me. I opened my eyes and felt my soul try to leave my body when I thought I saw a dark figure on the fire escape outside my window.

I sat up suddenly, drawing the bedding back up to my chin, as if I could use it to protect myself.

When I looked again just a second later, the figure was gone.

I let out a deep breath, the one I'd taken in anticipation of screaming my head off. But there was nothing there. I'd imagined it. Hadn't I? But if the figure was sort of man-shaped . . . could it have been Michael Adderly?

I felt like I was losing my mind. I fluffed my pillow a few times and then rolled over, trying to fall back asleep. Sleep came less easily than it had the first time, but eventually I drifted off, and by morning, the memory of the figure outside my window had faded almost completely away.

Chapter Nineteen

Monday afternoon, I walked into Chris Street and there was Billy, standing at the bag check in black jeans and an Ant-Man t-shirt, looking more cheerful than I'd ever seen him.

"Billy!" I shouted, rushing up to hug him.

"Jeez, Maddy," he said, shrugging me off. "Didn't anybody ever teach you about personal space?"

"Are you okay? What happened to you?"

"What do you mean?" He looked seriously confused.

"What do you mean, what do I mean? You disappeared!"

"What? Oh, that. I just got tired of that guy. That professor prick. I was bored. So I bolted." The words came out smooth, almost rehearsed.

"No," I said. "That's *not* what happened."

"Sure it is."

"Billy," I said, "I saw you with the corpse!" Or saw it with you, more properly, but whatever.

"Corpse? What corpse? I think I'd remember a corpse, Maddy," he said, with a mocking grin.

That made me want to punch him. The hell? How could he not remember a corpse, especially one that came to life and bit him? I frowned. I needed to clock in for my shift. "You stay right there," I said.

He held his hands in the air. "Whatever you say, officer," he said. "No problemo."

I opened the door to the office. "Hi, Mac." Preoccupied with our next week's comics order, Mac grunted in response before I walked back to the front of the store.

"Okay, out with it," I said, giving Billy my fiercest look. "Tell me what really happened to you."

"There's nothing to tell, Maddy. I split and started hitchhiking my way back to the city. Got a lift and here I am." He fiddled with a playing card half while he spoke. The King of Hearts, also known as the Suicide King because the king appears to be sticking a sword in his own head. I'd played a lot of card games at Spring House. There'd been many arguments about whether the king was killing himself or being assassinated. Crazy people like to argue about odd, morbid things.

"Why are you being so weird about this?" Billy asked.

"Oh, I don't know, maybe because my friend disappeared in the middle of a ghost hunt?" *Not to mention got kidnapped by a vampire*, I didn't say. "You really don't remember the corpse?"

"Corpse? Are you kidding me? I think I'd remember a corpse, Maddy."

"You said that already." He'd said it in the exact same way in fact, with the same emphasis on my name at the end. Which was creepy. It sounded . . . off. Like a phrase he'd practiced, trying to make it sound natural.

"What?"

"You already said that you'd remember a corpse."

"I did?"

"Yeah."

"Well, I would."

"It was Michael Adderly, Billy."

He gave me a skeptical look as the front door opened and a customer came in. Billy collected the guy's backpack and handed over half of the King of Hearts, carefully clipping the other half of the card to the backpack and stowing it beneath the counter.

"Wow, your imagination has really gotten the better of you," Billy muttered, coming out from behind the counter and sauntering in the same direction as the guy who'd just come in. It was Mac's policy. If there was no one working the back, whoever was on bag check needed keep an eye on the customer to make sure he didn't steal anything. Our conversation would have to wait.

I stood behind the register and tried to consider Billy's version of what had happened.

No. I'd seen Michael Adderly. I'd recognized those eyes, that nose, the hair. It was him. And he wasn't just a corpse. Michael Adderly was, well, if not quite alive, at least he was walking around.

Just say the word, Maddy. Vampire.

If Michael Adderly was a vampire, didn't vampires spread their vampness by biting people? Maybe Billy was a vampire right now, and just didn't know it. I searched my brain for what I knew about vampires. All I could think of, aside from being dead, having fangs, and drinking blood, was powers of mind control. But what else?

I went to the comics and graphic novels. *Morbius: The Living Vampire. Vampirella. Man-Bat. Greenberg the Vampire. Dracula: A Symphony in Moonlight. Vampires: The Living Dead.* I flipped through the pages looking for commonalities. Lots of capes. Lots of fangs, and pale faces, and bloody necks. One black and white image showed a fierce-looking vampire dude. His piercing eyes stared over the edge of a black cape, his eyebrows like evil caterpillars. Whoever that was supposed to be. Dracula, probably. In the next frame, a frail maiden in a white nightgown swooned. The vampire mind-whammy. Total hypnosis. Like Obi Wan saying, "These aren't the droids you're looking for." Except that Jedi aren't vampires. At least, I don't think they are.

From my skimming, it seemed like my knowledge lined up with what pop culture had to say: all vampires drank blood and were super strong. All of them were pale, too. Michael Adderly definitely fit the profile. But Billy had always been pale. Weirdly, he looked slightly *less* pale now. In fact, now that I looked more closely at him, Billy looked kind of healthy. The dark circles that usually lingered beneath his eyes were gone. He had a bit of color in his cheeks, if such a thing were even possible.

The customer he'd followed came up to the register with a few comics. I hit various keys on the register and took his money, then collected the half King of Hearts and returned his backpack to him. He left.

"Are you feeling okay?" I asked Billy when we were alone.

"I feel fine," he said.

"You never feel fine."

"Since when?"

"Since as long as I've known you."

"Maybe it was the winter doldrums."

"Winter doldrums? Who *are* you?"

"I'm Batman." He grinned.

"Hey, speaking of: who are *you*? Do you really have amnesia? Why didn't you ever say anything?"

"I'm sorry I never told you. There just isn't really anything to tell. I really have amnesia. I have hospital paperwork to prove it."

"So you aren't on the run from someone?"

"What? No! What would make you even think that?"

"I don't know. No reason." Billy shrugged and put his hands in his pockets.

A customer came in, then another. Multiple customers came and went, so I had little opportunity to question Billy further. Mac left an hour before closing, leaving Billy in charge.

Moments after Mac left, Billy sidled up next to me at the register. "Oh, uh, are you still dating Derek?" He said it casually. Almost *too* casually.

"I don't know," I said.

"I don't think he's any good for you, Maddy."

"Really? I thought you got along with him." There was something off about the way Billy was behaving—strangely curious and conspiratorial. It wasn't like him.

"Yeah, I don't know. Personality type. Kind of a boring dude. You can do better. I'm just looking out for you, you know?"

"You're being weird," I said. "And I don't want to talk about it with you, okay?"

Then a regular customer came in to pick up the comics we'd been holding for him for a while and we dropped the subject.

He counted my register while I swept up, and we left together. He was wearing an olive green hoodie over his Ant-Man t-shirt. Something about the hoodie struck me as off, and then I realized why: he'd left his signature leather jacket behind in Sleepy Hollow. I'd last seen it hanging on the coat rack right before I'd left.

Now I had him.

"Hey, where's your Wolverine jacket?" I asked.

"It's at home," Billy said.

"But I saw it at the Adderly House after you disappeared."

"Nah, I went back for it. It's at home." His voice

sounded dull and affectless. Almost robotic.

He pulled the security gate down across the storefront while I waited awkwardly, trying to figure out why he was lying. "What are you up to tonight? Going to Doc Holliday's again?" I asked.

"Nah, I've got class tonight." Again with the same dull, rehearsed tone.

"Class? At, what, 2am?" I asked, immediately suspicious. The Billy I knew didn't take classes. The Billy I knew said college was for suckers.

"Yeah, you know New York. The city that doesn't sleep? I'm taking it at King's College."

"Taking what?"

"English."

"What kind of English?"

He frowned. "I don't know, just English."

"Billy, you speak English. It's not like taking a foreign language. What are you reading?"

His face took on a vacant stare before he shrugged and answered, "Books."

"Books? What books?"

He blinked a few times, and said, "I don't know, there's this book I have to buy. I didn't get it yet. Why are you asking me all of these questions anyway?" He pinched the bridge of his nose. "Man, you're giving me a headache."

"Billy, you don't believe in college."

"Well, college believes in me, maybe. I don't know. I'm into it."

"You're into it," I echoed.

"Yeah."

"I'll believe that when I see it."

"Suit yourself."

"Suit *your*self!"

"I will!"

"Good!"

Billy walked away from me on Christopher Street without even saying goodbye.

So I followed him. Because what else was I going to do?

I wanted to shadow Billy surreptitiously, hiding behind an open newspaper, stooping behind mailboxes, and jumping inside phone booths, but it wasn't necessary (and there aren't any phone booths in the West Village anyway). Billy never looked behind him once.

Staying about a hundred feet back, I trailed him into the subway, where I jumped on the same train but in an adjoining car so I could keep an eye on him through the window. He sat staring straight ahead with his hands on his thighs. He didn't take out his phone and play with it. Now that I thought about it, I hadn't seen him check his phone all night long, which was definitely not like Billy.

He exited the train at the 34th Street station at Madison Square Garden and began walking east. Throngs of drunk tourists in black concert shirts crowded the station and sidewalks. I almost lost him, but then caught a glimpse of his olive green hoodie and rushed ahead to catch up, weaving in and out of the crowd like a frog dodging cars in a video game.

A few blocks later, at the corner of 35th and 5th, Billy passed a pair of fancy art deco revolving doors and went in a side door. The words EMPIRE STATE were carved onto the building. Wait a second. Had Billy just walked into the Empire State Building? It was hard to tell from street level. I couldn't even see the top of the building from here. What the heck was in there? Could there really be a college inside? I waited a minute and went in through the same door.

The brown marble lobby shined as if it'd just been polished. All very brown, with streaks of cream throughout. Who thought brown was a good color for the lobby of the most famous building in the world?

A gray-haired security guard in a blue uniform sat behind a desk, looking tired. "Um, hi?" I said. I hated how nervous I sounded.

"The tours are closed. Are you visiting someone?" he asked. I nodded. "Sign in, please," he said, pushing a clipboard at me. A chained pen hung from it. The form had multiple columns labelled NAME, VISITING, ROOM, TIME IN and TIME OUT. The last entry on the list was *Billy Stickler*, written in a spidery handwriting. Beneath "Visiting" he'd written "Kris Kong" and beneath "Room" it read "SB2."

Who the heck was Kris Kong? Maybe his professor? I dutifully wrote my name under Billy's with the same name and room. "I'm going to need to see some ID," the guard said, stifling a yawn. His shiny blue name tag read "Sgt. Keene."

"I'm sorry, but can you tell me how to get to SB2? Is that King's College?"

"King's College? Nah, it's not here anymore. They moved downtown a few years ago. It's right by the New York Stock Exchange now."

"So what or where is SB2?"

He squinted at me. "Do you have ID or not?" There was no way this guy was going to take my Spring House Resident Pass as ID.

"No, I . . ." I shook my head frantically, thinking quickly. "My boyfriend has my wallet. Billy. We had a fight. He just came in here and—"

"No ID, no entry. You'll have to wait for him."

"But—" I began, as the shrieking of a klaxon alarm jolted him out of his seat.

"You stay right there," he ordered, pointing at me. He picked up a walkie talkie and jogged down the hallway to the right, barking questions into it as he ran around a corner.

Fuck it.

I hustled down the corridor to the left and then to the right, following arrows to ELEVATORS. A brass mural of the building flanked by American flags stood at the end of the hall. The klaxon continued screeching as I passed an alcove housing a large potted plant.

A very large potted plant. It struck me as odd. And I had a very strong compulsion to go back to that plant and alcove. Even though I'd already passed by, it was like my feet were already trying to get me to turn around. I felt that the plant and the alcove were important somehow. It was eerie. I can't explain it any other way. So I went back.

The big green plant held many leafy fronds. Plastic or real? I grabbed a lower leaf and it felt fake. Plastic and smooth. Below it, I could see scratches in the gloss on the brown marble floor. Dull scratches in a semi-circle, as if the planter had been dragged repeatedly from the alcove. The alarm continued its wailing. I looked back and forth down the hall, but no security guards were coming this way.

An unobtrusive brown curtain hung behind the plant. The color matched the walls perfectly, down to the marbled cream pattern. I almost hadn't realized it was there. I pulled the plant out and pushed the curtain aside to find a door-sized wall of brass Xs. It was the metal cage door of a small old-fashioned elevator, its door only about three feet across.

I slid the accordion-style door open and stepped inside. The elevator was small, with enough room for maybe four people if they all squished together uncomfortably. For some unaccountable reason, the flutters in my stomach began to move into my chest—a migration of butterflies into my heart. This was excitement and anticipation, not fear or worry.

There were three black push buttons marked B,

SB1 and SB2 respectively. The alarm suddenly stopped. I could hear the squawking of walkie talkies in the distance. I quickly pulled the plant back into the alcove and closed the metal gate as quietly as I could. Then I hit the button for SB2 and felt my stomach give a little lurch as the elevator slowly began its descent.

The B level looked vaguely like an old mall, with wide hallways, glass storefronts, and an escalator going up. The lights were on, but the storefronts and halls were completely empty.

Brightly lit by fluorescent bulbs, SB1 level revealed an area under construction, with slabs of particle board covering the partially built walls. A faint scent of sawdust lingered in the air as the elevator car continued downward. It reminded me a little of the scary basement bunker we'd found under the Adderly garage, and I shivered.

And then there was SB2. A long, brown-tiled hallway lit at intervals by bare bulbs from the ceiling. Closed doors lined the hallway, a new one every ten feet or so. The elevator came to a shuddering stop, and I pulled the door aside. It was surprisingly quiet; the door, I mean. You'd expect an ancient metal elevator gate to squeal, but it slid silently, as if it'd been oiled recently.

I stepped out and caught a whiff of musty odor that wasn't quite covered by a lingering scent of bleach. The hallway of doors and bare bulbs loomed, almost seeming to stretch like I was looking into a funhouse mirror that made things look farther away than they really were. I listened. I heard nothing except for the squeak of my sneakers on the tile.

The first three doors on either side were unmarked, but the fourth one had a placard that read KRIS KONG, ESQ. I hesitated, then put my ear against the door. Nothing. Either the door was too thick to hear anything, or no one was home. I slowly tried the knob. It was locked. I wondered if I should knock.

The door on the other side of the hall was marked JANITOR, which seemed to explain where the bleachy smell came from. But once again I had a weird, nagging feeling that there was something important here, something hidden. It didn't make any sense. There was no way I had ever been down here before, was there?

That knob turned, and a buttload of mops, brooms, and buckets crowded the small closet, all leaning right. Shelves of cleaning products, brushes, and boxes lined the right wall. The left wall was strangely bare. *Why?* The butterfly migration swirled in my chest once more. Then I saw it: a small rectangle, barely noticeable, at waist height. I traced its raised edges with my fingers. It was about the size of a credit card. I touched the top center, and it flipped open with a metallic *clink*, exposing a small metal lever, like an awkward handle. First I pulled, then I pushed, but nothing. Then I slid the handle to the right, and the whole wall moved, revealing a dark passage. A secret door. In a janitor closet. In the sub-basement of the Empire State Building. That I had maybe somehow known was there. I could hardly believe it.

I heard a tinny, jazzy instrumental version of "Pop Goes the Weasel" playing softly somewhere. The dark passage opened into a much wider room, dimly lit. I took in an impression of ripped fabric-covered pillars, a tarnished tin ceiling, faded red banquette seating with dusty tables, a ruined parquet floor, a crystal chandelier covered in cobwebs, and a long bar with a complement of stools on the back wall.

Sitting on the bar inside a glass was a brightly lit smartphone, and the tinny music seemed to emanate from it. Two feet away, Billy sat on one of the stools, his mouth feeding from Michael Adderly's wrist.

CHAPTER TWENTY

ADDERLY'S EYES WERE CLOSED AND BILLY WAS utterly focused on his task. Suddenly the vampire's head turned toward me and his eyes flew open. I must have made a sound. I mean, he hadn't smelled me, had he?

In a split second, Adderly grabbed Billy, pulling him behind the bar. The two disappeared into a dark doorway I hadn't noticed. The smartphone still lay on the bar, continuing to play its song.

I used a stool to leapfrog the bar and lunged through the doorway. Stairs led upwards and I climbed them. I heard a door slam somewhere above. Three flights later, I emerged into the shiny brown lobby again. *DING* went an elevator down the hall. I ran again, my sneakers screeching on marble as I rounded the corner. Outside the elevator bank stood Sgt. Keene. With his mouth agape and his eyes staring wide, he didn't react to me at all.

The display above one set of elevator doors marked OBSERVATION DECK showed the numbers going up. I entered the next one and pressed the button and the car shot upwards, leaving my stomach in my Converse All-Stars. *Come on, come on.* I breathed deep and fast, winded after my run. The elevator took about a minute to reach its destination, slowing at first before stopping. The doors *dinged* open and I spilled out into a glass box. The walls were glass and the observation deck was outside. Billy, his back to me, stood at the protective fence at the edge, looking out over the city lights.

I didn't see Michael Adderly anywhere.

I pushed open the glass door. Billy had his hands on two bars of the security fence. I walked down the ramp toward him. Something moved above and behind me. "Chris," it said in a choked whisper that sent my pulse racing. I whirled around.

There he stood. Michael Adderly. The piercing blue eyes, the imperfect aquiline nose, the supple mouth. Where had he come from? The flagpole jutting from the side of the building, twenty feet up? He wore dark jeans and a button-up shirt with the sleeves rolled up his forearms. He was painfully handsome. My chest and throat tightened inexplicably as I gazed at him.

"You know I thought you were dead," he snarled. "All those years. Pining for you. I thought you'd died like the others, but you woke me, and stalked me, and now here you are. Here you are, still young. After all these years. Why, Chris? What did they offer you? Was it Thisbe? The Crone? The Viscount? Who do you belong to?"

"I don't know what you're talking about. I only

281

belong to myself."

The wind stirred his hair and the flag overhead flapped noisily. "Yes, they make you believe that for the first decade or two, don't they? But you should have learned by now, my girl, they're all users. They will use you as long as you have a purpose, and then flush you away the minute you outlast your usefulness. Is that what happened? Did you wake me to cry wolf now that your master has bored of you?" he sneered. It made him ugly for a moment.

"I told you I have no idea what you're talking about!" I cried. "I don't have a master and I don't know who Chris is!"

"Was it Irina? Did she get to you?"

"All I know about Irina Van Horn is that she killed Tamara. I know that now. That you didn't."

"Poor Tamara," he said, with a sad sigh. "I thought Irina—but how do *you* know? Why this façade, Chris? How can you say that you don't know me? How do you know she killed Tamara?"

He was so mercurial—one moment angry, the next sincere. But if he was sincere, if he wasn't a murderer, why was he keeping Billy? Controlling him?

"Look, all I want is for you to let Billy go."

"Ah, yes, *Billy*. I appreciated that you brought me a meal. Though not a very happy one." He frowned a moment, looking from me to Billy. "Come here, William," he commanded. Billy turned from the security fence, moving mechanically toward us.

"No!" I shouted. "Just stop. Leave him out of

this!" I thrust my right palm out, fingers spread wide. The gesture was meant to emphasize my meaning. To tell Adderly to stop. I could feel my hand shaking, thought I couldn't tell if it was from fear or anger. I could feel the hot blood pumping through the veins in my arm. My fingertips pulsed with heat.

Adderly's face softened for a moment and he took a step forward. My heart sped up and my breathing did too. He came closer, and my hand brushed his arm.

And the arm caught *fire*.

Flames burst from his shirt sleeve.

He moved. It was a blur. Past me, to Billy, and then away.

I was so busy trying to figure out what had just happened that I was surprised when my thigh felt hot.

I looked down and realized my jeans were smoking. I screeched and beat the spot with my palm. *Is my hand on fire?* I held it before my eyes, seeing tiny flames lick from my thumb, forefinger, and middle finger. Yet I felt no pain. *This can't be happening.* I flapped my hand against my shoulder and looked again. The flames were gone.

"How did you do that?" came Adderly's voice from above. His sleeve was scorched and Billy stood beside him. They were both up there now, standing on the horizontal flag pole like tightrope walkers. How did it hold both their weights? Adderly stared at me, his eyes gone completely black. No iris, no pupil, just black.

"You're asking me? I have no idea. I thought you did it!"

"Shall I kill the boy then?" Adderly dangled Billy off the edge.

"No, no, please! I'll do anything."

"Anything? My, that's a tempting offer." He smiled an insincere smile and I saw fangs.

"What do you want?"

"I want the truth!" he shouted.

"The truth is that I don't know! I don't know anything! I have amnesia. Didn't Billy tell you? Didn't you ask him? Why don't you ask him now?"

"I did ask William about you. He seemed quite enamored of you at the time. He said your name was Madison and that you were hiding from someone."

I gaped at him. "Hiding from someone? I'm not hiding from anyone! I just don't know who I really am!"

"William, is that true? Is your friend hiding from someone or not?"

Billy's face didn't change at all from its blank expression. "I don't know."

Adderly's brow furrowed in consternation. "That's not what you said before, William. Which is it?"

"I don't know," Billy said again, his tone flat and lackluster.

"Please, how can you expect him to know anything when you have him all zombied-up like this? Just let him go."

Adderly pointedly stared at me as if I'd just done something interesting. "Why should you care what I do with him?" he asked.

"Because he's my friend and you're controlling him and it's not right."

"Since when do you care about what's right?"

"I don't know what you think you know about me. I will not help you or answer you in any way until you unzombify him and let him go."

Adderly sighed. "Very well." He took Billy by the shoulders and stared into his eyes. "William, I release you."

It was like watching someone wake up, except that Billy wasn't asleep. Suddenly, the real Billy was back behind his eyes, and he almost lost his balance. Adderly steadied him.

"What the actual fuck?" Billy exclaimed.

"Language," Adderly said.

Billy blinked a few times. "Wait a second, I remember . . . you . . . you drank from me? You made me drink your blood . . . You controlled me!"

"I saved your life," Adderly said. "I'd think you'd be more grateful."

"Grateful!? I was your slave! You took my phone, my jacket, my free will. You turned me into a spy for you!" Billy tried to pull away, but Adderly held him there.

"Careful now," he warned. "Perhaps you should try talking to him," he said to me.

"Billy," I said.

"What the fuck, Maddy? What are you doing here?"

"I followed you. I'm here to help you."

"Help me? You can't help me. I'm a slave to this . . . this . . . thing."

Adderly frowned. "Maybe I shouldn't have saved your life. I could change that, you know."

"Billy, just answer his questions. Tell him everything you know about me."

"What? I'm not telling this guy anything."

"Convince him," Adderly growled, lifting Billy off his feet.

"Please don't hurt him!"

He placed Billy back on his feet again. "You really do care what happens to this boy?" Adderly's brow furrowed.

"Will you let him go?" I asked.

"Will you tell me everything?"

"Just let him go," I pleaded.

I saw it happen. First, Adderly released him. Then I heard Billy's words, and then it happened. In the blink of an eye.

"You know what? I'd rather be dead than anyone's slave." And then with a running leap, he dove over the security fence.

"Damn," said Michael Adderly. Our eyes met for a moment. In one bound, he was at the end of the flagpole. "This isn't over," he said. Then he dove off the building.

I rushed to the fence. A blur of movement below, then nothing but the brightly lit night streets of New York City.

CHAPTER TWENTY-ONE

I RUSHED TO THE ELEVATOR AND TOOK IT ALL THE way down to the lobby. Sgt. Keene was back at his post, writing on a clipboard. "Goodnight," he said as I pushed the door open and ran out to the sidewalk.

I don't know what I expected to see. Billy's broken body splattered across the sidewalk? Michael Adderly floating in mid-air? The two of them doing a tango down 35th Street?

Whatever I'd been expecting, I didn't see it. Just cars on the streets and regular people on the sidewalks, trying to get wherever they were trying to get to.

I stood with my back against the building for several minutes, letting the pounding in my chest subside, thinking about everything that I'd just seen, just heard, just done. It made my head ache.

The next morning, I rolled over and stretched, slowly sitting up, before freezing in mid-yawn. I didn't freeze literally, because I didn't turn to ice, but it was cold in the room—much colder than it should have been, because my window was open. Not wide open, but a few inches. It had been closed when I went to sleep.

And that wasn't all. My dresser drawers were open. My desk drawers were open. My laptop was open. Papers were all over the desk. Clothes lay all over the floor. Every piece of furniture in my room that might conceal any object at all had been opened, and presumably, searched. What for? I fought the rising feeling of panic in my chest and tried to calm my breathing.

I could have sworn my window was locked. Would have sworn it.

But what good is a locked window against a vampire?

With dread, I looked down at my tank top for bloodstains and then went to the bathroom mirror to check my neck, sighing with relief when there were no marks there.

Then again, he'd bitten Billy and Billy didn't seem to have any bite marks either. Then again, he hadn't killed Tamara. Did I need to be worried about Michael Adderly?

I stared steadily at myself in the mirror. My eyes looked big and scared. "It's okay," I told myself. "Just go back in. They can't come out during the day, right? Go back in there and clean up." I took a deep breath and returned to my bedroom.

I found my hospital discharge papers with my diagnosis, dissociative fugue, on top of the pile. I stacked the papers neatly and put them away with the rest of my unanswered questions.

One answer arrived three nights later. There was a note waiting for me on the kitchen table when I got in from work. "Package for you, Maddy," the note read in Kara's handwriting, with an arrow pointing down. On the floor was a large brown cardboard box, about three feet by three feet by one foot. The apartment was quiet as I examined the box. *No return address. Postmarked today in Brooklyn.* There was definitely something weighty inside, though I couldn't imagine what.

I clicked on my small bedside lamp and used scissors to open the box. I pulled out the wadded up brown paper stuffing and found a surprise beneath: a wooden box with speakers in the front and a hinged lid. Inside was a Victrola record player. Who had sent it? I pulled it out and gasped at what I saw beneath. A record in a sleeve: Michael Adderly's single, produced by Romeo Records: "The Kiss" played by Les Elliott and His Orchestra.

I moved the record player to the top of my bureau and plugged it in, then carefully slid the shiny black record from its jacket and placed it on the turntable.

I held my breath when I put the needle on the record's outer rim. The static-filled white noise of the recording gave me goosebumps.

And then he began to sing.

Once again, I was transported. This time it was from the four walls of my bedroom to some non-place inside my mind, an empty labyrinth of hallways filled with fog and blurred images, feelings that had no context, no faces to identify, but that voice, something about that voice, made me feel that there'd been a terrible mistake. I knew that voice. I had lost that voice. Something awful had happened. I just knew it.

The song came to an end and my cheeks were wet with tears. I picked up the paper sleeve to put the record away and a folded piece of newsprint fell out.

The edges were yellowed with age, and it was heavily creased, as if it had been folded and refolded many times. I sat down on the bed and opened it in the light from the bedside lamp, only to find myself staring at a black and white photo of . . . me. The hair was a little shorter, but the wide smile and high cheekbones were the same. It was me. Maybe a little younger, but me, wearing a flowered top, in a newspaper clipping. The headline read "MISSING." Beneath the headline was the following text:

Name: Christina Marie Taylor

Sex: female

Age: 18

Hair: blond/strawberry

Eyes: blue

Height: 5'9"

Weight: 135 lbs.

Details: Last seen wearing jeans, a black V-neck sweater, and a pair of black Converse sneakers, in SoHo in the company of a man with longish brown hair. Reward offered for information leading to her being found.

Missing Since: Tues. Oct. 13, 1987

My mouth dropped open. It couldn't be. Was it a typo?

The top of the newspaper cut-out read October 19, 1987. Could someone fake a newspaper? The reverse of the page was a part of the "for sale" section of the newspaper. It seemed real enough.

I read the description again. The details, what Christina was wearing . . . It was the same outfit I'd had on when I found myself standing on Madison Avenue.

Christina had disappeared in Soho . . . seen with a man with "longish brown hair." Could it have been Michael? Soho . . . Raoul's restaurant was in Soho.

Christina. Christina Marie. It didn't sound familiar. He'd called me "Chris." Maybe it was a nickname for Christina.

But the year—1987? If I was eighteen in 1987, then I'd be . . . forty-eight now? I sure as hell didn't look forty-eight. And the date, October 13th, was the same as when I'd come to. Almost thirty years later. Nothing made any sense. It was impossible.

I rushed to the mirror to search my face, fearing it had somehow changed. But the same young face stared back from the shadows, pale and lost, like a half moon reflected in a dark body of water.

THE END

Madison will return

in

INTO THE DARK MARKET
Book 2 of the *Madison Roberts* Series

APRIL 2020

ACKNOWLEDGEMENTS

THIS SELF-PUBLISHING ENDEAVOR HAS BEEN IN THE works for several years and I am glad to have pushed this hapless bird out of the teeming nest that is my brain.

I could probably thank every person I am connected to in real life and through social media, because surely each one has contributed in some small way to any given portion of this project: by responding to my woes, making me laugh, or sharing some pithy meme that uplifted my spirits. However, I'd like to thank the following individuals for their assistance in getting this particular book out there.

The first person I'd like to thank is my editor Marcel Leroux, whose keen insight on dramatic structure and tough love on redundant nods, movements, and phrases helped this book find its final form. Any mistakes or typos that remain are most definitely my own.

I am also grateful to my cover illustrator Steven Novak, who deserves a medal for his endless patience and an award for his amazing artwork.

I've had a remarkable group of beta readers who shared their thoughts, opinions, and confusions during the writing and revising process (some of whom read multiple drafts!). I wouldn't have felt confident enough to put the book out there without your feedback and encouragement. Thank you: Staci McGranaghan, Diana Ballard, Evette Alvarado, Amy Marcoux, Tina Hudec, Janelle Lannan Schittone, Miriam Lover-Williams, Lindsay Wisneski, Sheri Sikes, Melissa Grzybowski, Karsen LaRue, Marta Gregory, Kat Redfern-Shaw, Alexei Esikoff, and John Sisson.

For advice, helping with research, publication readiness, marketing plan, and other support, I thank: Sean Clarke, Michael Boucher, M.J. Heiser, E.J. Runyon, Jimi Ripley-Black, Alyssa Naley, and Christy Decker. Thank you, also, to Amanda Van Horn for the loan of her last name for one of my characters. I'd also like to thank indie publisher/writer Anna Castle, who—when I revealed my anxieties about self-publication—told me, "Just jump!"

Last but certainly not least, I need to thank my husband, Sam Garrett, to whom this book is dedicated. Sam has been a tireless cheerleader, writer's therapist, cat wrangler, head chef and housekeeper, as well as parent-and-midwife to the concept of this book. He has supported me in countless ways, taught me to be kinder to myself and my words, and loved me when I felt least loveable. I would not, and could not, have written and published this book without him.

Finally, I want to acknowledge my research materials. For those who are curious about ghosts and haunted locations, check out Loyd Auerbach's *ESP, Hauntings and Poltergeists: A Parapsychologist's Handbook* (1986), S.E. Schlosser's *Spooky New York* (2005), and Dolores Riccio & Joan Bingham's *Haunted Houses USA* (1989). I'm sure there are newer books out there on the topic; these happened to be on my shelf.

Readers who are interested in the history of Dutch architecture in New York might enjoy Maud Esther Dillard's *Old Dutch Houses of Brooklyn* (1945) and Helen Wilkinson Reynolds's *Dutch Houses in the Hudson Valley Before 1776* (1965). Fans of Art Deco design will love the photos in Patricia Bayer's *Art Deco Interiors: Decoration and Design Classics of the 1920s and 1930s* (1990) and Theodore Menten's *The Art Deco Style: In Household Objects, Architecture, Sculpture, Graphics, Jewelry; 468 Authentic Examples* (1972). These books, borrowed from Brooklyn Library, were instrumental in helping me establish the look and contents of Adderly House, with one exception: the attic portrait of Catharina Van Horn was inspired by Bartholomeus van der Helst's painting *Anna du Pire as Granida* (1660).

Made in the USA
Lexington, KY
11 November 2019